Payback

*Sometimes your past
won't let you go*

Geoff Palmer

PS

PODSNAP PUBLISHING
WELLINGTON, NEW ZEALAND

Podsnap Publishing Ltd., 17 Moir Street, Mt Victoria,
Wellington 6011, New Zealand.

ISBN:
978-0-473-34886-1 (paperback)
978-0-473-34887-8 (ePub)
978-0-473-34888-5 (Kindle)
978-0-473-34889-2 (iBook)

COVER DESIGN BY MELODY SIMMONS

I

ONE

Solikha Duong was nine years old when she killed two men. She was a pretty child, and that was their undoing.

Village life in northern Cambodia consisted of long days and hard work. Everyone helped where they could, young or old. That's what a villager did. The communal storehouse never emptied and there was still time to play in the lush green fields and the forest fringes that surrounded them. Time for games and laughter. Time for stories around the brazier at night and growing sleepy in her mother's arms.

Then something changed. Her parents went to market one day and never returned.

Old Aang told her, her eyes heavy with grief, her arms full of comfort, but Solikha didn't really understand. How was it possible? She'd seen death before, of course. Mr Aang and Old Nhek and baby Sann. But death visited the very old or the very young, not vital people like her parents.

Then they brought the bodies back.

Shrouded outlines. Formless. Surely not real people? They were laid out on a low mound in the meeting hut, surrounded by fresh leaves and rumdoul blossoms, lit by candles. She was allowed to visit, to touch, to say prayers, but not to see their faces. That was strange. Mr Aang and Old Nhek and baby Sann had been laid out in such a fashion, but swaddled from the neck down, not wrapped from head to foot. She placed a flower, lit a candle, said a prayer, but did not understand until the van that delivered them returned two days later. The mangled bicycles told the story more eloquently than the mangled bodies. A narrow lane, a drunk driver, a speeding truck...

Six days later she was sent away, to an uncle in the north. To a man she'd never met before and a village she'd never seen. A village where few people could afford bicycles and where there was little time for play or stories. Where the communal storehouse was often empty, and where one more mouth to feed added to life's burden.

She worked in the fields with the others and tried hard to prove her worth, but it never seemed enough for her sharp-tongued aunt and taciturn uncle. Two months later, when men from the south came and swapped money for her, it was almost a relief to get in their truck.

A new life, they said. A better one. Solikha just wanted her old one back.

There were three men in the cab. A driver with a pockmarked face, a simple boy who did the menial work, and a muscled man with hair dyed the color of fire who seemed to be in charge.

The journey was long. A nightmare of rutted tracks with nothing but a hard wooden bench for sitting on and the hard wooden floor for sleeping. Every day more people joined them. Young women mostly, older than Solikha, but not by much. A few boys too. They hardly spoke. Like her, they were wary, but when they did exchange a few words, the dialects and accents sounded strange.

The interior of the truck sweltered from the heat and the press of bodies. Condensation clung to the canvas roof and ran down the canvas sides. Solikha kept to her corner at the front. It was a good spot because a little air came up between the boards when they were moving.

They stopped. Again. The truck was already full. Surely they wouldn't take on any more?

Solikha lowered herself to the floor and peered through a gap between the boards. Something was happening outside. Something important. She saw a guard post and a barrier arm. A man in uniform. Flame Hair beckoned to him and they talked together quietly. Money changed hands, a fat wad of it. The barrier was raised and the truck moved on.

The journey grew easier after that. She could hear it in the sound of the wheels and the note of the engine. The bump and grind of rutted tracks became a steady hum, and the breeze through the gaps in the boards increased, lightening the air inside.

Outside, the little she could see of the world changed too. Forest gave way to fields interspersed with houses, shops and buildings. And people! Hundreds of villages worth. Thousands. So many it seemed beyond belief.

They stopped for one final addition, a cheeky boy in a torn blue shirt. He appeared to amuse the truck men because he called to them as they closed the tailgate and retied the canvas flap. He said something to the children at the back that made them smile. But Solikha didn't understand his words and didn't care. She'd been huddled in her corner for four bruising days now and was groggy with fatigue.

After another endless day on the smooth road—fields and villages giving way to tarmac and a sea of cars and trucks—they arrived to night lights and the bustle of a crowded market street. The air smelled of rotting fruit, drains, and an undertone of something darker she could almost taste. Like grit between her teeth. People bellowed in a strange tongue, beckoning and shouting. In the distance, she glimpsed towering buildings filled with light and guessed this must be a city.

They spent that night and most of the next day in a bare concrete room with just a water barrel and an open toilet. It was a relief from the constant noise and movement of the truck, and at last she had room to stretch and walk about.

Late the following afternoon, the truck men reappeared and herded them out with bamboo canes, slapping and poking at them as is if they were cattle. Flame Hair laughed and grabbed at some of the older girls in ways she knew he shouldn't.

Solikha shielded her eyes from the sudden sunlight and found herself in a closed courtyard with high concrete walls. They were lined up shoulder to shoulder, pushed into place with stabs of the bamboo canes.

The yard went quiet. The truck men stiffened and stood a little straighter as three strangers strode in wearing tan pants, white shirts, brown shoes, and sunglasses. They fanned out, facing the weary collection of women and children, and were followed by a large man in a dark blue suit. His shirt was the color of barley husks, open at the neck, and his black shoes had a lustrous shine. He turned cold, appraising eyes on them, standing with his legs apart, hands resting on his hips.

He looked from one end of the line to the other, then his gaze returned to linger on a girl beside Solikha. A girl twice her age whose hand and forearm were withered and scarred. A burn. Perhaps a fall into an open fire. Solikha felt her shrink back, trying to hide her damaged arm behind her skirt.

Cold Eyes snapped something. Flame Hair pursed his lips and replied respectfully, moving to pull the girl out of line. She stood trembling as Cold Eyes looked her up and down, his lip curled in disapproval.

Flame Hair leaned close and said something in her ear.

The girl looked back, shocked.

He raised an eyebrow, nodded, his expression reasonable.

She shook her head.

He shrugged, sighed, and tossed his bamboo cane to one of his friends. Then he whirled back and lashed out, tearing at her thin cotton blouse, baring one breast for a moment before she could cover it with her withered arm. She tried to draw away, step back to the wall with the others, but he seized her and dragged her forward, yelling the words in her face.

She pushed him off. He staggered, almost fell.

The courtyard went deathly still.

Flame Hair snarled, glanced at Cold Eyes, and received a faint nod in reply. He spoke again, gesturing this time so that even those who didn't hear his words would understand. He wanted her to undress.

She cowered and held her ripped blouse tighter.

His temper vanished, and he shrugged again, seeming to accept this. The girl relaxed a fraction. Then he suddenly exploded, lunging and grabbing her by the hair, dragging her head down as he brought his knee up sharply. They met with a dull crack, and she staggered back, her jaw askew, blood welling from her mouth. He kicked her legs away. She fell, landing on her back, and he slammed his heel into her face.

He raised his boot to strike a second time, but Cold Eyes said something, and he paused, lowered the boot slowly, wiped the blood and tissue off on the girl's torn blouse, and stepped back.

Cold Eyes stared at the others, then down at the crumpled heap on the ground, then back at them, his face expressionless. The message clear: do what you are told.

* * *

Later, they came for them individually. One of the older, prettier girls first, then another, then the cheeky boy. Not so cheeky now. By the time they led him away, he looked as frightened as the others.

Each time the door closed, a collective sigh ran around the room. Each time it opened, all breathing ceased.

It opened again and Flame Hair stood looking them over. Then he pointed to Solikha and jerked his thumb.

She didn't think her legs would carry her across the room. She could feel the apprehension—and relief—in the others. A tight knot formed in her chest. But she was a village girl from Trasek Chrum and there was a song they sang in the fields as they worked, her and the other girls. A taunting song for the boys: how they were twice as good, and twice as tough, and never cried. She sang the words in her mind as she went towards him.

He took her by the wrist and led her out. Through an alley, across a street, then into a building through a side door. She glimpsed a maze of lighted rooms, smelled cooking, candle wax, and sandalwood. Heard pop music—a pounding beat—the sounds of laughter and dancing.

Flame Hair rapped on a door. It opened, and she was given over to a matronly woman in a red shawl who smelled of sharp perfume and cigarettes. She looked Solikha over with a weary eye and directed her to a bathroom. There she was made to bathe and wash her hair.

Solikha stood huddled in a thin white towel while the woman flicked through a rack of dresses, drew one out, held it against her, put it back and found a smaller size. The dresses were all the same. Like uniforms. The fabric was coarse, but the pattern was a gay swirl of bright flowers in orange and red. Striking. Distinctive. It was cotton, close-fitting at the top, with a flared skirt and button-down pockets on the bodice. It was pretty. Solikha had never had a brand-new dress before.

The woman tucked a pink flower in her hair, but gave her nothing else, no underthings, and Solikha didn't have the words to ask. She wouldn't have done so anyway. She was shy and the woman was brusque and businesslike, but not, she sensed, unkind.

Instead, she tried to focus on her good fortune. She'd been frightened when Flame Hair took her from the concrete room, but now she'd bathed and had a new dress and a flower in her hair. Memories of the cramped, unpleasant journey were already fading, and for the first time in many days Solikha felt a ray of hope that this new life might not be so bad after all.

The woman in the red shawl pulled a string that rang a distant bell. Another man appeared and led Solikha away. Not one of the truck men. He was better dressed but had a distant air. He held her by the wrist, lightly, like a guide, and she followed him up a narrow staircase, down a corridor, then along a wider passage with closed doors to her left and bare light bulbs overhead. Muffled screams came from behind one of the doors. Plaintive and pitiful. The man didn't pause. Solikha did, for just a moment, and his grip tightened around her wrist. He jerked her forward. On towards a door at the far end, which stood ajar.

TWO

"Well lookee here," a voice called from the cruising car.

Alice Kwann kept walking.

"Hey little lady, you want a *ride*?" The last word was drawn out and accompanied by snorts from the car's other occupants as it kept pace with her.

Alice Kwann kept on walking.

"Cos if you do want a *ride*, we'd be happy to oblige."

Alice considered her options. Three hundred yards of unlighted sidewalk lay ahead, but there was still a little light in the sky. Even with her injured ankle she'd cover the distance in a minute or so.

"I'm fine, but thank you," she said to the leering face in the car window.

Her reply silenced him for a moment. He'd expected to be ignored, it seemed.

She checked out the car. Old, big and domestic. The color looked blue or black in the twilight, but she was more interested in the occupants. Three guys. Young, beefy types. Football players who hadn't made the team, perhaps. There was one in the rear seat, two in the front. Their windows were down. The evening air was mild.

"Only, you look like you really need one." The speaker was the front seat passenger. Sandy hair, bull neck, a star-shaped tattoo below his right ear. He turned to the other occupants of the car. "Don't you think so boys?"

The boys muttered their ascent.

"I'm fine," Alice repeated.

The car wavered a little, edging closer to the sidewalk. A patch of loose gravel crunched beneath its tires.

"Well, that ain't very friendly. You being injured 'n' all."

Two hundred yards.

Alice tried to quicken her pace, but her sprained ankle gave her a painful jab.

"We're just being neighborly, ain't we boys?" The boys confirmed it. "We're always neighborly to runners out here. It being a quiet road and all. 'specially injured runners. 'specially when it's getting on for dark."

His tone changed. Took on an edge. Like he was licking his lips as he spoke.

A light came on. The guy in the back seat had a torch.

"That better?" A second voice. Thinner. Reedier. "We can light your way, at least. That'd be neighborly, wouldn't it?"

But they didn't light her way. The beam played over her bare legs, hovered on her shorts and T-shirt, flickered in her face. It was bright. She raised a hand to shield her eyes.

A hundred yards.

The beam dropped, lingering on her torso.

"Yeah, right neighborly," the first voice said, its tone lower, its edge edgier.

Alice felt the pounding of her pulse. Braced herself.

Seventy-five yards.

Streetlights wouldn't give her much protection, but at least she'd be able to see what she was dealing with.

The front seat passenger said something to the driver. The car sped up for a second, then swung in front of her, mounting the curb and angling across the sidewalk. While the vehicle was still in motion, the two doors on the right flew open and the two passengers stepped out.

Or tried to.

Alice was ready for them. She leaped at the front door, catching its outward swing with the sole of her injured foot and slammed it back against the first guy's ankle. He let out an explosive "Fuck!" and fell back in the car.

Alice muttered something similar. The blow jarred her sprain and made her stumble.

The second guy, the guy with the torch, kept on coming, then the car stopped completely, blocking her way. She heard the parking brake engage and the driver's door open as the third guy stepped out to join his friends.

Alice considered her options. The way ahead was blocked unless she leaped the hood and ran. But with her ankle? They'd be after her in a flash. Besides, they had a car.

To her right was a stone wall set with high metal railings. Square, iron, narrowly spaced. A park of some sort. No exit there unless she vaulted it and ran. But again, running was out of the question.

To her left, beyond the angled car and the two-lane blacktop, was an open field settling into darkness. A new housing estate dotted with construction materials and freshly dug trenches. Some shelter there, perhaps. But for one woman against three burly guys?

The only other option was back the way she'd come.

Back out of town. Deeper into darkness. That was no option at all.

The guy with the torch hesitated, playing his beam over the guy in the front seat. He'd missed what Alice had done. "What happened, Big Jim?"

"Bitch!" Big Jim said as the driver came around the hood. "Get her!"

Alice lashed out with her foot again, caught Torch Guy's hand, heard a crack and sent the light spinning away over the trunk. Another cry of "Fuck!" Then the driver seized her from behind. He caught her around the waist and dragged her back off balance. She fell against him, her shoulders to his chest. He grabbed her wrists and dragged her arms out wide like she'd been crucified. He was her height, but strong. Obviously worked out. She felt the flex of muscles against her shoulder blades.

Big Jim recovered, threw the door wide, and used it for support as he hobbled out the car. Torch Guy recovered his torch and they regrouped around her.

"Now that *weren't* very neighborly," Big Jim said, his face close to hers in the fading light. He was sweating slightly. His breath smelled sour. "Let's see what we've got here."

The driver dragged her arms out wider. Alice felt like an insect specimen pinned in a display case. Bad analogy, she thought, feeling his excitement hard against her butt.

Torch Guy played the torch on her face. Alice squinted.

"Chink, huh?" Big Jim said. "Slanty eyes. A gook. You speaky Chinee?"

Alice said nothing.

"Never had a chink before. You Davy?"

"Nup," the guy holding her said.

"Cos you know what they say about the slanty eyes?" His face was real close now. "They say *it's* slanty too." He jammed a hand between her legs.

Alice nodded sharply. Her forward motion was restricted by the proximity of Big Jim's face. Not much room to build up momentum. Still, the head-butt was enough to make him stagger back and give her room for a full return swing.

Alice knew a human head weighed around eleven pounds. She pitched hers backward, dropping her shoulders as she did so to increase the force, and the full eleven pounds of her skull, traveling at speed, was only stopped by the bridge of driver Davy's nose.

The two small oblong bones that form the nose are designed to support the cartilage that hangs below them, not absorb shock, so they shattered at once. And because Davy's head was turned slightly to one side, they shifted with the impact, dragging broken bone edge over jagged bone, dislocating the nasal septum. That probably accounted for the scream he let out, surprisingly high-pitched. Not that Alice paid it much attention.

Big Jim came back at her, one hand to his forehead where she'd cracked him, the other grabbed her T-shirt. But her hands were free now. She bunched her right fist, raised the knuckle of the middle finger half an inch, and punched at his eye, a quick, hard jab. Blunt knuckle met soft tissue. He howled and reeled away, half-blinded, cradling his head with the pain.

The guy with the torch drew closer to get in on the action. Then he backed away as the beam traveled over one friend then the other. Davy's nose, bent sideways, was gushing blood, but he seemed powerless to stop it. Each time he raised his hands to staunch the flow, he groaned and flinched and reeled at the pain from the dislocation. Big Jim was cradling his head, bent almost double, his ass against the side of the car, but he was urging Torch Guy on. "Get the bitch. Fucking get the bitch!"

Alice gave Big Jim a high kick to the head to shut him up.

Torch Guy backed away as if a dangerous animal had been unleashed. Which, in a sense, it had. He held the torch out like a protective shield, the beam aimed in her face. Alice shaded her eyes and continued to advance. He backed up further. Then his heel caught the edge of the sidewalk. A moment of imbalance. Alice charged.

The torch was long, chrome-plated, four D-cells stacked end-to-end in the handle, blooming to a mushroom shape around the bulb and reflector. She snatched it from his hand and swung it back in a wide arc, clipping him across the side of the head. Then she reversed it and brought it back for the forehand swing. The mushroom-shaped top slammed against his right cheek bone. The glass shattered. The bulb went out. The guy staggered and fell to the sidewalk.

Now what? Alice thought. Three down. None out. She still had to get away.

She could hobble-run with her injured ankle, but her motel was still at least a mile off, and the injured men would soon recover—at least some of their faculties. Big Jim might have trouble seeing straight for a day or two, but the driver could still drive with a busted nose, and she really didn't know the state of Torch Guy. They'd track her easily. The streets were wide and empty. Maybe they'd just run her down.

Take the car, leave them stranded, then abandon it in town.

The driver's door was open, the interior light on, but she saw at once the keys were gone. A natural habit. Automatic. Take the keys out when you shut off the ignition. It would require a deliberate effort on the part of most drivers to leave them where they were. And Davy's mind had been on other things.

"Fuck, man. I need a doctor or something," the driver muttered. "Where are you guys? Big Jim? Rick?"

They were recovering. She had to be quick.

There was a pack of cigarettes on the dash. A lighter in a tray on the console. The interior was littered with the discarded shells of takeaway containers, mostly cardboard. Alice swept an armful under the driver's seat and flicked the lighter. An orange tongue of flame licked along one edge.

"What the fuck?" Torch Guy staggered out of the darkness, his face still cupped in one hand, drawn to the glow like a moth to a candle. Alice feinted, jabbing at his damaged cheek. He lurched back. She slammed the door to fan the flames, and the glow brightened as the underside of the driver's seat caught light.

There's lots of flammable material inside an automobile. Seats stuffed with foam padding, nylon carpets, plastic trim and fittings. Once a fire starts, it's hard to stop.

Alice hobble-walked away as black smoke began billowing from the open windows, a sure sign the seating foam was well alight. The glow subsided for some seconds, then burst out again with renewed energy as the plastic dash and trim reached combustion point. By the time she looked back from under the first streetlight, the whole of the interior was boiling with orange flames.

THREE

There were three men in the room. Westerners. Solikha had seen men like them before in the big village, but only from a distance. One was young and good-looking. One was old, like Mr Aang. And one was very fat.

The door closed behind her. Solikha looked around. The man who led her there vanished. The old one locked the door and pocketed the key, smiling at her as he did so.

The room was grimy and sparsely furnished with a single bare bulb in the center of the ceiling. A curtained window, two chairs, a bed without sheets—just a plastic-wrapped mattress. There was a bottle of liquor on the sideboard, a bowl of fruit, and a dusty black telephone. An oversize sports bag lay in one corner. Fat One unzipped it and took out lights, a camera, a tripod and set them up. When he was done, he and Old One took the chairs while Young One settled on the edge of the bed and beckoned to her.

Solikha approached hesitantly.

Young One said something. Smiled. A greeting, obviously.

She returned her own and bowed politely, despite the

fluttering in her chest.

His smile broadened. He beckoned her closer, took her by the shoulders, and turned her gently, so she faced the camera, lowering his face till it was next to hers. Then he pointed, coaxing her to do the same, making a game of it.

At first, she was uncertain, so he took her arm, extended it, and pointed her index finger. Then he let it drop and gestured, clearly wanting her to do it on her own. She did so. He seemed pleased.

He said something to her, and she looked into his face, into gray-blue eyes like pools of cool water, and a broad smile of astonishingly white teeth. An infectious smile. She caught it and smiled shyly back.

He gave her a little shake. Affectionate. Complicit. He held her between his spread legs, his hands lightly resting on her hips. His hands were warm.

He nodded back towards the camera, but she couldn't see it now. Or Fat One or Old One. The lights facing her were on. Bright. She blinked. They'd disappeared behind the wall of light.

Young One squeezed her gently as a cue, and she lifted her arm and pointed just as she'd been shown. She looked at him. Was that right? He smiled and nodded and tickled her briefly, then pushed her hand down. He gave her the cue again, and she raised her arm of her own accord, looking back for his approval. He smiled and nodded and tickled her. She laughed out loud.

He tickled her again, making her squirm, then pulled up her dress. She pushed it down, remembering there was nothing underneath. He made to pull it up again. She pushed his hand away. He waggled his fingers. Another game, but she didn't like this one so much.

As she swatted his right hand away again, his left shot in and whipped her skirt up high, past her waist, baring her lower half completely. She squealed and struggled, but his right hand clamped hard around her chest. He fumbled with himself with his free hand, then reached around, caught her right knee, dragged her back and pulled her down against himself. She screamed and struggled, but his warm hands held her tightly.

The lights dazzled and the nightmare and pain went on and on. He threw her face down on the bed and did it again from behind. Held her under the arms and slammed her against the wall. Shoved the vile thing in her mouth. Then he threw her aside, bloody and bruised, and left her sobbing on the bed.

The lights went out.

* * *

Pain and shock deadened her sense of time. She couldn't have slept. Perhaps she'd fainted because things were different when she came to her senses. Young One was gone. Old One and Fat One were sitting at the sideboard drinking liquor and looking at the tiny screen on the back of the camera. She could hear herself, her screams. Tinny from the tiny speaker. They sounded lost. Pitiful.

Fat One was eating fruit. Papaya. Peeling and slicing it with the blade of a flick knife. He saw her stir, saw she was awake, and held out a slice. She was hungry. The fruit looked golden and delicious, but she shook her head.

Old One looked up from the screen, saw her curled naked in the corner, and said something to Fat One. They laughed. Fat One picked up the camera and put it back on the tripod. The lights went on again.

Solikha cried and cowered, scampered at the hard mattress, trying to get away, trying to force herself through the unyielding wall in the corner of the room, but Old One grabbed her by the ankle and dragged her back, bent her double over edge of the bed, jammed her face down against the clammy mattress and did something even worse.

Fat One came next. There were no lights, no camera now.

He took off his belt and wrapped it around her neck, buckling it like he was buckling his discarded trousers. He tightened it. And tightened it again. Her hands went to her throat, trying to tear it free, trying to relieve the pressure, but she couldn't. She couldn't breathe. She felt faint. Lights swam in her eyes. He was doing something else to her down below, but that was incidental to this struggle for life. For a single breath.

It was then she realized something.

Huddled in the corner when Young One was done with her, she'd prayed to join her parents. To join Mr Aang and Old Nhek and baby Sann, and all the others in the spirit world. But they wouldn't let her. Now she realized why. She wasn't ready. In spite of everything, she wanted to live.

Just as she felt the blackness sweeping in, just as her eyes rolled back in her head, he released the belt. Air and life swept back into her. She gasped and shuddered uncontrollably. Heard a distant groan. It seemed to excite him because whatever he was doing to her became more frantic for a while. Then he moaned and began tightening the belt again.

This time, she fought her instinct. Tore her hands away from her throat and jabbed them at his leering face instead. A lucky shot. An eye. The leering face leaped back with a cry. The belt went slack. She leaped to her feet, raced for the door and seized the handle.

Locked.

Angry voices sounded in the room behind as Solikha tore at the handle, battered on the door and cried for help.

No one came.

Old One caught her from behind and dragged her away, one arm looped around her waist, the other fighting down her flailing hands and kicking feet. She didn't make it easy. She might be small and slight, but she fought like a demon.

As he hauled her back towards the bed, he swung her past the sideboard. Fat One had stabbed his flick knife into an uneaten papaya. It stuck out, upright. She snatched it up in her small fist, caught it by the handle, and brought it down hard, into the thigh of the man behind her. It was sharp. It went in deep. He screamed and let her go.

She dropped to the floor, landing in a crouch, still holding the knife. Old One was yelling, clamping hands around his wound as blood pulsed between his fingers. Fat One turned. He hadn't seen what happened. The palm of his hand was still pressed against his eye.

Old One called for help, must have told him what she'd done, because Fat One stared at her, a wary look in his one good eye.

Old One urged him on, to get help perhaps, but Solikha

stood between him and the telephone. Between him and the door. And they all knew the door was locked.

Rolling sideways on the bed, Old One gestured to the pocket where he'd put the key, not daring to reach for it himself, not daring to move his hands because there really was a lot of blood. It welled up through his fingers. He couldn't seem to stop it.

Fat One stared at it like he was in a trance, then something kicked in, a sense of urgency perhaps, and he rushed towards the bed and fumbled for the key. He had one hand in Old One's pocket when Solikha struck.

She lashed out blindly, seeing the fat expanse of neck, aware of the belt still wrapped around her own. A rapid down-stroke then an up. A jagged X to mark the spot.

Fat One froze and gurgled as blood spurted like a fountain, thundering down onto the plastic-wrapped mattress, spattering the walls and pooling under Old One.

Old One howled and pushed himself away, kicking back in panic, heels slipping on the slick surface, tearing his own wound in the process. But Fat One said nothing, did nothing, just gurgled and sank face down on the bed.

A human body contains eight pints of blood. One hundred and twenty-eight fluid ounces. Each heartbeat pumps one-fiftieth of that through the carotid arteries in the neck. A pint every six beats. At a resting rate of sixty beats a minute, a severed carotid bleeds dry in under a minute. Fat One hadn't been resting. He was unconscious within fifteen seconds. Dead within thirty.

Solikha was a village girl. She'd seen blood before. She'd watched the slaughter of pigs, helped in the slaughter of chickens, but she'd never seen so much of it in one place.

It pooled around the bodies of the two men, dribbled onto the floor in a thick black-red stream where Fat One's weight held the mattress down, and congealed on the walls where the spray had hit them. And all over her, she realized. She dropped the knife and screamed.

Her screams went on and on. Her screams went nowhere. They were used to screams in that place. Screams meant good business. Screams meant their customers were enjoying themselves.

* * *

She couldn't tell how long had passed, but the sky outside was growing lighter. She'd wrapped herself in one of the curtains and huddled in a corner of the windowsill, her face pressed against the cool glass, her view of the room shielded by the fall of fabric. Her limbs were stiff, her body ached inside and out, and she began to cry again at the recollection of what they'd done to her. But as the first shafts of a new day shone through the glass, she was filled with fresh resolve. To endure. To survive. To escape.

She pulled back the curtain, let in light, and looked around the room.

Old One and Fat One were dead. There was no doubt of that. Bled out like stuck pigs. It was what they deserved. She looked at them coldly. Fat One face down, half-drowned in blood. Old One backed into the corner, the same corner she'd tried to claw through herself, his face a rictus of pain and fear.

She padded across the floor, naked, her feet sticking in

places where the blood had spattered. Her floral dress lay across the back of one of the chairs where Young One had thrown it, but she walked on, skirting the congealing puddle by the bed, to the tiny bathroom opposite the locked door.

She used the toilet. It took an age because of the pain. When she was done, she stood at the sink and splashed herself with cold water, all over, rinsing clean before drying herself on a grubby hand towel.

She steeled herself and went back into the room, keeping her eyes averted from the men. She took up the dress, slipped it on, and went back to the door. It was locked of course. Old One still had the key in his pocket. But what if he didn't? What if she could open it? The men outside would see her, stop her. Then they'd see what she'd done. How could she explain it?

She couldn't.

There had to be another way.

She went back and saw Fat One's bag, open, the video camera on top. She picked it up, remembering how Young One had made her point at it, made her smile and laugh before he... did those things to her. She'd trusted him. Thought he was nice. Thought she'd found a friend.

In a flash of rage, she hurled the camera down against the floor with all her might, smashing it against the concrete. Bits flew off it, the lens broke, and something popped out one side. A small black plastic cassette. She stooped and picked it up.

The cassette looked like a miniature version of the ones she'd seen in the big village her parents took her to sometimes. They held cartoons and funny films. An elder would put one in a machine and pictures would show on a television screen to entertain the children.

Did this contain pictures of her?

It didn't seem likely. How could a little box like that hold moving pictures? She wasn't sure, but after a moment's thought she slipped it into the pocket of her dress.

Fat One's trousers lay on the floor, their cuffs soaking in the pool of blood. There was a bulge in the back pocket where she could see the corner of a wallet he wouldn't need anymore. She drew it out and rifled through the wad of notes. The money looked strange. Brightly colored banknotes similar to ones from her own country were mixed with dull green ones with writing like the writing on the cartoons and funny films. She took it all, stuffed it into the other pocket, and bent to put the wallet back.

A card fell out. Fat One's picture and more of the video writing. An identity card of some sort. Like the ones policemen and government officials carried. An important document. Possibly valuable. She took it too and went to the window.

The rising sun was an orange ball just breaking the horizon, shimmering in the early morning mist. She drew back the curtain and opened the window, letting in the hum of the city. Distant sounds of traffic mingled with the crowing of a cockerel from the shacks and shanties clustered down below. The room was on the fifth floor, too high to jump, but a rusting fire escape ran beneath the window. It was ancient. Looked unsafe. The handrail opposite flapped loosely from a rusted joint. She looked up. The anchor points of the platform for the floor above were flaky with rust. Long ocher tears ran down from them, staining the side of the building.

She slid out, but the platform creaked so ominously that she snatched her legs back and crouched on the windowsill, wondering what to do. Then she looked over her shoulder, back into the room at the men she had killed, and saw she had no choice.

FOUR

Alice stood in the shower and debated what to do next. Not that she had many options. The Greyhound bus that should have delivered her to Sacramento had broken down in a patch of nowhere fifteen miles east of Winnemucca. A replacement bus was on the way, but it wouldn't reach them until morning. The holdup hadn't bothered her unduly. After six hours in a seat from Salt Lake City, and with the prospect of six more to her destination, it was good to unkink and unwind. The company had put her and the other eight passengers up in a local motel just off I-80. Nothing fancy, but adequate. She'd been in worse.

She could call the cops. But she knew how small town cops worked and didn't want the hassle. She'd spend half the night being interviewed and filling in forms. Would have to stick around at least another day to give evidence and talk to the prosecutor. Besides, she didn't know the standing of the guys she'd hurt. Maybe they were local hoods and the cops would be happy to see them banged up. Or maybe they were the sons of prominent citizens.

Besides, she was on vacation.

She shut off the water, her mind made up.

Her first inclination had been to move on right away, to put some distance between her and them, but there was no way of moving on and nowhere to move on to. Upstate Nevada was pretty empty. She could rent a car. Maybe. But that would be like running away. Like the assholes had won after all. Alice had long ago decided that assholes would never win again.

* * *

"Hear them sirens last night?" the old guy at reception said when Alice returned her key.

"You told me it was a quiet town."

"It is. It's them passing-through folk."

"Like me?"

He grinned at the pretty Asian woman in front of him, neatly dressed in cotton pants and blouse. "Yeah, I see'd you was trouble the moment you hit town."

She smiled. "What was it?"

"Bikers, they're saying. Beat on some of our guys and torched their car. A classic too. "68 Ford Custom 500." He shook his head.

"How about the guys?"

"They'll mend. Car won't."

That, Alice thought, might be a problem. They'd be sore today, in more ways than one, and it wouldn't take much to figure out she was passing traffic. Still, her bus was due at ten. She only had an hour to kill.

"How big is this place?" she asked.

"Winnemucca? Round about seven thousand folks."

They might be out there now, checking the motels. But they'd be looking for a driver. Hardly anyone took the bus these days.

The old guy pointed out a shortcut to the depot off the back of the motel's parking lot. Alice thanked him, shouldered her pack and tested her ankle. She'd put a compression bandage on it last night, packed ice around it from the machine in the lobby, then stuck her leg up on the bed while she lay on the floor. Rest, ice, compression, elevation. RICE. It seemed to work. Not perfect, but it was definitely on the mend.

She checked her backpack in at the depot then crossed the road for breakfast at a diner called The Little Ray of Sunshine. She found a booth near the back and settled where she could keep an eye on the bus station. A sour-mouthed, sharp-faced waitress—who looked nothing like a little ray of sunshine—took her order. When she was done, Alice stretched out and rested her sprained ankle on the seat opposite. E for elevation.

Then the three guys walked in.

She could tell it was them. One had a wad of gauze taped over his left eye. One had a blue plastic splint taped over his nose. The other had a bruised cheek. Rick. Torch Guy. He was very solicitous. Found his buddies stools at the counter and appeared to be buying. It was like he was trying to make up for his lack of injuries.

They seemed bigger in daylight, a little older than she'd guessed. Late twenties, perhaps. Muscled but heavy, already carrying a few more pounds than they should. It showed in the lines of their jaws and the profiles of their bellies. Their size didn't bother Alice because size rarely correlated with speed. In her experience, it was almost an inverse square thing. Bigger equals slower. Like dinosaurs. But two things did bother her. There were three of them and one of her, and a few hours earlier she'd beaten the crap out of all them.

"Back again?" the sharp-faced waitress said. "Y'all settling in for breakfast this time?"

"I guess," the one with the taped up eye said. Big Jim.

"No sign of them bikers, huh?" She set out three cups and poured coffee. "Reckon they'd've skipped town by now."

"Reckon you're right."

So they had been out looking for her.

Alice checked her watch. The replacement bus was due in twenty minutes. Depending on how long they took over breakfast, it could be cutting things fine. But they hadn't seen her and were unlikely to confront her in public. Not in broad daylight.

Still, she hunkered down and scoped the place out. There was one way in and one way out. Just the double doors past the register at the end of the counter. No rear exit. Unless she vaulted the counter and went out through the kitchen.

She angled herself in the booth to wait them out, wishing she had a newspaper or a magazine. Something to sit behind.

Two more passengers from the stranded bus entered the diner, a middle-aged couple. They paused at the entrance and looked around. Alice tried to catch their attention and wave them over, figuring on safety in numbers, but they didn't notice her in the back corner and took a table by the window.

A guy in overalls with an auto parts logo on the back

came in for a take-out. While the waitress bagged donuts, he leaned on one elbow and talked to the guys at the counter. There was a recollection of last night's troubles. A story about a gang of bikers and their valiant but doomed defense. The guy nodded and shook his head in all the right places. Then the waitress handed him a bag and a cardboard tray of take-out coffees, and he handed back a twenty.

"So what are you doing down town?" Big Jim said.

The auto parts guy explained about the broken-down bus. About a special order coming in from Salt Lake City on its replacement. He took his change, thanked the waitress and left.

The three guys at the counter exchanged glances and leaned together in a huddle. Then the one with the bruised cheek—Rick—sat up, swiveled on his stool, looking around the diner. A whole three hundred and sixty-degree turn just as the sharp-faced waitress, carrying a Bunn flask, leaned in to top up Alice's coffee.

They came as a group after the waitress was done. Two slid into the booth beside her—Rick and driver Davy—while Big Jim took the seat opposite.

Alice didn't react. Continued sipping her coffee. Big Jim clamped her outstretched ankle in a meaty hand. So much for E for Elevation.

"Morning," she said.

"Bitch," he hissed.

"Bikers, huh?" she said. "What would people say if they knew it was just a weedy girl? Perhaps I should call the waitress back and tell her what a bunch of pussies you really are."

"Why don't you try that?" Big Jim said. Then he called

loudly, "Oh Doreen, nothing more here for the moment. OK?"

Something passed between them. A look. An understanding. After that, the booth seemed to be off Doreen's radar.

Big Jim smiled.

"You owe us, bitch," Davy said. His nose splint made the words more comical than threatening. "You wrecked my car."

"Wasn't much of a car."

"I was restoring it."

"So start again."

Alice reached forward and set down her cup. She moved a little faster than normal. The three guys tensed. Just a fraction, but it showed they were wary of her. A good sign. About the only positive sign in this whole mess. She should have listened to her own advice and moved on last night.

Big Jim leaned across the table, fixing her with his unpatched eye. "I got an idea. How about we let you go?"

"Oh, were you detaining me? I was just finishing my coffee."

"You can go. Right after you pay off Davy for what you did to his car. I reckon two thousand ought to cover it. There's a cash machine right across the street."

Alice considered. Two thousand for that heap of junk? She wasn't going to haggle. Or pay. But any place out of this booth would give her a fighting chance.

"OK. Let's go," she said.

"Before we do, we reckon you owe us all a little compensation too."

"And what form would that take?"

"I think you know." Big Jim reached under the table and unzipped his pants.

FIVE

Solikha kept her hands on the windowsill, balanced lightly on the soles of her feet, and lowered herself to the fire escape. The platform groaned quietly as her weight went on it and something underneath shifted. She tensed, hands still on the sill, ready to drag herself back inside if it gave way, but it settled and seemed to hold. Pressed close to the building, sliding one foot after the other, she edged to the far end where a ladder led to the floor below.

The ladder was as rusted as the platform, its rungs eaten through in places. She inched down, careful not to put too much weight on each rung, feeling rust flake off and fall away beneath her hands and the bare soles of her feet.

The fourth-floor platform was in better repair, but its ladder was at the opposite end. She edged across. The rising sun glinted in the grimy windows making it impossible to tell whether the lights inside were on or off, or even whether the rooms were occupied. She kept low, ducked beneath each sill, moving with the stealth of a cat stalking a bird. There were six windows. Six rooms in all.

Six more like her?

The ladder to the third level was in better condition.

She slipped down it quietly, dropping into the shadow of a neighboring building. The sun wouldn't reach here for a half-hour yet, and she was glad to be out of the glare. After a pause to catch her breath, she made her way across to the next ladder, keeping low, counting off the windows as she went. One, two, three, four...

As she passed the fifth, she was arrested by the sound of low sobs.

One more like her?

Straightening, she pressed herself against the building and inched back.

Through a torn curtain, she made out a tiny room and a boy pressed against the glass, one hand outstretched, as if to reach through it to the outside world. She recognized him at once. The cheeky boy from the truck. Not so cheeky now.

She studied him through the steel-framed window. It was open a quarter inch, but there it had frozen, scaly with rust.

She reached across and tapped a fingernail against the glass.

The sobs stopped immediately.

She waited. Heard him move. Saw the tips of his fingers appear around the rusting frame. Both hands. They shook and pushed it, but it remained frozen, as solid as if it had been welded in place.

Solikha drew a breath, swung out and revealed herself, a finger hard against her lips. The boy sat back, startled, but he must have recognized her because his fingers reappeared around the frame, and he whispered something through the gap.

She didn't understand the words, but she didn't need

words to sense his desperation.

She signaled. Made hand gestures. Their combined strength, perhaps?

He pushed. She pulled. The window creaked, lost some flakes of rust, but remained fixed in place.

More gestures. Could he smash it?

A startled look followed by a pointing finger and a shaking head. She guessed there were men outside his room. Any sound would bring them running.

She looked around the fire escape, searching for some sort of tool. This platform was more solid than the one two floors above, but the rail was just as rusted. She held up a hand, signaled. He should wait, then tiptoed back to where the ladder emerged from the floor above.

The upper bar of the handrail there was rusted through at one end. A round piece of steel four feet long. She gripped the loosened end and worked it back and forth, feeling the movement grow easier as the welded joint flexed and bent. There was a faint snap. The freed end fell to the lower rung, landing with a sharp metallic *clack*.

She grabbed the bar and pressed herself against the building, keeping low, worried the sound would draw attention.

Nothing stirred.

A distant rooster crowed.

Solikha let out her breath and headed back to the boy's room.

He was pressed against the glass, head angled to one side, desperate to see where she'd gone. His face relaxed when he saw her returning.

She forced one end of the bar into the gap between the

frame and window, used the side of the sill as a fulcrum, and pressed on the lever formed by the other end. It was a familiar technique. The men of the village often used levers to move large stones or heavy objects.

The window frame groaned. Flakes of rust fell from its edges. Several larger chunks too. There was a creak, then a crack like the snapping of fingers. It sounded like a pistol shot in the dawn air. Solikha ducked. The boy looked over his shoulder at the door.

Nothing happened.

The rooster crowed again.

She set the bar down and examined the window. The lower hinge had broken. Sheared off completely. And the upper hinge was loose. If that went, the whole window would fall out.

She put her hands under the bottom edge and pulled out and back. The frame shifted and twisted, dislodging more chunks of rust and forcing her to support the window's weight. As soon as the gap was wide enough, the boy slithered through and dropped onto the fire escape beside her. Then, between them, they eased the frame back into place.

It was twisted now and wouldn't stay shut. The bottom edge kept sliding out, threatening to drag the whole thing with it. Frame, window, glass and all would go crashing down into the yard below.

Solikha took up the metal bar again and wedged it between the bottom of the frame and one of the handrail supports. It wasn't a good fit. Only just held. But it would do.

They edged away and took the ladder down to the

second floor as a light went on below them. A torch. Someone had been snoozing in the yard behind the building. They could see his sleeping mat through the metal mesh they were standing on.

The torch beam shone at the ground around the mat. The bare concrete was dusted with flakes of rust along with some star-shaped impacts where larger chunks had fallen and burst on the cement. He turned his face up to the fire escape and raised the torch, playing it along the outer edge of the landing on which they were standing.

Solikha and the boy pressed flat against the building.

The beam swept past them, moving higher, but it was too feeble to pick out any detail. She glimpsed the man's face as he swung back and forth. One of the truck men. The older one with the pockmarked face.

He muttered something and went to the back door, pounding on it with the butt of his torch. That was their cue. They moved quickly to the far end of the platform and the final length of ladder, a shortened segment that ended eight feet from the ground. There was another, longer section attached to it, meant to slide down when weight went on it, but it was rusted in place.

They heard the back door open and the sound of voices. Flame Hair came out, looked at the pocks of rust, went back inside and returned with a bigger torch.

Solikha climbed down the stump of ladder till her feet reached the lower rung. Then she took the weight on her arms and lowered herself further till she was hanging at full stretch. That made the drop only four feet, not far at all, and she landed silently, scissoring her legs to take the impact before rolling into deeper shadows behind some trash cans.

The boy hesitated. She waved him on.

There was a click. A bright beam flooded the area. The space behind the building was bare concrete, stacked with produce and crates of bottles. High walls surrounded them on three sides, capped with broken glass. There was no way out here, only through the building itself.

The light moved from side to side, throwing the upper levels of the fire escape into sharp relief as it crisscrossed back and forth. The boy moved, copying Solikha's descent down the shortened ladder as the torch beam paused at the third level, stopping at the sagging window frame and its metal prop.

The two men exchanged words. Flame Hair yelled something at the open back door, calling to a third man, swiveling and lowering the torch as he did so, catching the boy just as he dropped from the ladder.

There was a moment's startled silence. The boy landed smoothly, got to his feet, dusted off his hands and shielded his eyes from the glare. He said something and ambled towards them, looking for all the world like he belonged there. From where she was hiding, Solikha saw the men exchange puzzled looks. Flame Hair snapped something. Sharp words. The boy laughed and replied lightly.

He was bluffing them.

A brief interrogation followed. The boy stood calm and confident, hands on hips. He was getting away with it! Then a light went on in the third floor room where he'd been, and they heard a muffled exclamation as a face appeared at the window.

The boy went to run, but Flame Hair grabbed him by the arm. Solikha leaped from her hiding place, hurling the only weapon she could find—a metal trash can lid—that caught Flame Hair a glancing blow and made him stagger.

As it clattered to the ground, the figure at the upstairs window pushed it open, dislodging the metal bar and sending it spinning to the ground. A second later, the damaged window—frame and all—followed, bouncing off the fire escape and landing just behind them, the glass bursting with the sound of a miniature explosion.

Flame Hair, still holding the boy, began shouting at the top of his voice. The man with the pockmarked face backed away, wary of more things falling from the building, while the guy at the upstairs window clambered out onto the fire escape.

Solikha found the fallen metal bar, grasped the end in both hands, and swung it low, catching Flame Hair on one knee. His shouts turned to a shriek of pain, and he released the boy. Solikha dropped the bar, shouted, and raced towards the lighted door.

There was a groan from the scaffolding overhead. The figure on the platform realized his mistake and dived back towards the window as a section of the fire escape peeled way, tilting and sagging. Crumbling supports popped from the wall, gathering momentum and bringing the whole lower section down around the men in the yard below.

Solikha ran, followed by the boy. She had only a vague notion of where she was heading, but if the back of the building was a dead end, the front must be the exit. But where was it? Which way? The place was like a maze.

She darted left and right down narrow service passages, past a kitchen, through a beaded curtain, then slowed, suddenly finding herself in a different part of the building.

The boy ran into her from behind. They staggered, held each other and looked about.

Beyond the bead curtain was a wide carpeted hallway with rooms running off it left and right. Muted lights, the smell of incense, textured paper on the walls. A grand staircase ran down from the floor above, fanning out at beneath a gleaming chandelier.

At the far end, across a marbled entrance, they saw two stout doors, closed and bolted. One had a grille set in it so that visitors could be inspected before being let in. They were manned by a stocky guard dressed like a hotel doorman who paced slowly back and forth.

The boy pressed a finger to his lips, seized Solikha's wrist and strode out into the hallway, dragging her along behind.

The guard looked around, a surprised expression on his face when he saw who he was dealing with. The boy said something, gesturing at Solikha. The man frowned, moved towards the bolted door, then hesitated.

The boy snapped at him and gestured over his shoulder with his free hand, like he was giving orders.

If she hadn't been so frightened, Solikha would have laughed.

Still eying them uncertainly, the guard unlatched the door.

Footsteps thundered down the staircase and there were calls and shouts from beyond the beaded curtain. The guard went to slam the door again, but the boy wedged it with his foot and shoved Solikha through, then followed her in a staggering run as they stumbled down three steps and raced out into the street.

Six

Alice took up her coffee again. It was fresh, but not very hot. Useless as a weapon. Pity.

Big Jim edged forward in his seat. The fabric of his jeans brushed her knee as he spread his legs. He gave her a challenging look. Superior. A half-smile playing on his lips.

Alice sipped her coffee and considered her options. She was backed into a corner. Literally. She'd chosen a rear booth to be out of the way, and that was a mistake because out of the way also meant out of sight. The middle-aged couple from the bus hadn't spotted her when they came in. If they had, they would have joined her. A fellow traveler; shared experience; a chance to bitch about the delay. Doreen the waitress knew she was there, but that was the waitress's job. And now Doreen had been told to look the other way.

Strike one.

The place was pretty much empty. Apart from Alice and the middle-aged couple and the three guys. It was work o'clock for those who had work. Too early for morning break, way too early for lunch, and still too early to expect much passing traffic. So the chance of the place filling up with potential witnesses in the next five minutes was practically zero.

Strike two.

And Alice wasn't carrying her work ID. If she had, this problem would just disappear. If she'd been carrying it last night, none of this would have happened.

Maybe.

But who packs their ID going out for a run?

OK, Alice did. But driver's license only. In case of accidents.

And who takes their work ID on vacation?

OK, Alice did. But that had been a last minute thing. People had a habit of not taking her seriously, so sometimes a little official ID helped. But this trip was strictly personal, strictly on her own time, so her ID was currently tucked away in the bottom of her backpack. And that was sitting on a luggage trolley waiting to be loaded onto a replacement bus at the depot across the road.

Strike three.

Alice looked at the guys over the rim of her coffee cup. Two options: over the table, or under it. Not much choice there. Six strong, kicking legs in a cramped space versus six strong arms in a slightly more open one. The broken nose would be sensitive, likewise the patched eye, but Big Jim still had a hand clamped around her ankle. That was really going to slow her down, whichever way she went.

The real problem was that she hadn't done enough damage last night. She should have put them all in the hospital.

Her hand on the coffee cup felt numb. She drew a breath, angry at herself. This was all her fault.

No, it wasn't. *Stop that shit!* None of it was her doing.

They got what they deserved last night, and they deserved what they were about to get now.

Rick—Torch Guy—the guy with the bruised cheek, was on her immediate left. He'd missed most of the action last night and had something to prove. Coming away without a medical endorsement of his actions suggested a lack of commitment. Which probably explained his bravado today as he leaned in, reached beneath the table and unzipped himself. "And when you're done there..." he said, squeezing her thigh.

Alice set her cup in its saucer and looked around at them. "Thanks for the offer guys, but this place already has a supply of toothpicks."

She reached over, picked one out of the holder and flicked her teeth with it.

It took a second for her meaning to register. Big Jim's smile disappeared.

"Hey, relax. I'm kidding," Alice said. "So you guys do this often? Pick on girls, I mean. Three on one?"

No one spoke.

"I'm only asking because I want to know if I'm dealing with first-timers."

They stared at her.

"Well?"

"You ain't dealing with first-timers," Big Jim said.

"Local girls?"

No one spoke.

"Passing strangers then. Like me."

No one spoke.

"They put up much of a fight?"

No one spoke.

"Hey, give me something here guys. I'm trying to figure out how rough you like it."

Rick looked from her to Big Jim and back. "You mean you'll give us what we want?"

Alice worked the toothpick. Drew it out, examined it, picked up another and licked the pointed end. Slowly. Making sure they registered the action.

"Maybe," she said.

The three guys exchanged glances.

"You didn't much want it last night," Big Jim said.

"You got to learn how to talk to a girl." Alice tugged her ankle from his grasp and lowered her leg to the floor. "Your initial approach could do with some work, you know." She turned to Rick. "So how do you like it? Submissive or spunky?"

"I like spunky. Like that redhead," he said to his buddies. "She put up a fight. She was fun."

Big Jim glared at him and shook his head.

"You prefer that, huh?" Alice said. "To someone who just lies there and takes it?"

"Hell yeah! Or them ones that beg you don't. They know you're gonna do it anyway. Dumb bitches."

"Shut up, dick-brain," Big Jim said.

"And do you tie them up or just hold on?"

"Depends on how feisty they are. That redhead, we had to tie her and hold her down. She was fun."

"Shut up, Rick."

"You got any pictures? I bet you have."

"Hell yeah!" He pulled a phone from his pants pocket.

"Jesus, Rick."

He switched it on and showed her, flicked through

image after image. A young redheaded woman, bound and brutalized. Clearly screaming. Three leering faces enjoying her torment.

Alice felt sick but forced an approving nod.

"No complaints?"

"Not when we tell 'em my daddy's chief of police and Davy's is the mayor." He sniggered. "Then they're just happy to let us see 'em out of town." He gave her a significant look. "Cos there's an awful lot of desert out there, you know?"

Alice knew. About a hundred thousand square miles of it in Nevada alone. A lot of space for lone travelers to disappear in.

"So," Rick set his phone on the table-top and zoomed the image out to show a whole album full of pictures. "You up for it or what?"

Alice glanced at the others then back at Rick. She could see the look in his eyes, the quickened pulse in his throat. He moistened his lips.

Over Big Jim's shoulder, she saw the replacement bus edge to the front of the depot, sunlight glinting off its plate glass windows. The driver came down the steps and opened the luggage racks in the side. Began loading bags from a trolley. She saw her backpack go in. She had ten minutes, tops.

"Why not?" she said. "I've got some time to kill. Where are we going?"

Big Jim grabbed her wrist. "You gotta prove your good intentions first," he said. "Right here. Right now." He turned her loose and sat back.

"Well of course." She smiled and slipped beneath the table.

Alice checked she had all she needed—travel pack, phone, bus ticket—then gritted her teeth and did what she had to do. Left hand, right hand.

Rick and Big Jim slid forward slightly at her touch, easing back in their seats. She positioned things carefully. Gave herself a countdown. Three, two, one...

Two toothpicks. Two thumbs. Two urethras. She pressed down hard. Two pairs of hips jerked back explosively, but only one voice cried out. A low, shocked gasp. "Jesus Christ!"

Alice wiped her hands on two pairs of jeans and pushed out past the third pair of legs. She stood, straightened, and brushed herself down.

Halfway down the booth, Rick and Big Jim were locked, half bent, convulsed with shock and pain. Rick still hadn't spoken, just made choking noises as his hand scrunched the tablecloth beneath it, drawing in the coffee cup and sugar shaker like they were being sucked towards a black hole. Their faces were like Halloween masks of horror.

Nose splint—Davy—stared at his friends then at Alice, his eyes showing a mix of puzzlement and fear. She took his splint between her thumb and forefinger and gave it a tweak. Just enough to get his attention. He gave a little nasal cry and tried to pull away.

"You see what I did to them? No, you didn't. And trust me, you don't want to know." Rick finally gave a low moan. "But if you don't sit there quietly, you'll find out. You understand?"

He swallowed, not taking his eyes off her.

She let him go, reached over, picked up Rick's phone, and walked out.

The waitress, Doreen, looked up as she passed the counter.

"Big Jim's paying," Alice said.

SEVEN

The sky between the buildings outside was pale with dawn's luminescence. Apart from the light of a few lamps and discreet neon signs, the street still lay in night's shadow.

The boy led, Solikha followed, and they ran on, not knowing where they were. He chose directions at random, concerned only with putting distance between themselves and their captors. They couldn't get lost. They were already lost. They just had to get away.

Solikha felt overwhelmed. She'd never seen a city before. Even the big village where her parents had taken her to watch television had no more than a dozen of streets, but here the streets went on and on. A vast interlinking web of alleys, lanes and thoroughfares. Some crowded, some empty, some jammed with traffic, some filled with market stalls. Several times she felt sure they must have doubled back by mistake, must be making another circuit of the same small area, only to find some new building or landmark or vendor she hadn't seen before.

Eventually, they found themselves at the side of a broad brown river with strange looking boats plying the waters like long-tailed fish. A market ran through the twisting streets nearby, and fruit and produce sellers were busy setting out their wares.

They stopped and regarded each other properly for the first time. He was a head taller than she was, broader too, but still with the skinny arms of a boy. He had a winning smile that lit his face like a ray of sunshine and his dark eyes were full of intelligence and mischief.

The boy was breathing heavily, but composed himself and bowed his head, saying something in a language she didn't understand, but she guessed his meaning well enough: Thank you.

He said something else then laughed. She told him she didn't understand, and he looked at her curiously. Then he tapped his chest, bowed again and said, "Chatri."

She nodded, bowed in return and replied, "Solikha."

* * *

Chatri was hungry. Solikha saw his eyes linger on the food stalls as they moved through the market and realized she was too. She hadn't eaten since the previous afternoon.

They paused in front of a fruit stall. Bananas, dragonfruit, mangos, lychees and custard apples were layered in a colorful array on three angled shelves. Chatri pretended to examine them then looked suddenly to one side, frowning at something in the distance. The fruit seller looked too, and as quick as lightning Chatri snatched two mangoes and flicked them back towards Solikha. She caught them, more out of surprise than anything, and a minute later they were round the corner in an alley, laughing and tearing at the sweet fruit, the juice running down their chins.

When they were done, he indicated they should try again at another stall and made to move on, but Solikha reached out an arm and stopped him. She unbuttoned the pocket of her dress, took out the bunched up wad of notes and held it out. Chatri's eyes widened. He wiped his hands on his shirt front and cupped them to receive the load.

He asked her something. She guessed he wanted to know where she'd got it, but all she could do was gesture with her thumb. Back there. He nodded in understanding and gave her an admiring look, perhaps thinking she was a pickpocket. Well, let him think that.

They squatted and flattened out the notes, separating them into two piles. The dull ones to one side, the brighter ones to the other. Solikha preferred the colorful ones in shades of blue, green, red and purple, all with the same picture of a scholarly looking man on one side.

Chatri squared the piles and folded them in half. He held the dull ones over his heart before handing them back, indicating they were valuable. Then he handed back the colorful ones, taking only a single green note from the top.

He tapped her arm and beckoned her to follow.

They dined at a roadside food stall, a cart built on bicycle wheels with signs she couldn't read. Stewed pork and rice, a dish Chatri called *Khao Kha Moo*. He held up his plastic fork and made her say the words. She tried them, feeling the strangeness of another tongue, and laughing at his pained expression at her first attempt.

They followed it with murtabak—thin pancakes filled with banana, egg, and condensed milk. They sat on the curb beside a stormwater drain. Chatri burped contentedly and pushed his plastic plate aside. Solikha ran a finger over hers to get every last morsel of the sweet, sticky filling. He looked at her and said something she didn't understand, but his smile spoke for him. For the first time in weeks, Solikha realized she was happy.

* * *

She didn't know how he found the old men, but she was rapidly learning that Chatri was streetwise and resourceful. His only tools were quick intelligence, a cheeky smile and an ability to assume a haughty manner. As if—despite his ragged blue shirt—he was lord of the district.

The old ones sat in groups in a dusty quadrangle under a sparse chamchuri tree. Sheets of corrugated iron had been tied to the lower branches to provide extra shade, making it look like a storm had just blown through. Some of the men were playing games on painted boards that she didn't understand. Others sat reading or talking. Chatri called to them in his cheeky, haughty manner and got their attention, then he pointed to his companion. Solikha shrank back, but he took her by the elbow and led her before them as if she was a special guest of the village elder. She glanced at the dozen pairs of eyes regarding her and respectfully dropped her head.

Chatri shook her arm and gestured. It took some seconds before she understood what he wanted. He expected her to speak. But surely not in front of all these venerable ones? She blushed at the thought and dropped her head again.

He shook her arm and nodded encouragingly, and suddenly she understood.

"My name is Solikha Duong," she began, recalling a litany from school. "My father's name is Atith and my mother Chankrisna. I come from the village of Trasek Chrum in the district of Malai in the province of Banteay Meanchey. My country is the Kingdom of Cambodia. Our capital is Phnom Penh and our Prime Minister is..."

A ripple of chatter ran around the men and a voice called, "Where are your parents, child?"

"With the spirits of the earth and air, sir," she replied, turning towards the speaker and bowing, even before she realized he was speaking her tongue. It had been more than a week since she'd heard it from another's lips.

"How do you come here?"

"In a truck, sir. Brought here by bad men." Her voice quavered at the words. And at his look. She could see he understood.

"Please sir, where am I?" she ventured.

"You are in Bangkok, child. The greatest city in Thailand."

She thought of the battered map on the classroom wall. Thailand was a neighbor, but Thailand was another country, and Bangkok was a long way from her home.

"You must speak Thai here," he told her. "No one speaks Khmer."

"But I do not know it, sir."

"Then you must learn it. Quickly."

There was some discussion amongst the men, and words with Chatri. Harsh ones. He looked chastened. Then the Khmer speaker said in her tongue, "You come on a truck with this boy?"

"Yes, sir."

"With truck men?

"Yes, sir."

"You run away?"

"Yes, sir."

He looked her up and down. "But from house, not from truck."

"Yes, sir." How did he know?

He shook his head. "You run from house. You should not. You belong to house now. You must go back. This boy is bad. He will make you trouble. The house men will make you trouble if you don't go back. The only place for Khmer girl is in the house."

Her breathing faltered. She felt the start of tears. How could he say that if he knew why they had taken her there and what they had done to her? She looked to Chatri for guidance, but his face was still pale from their rebukes.

"You have been with *farang?*" the man said.

She looked at him. She didn't understand.

"*Farang.*" He repeated and tapped his cheek. "Pale skin. Westerner. They use you?"

Her heart pounded in her chest. He knew everything.

She didn't answer. Couldn't. But she didn't need to. Her expression spoke for her.

The old man turned his head and spat on the ground, then spoke with the others. There was a consensus of nodding heads. Chatri tried to speak but was shouted down. Fingers were pointed. Arms raised.

"Khmer girl must go back," the old man told her. "Your

place is in the house. They will make trouble if you don't go back. They will make trouble for us if they find you here. Go. *Go!*"

EIGHT

A lice boarded the bus and took a rear seat. She nodded to the middle-aged couple from the diner, to the old black guy, and the two college graduates from the day before. The breakdown had turned strangers into passing friends.

Her hands still smelled of antiseptic handwash. So did the phone she'd taken from Rick. She'd wiped it down with paper towels in the washroom at the depot, wanting to rid herself of every taint of the three guys. For a long while she left it resting on the magazine in her lap as she sat staring out the window at the endless desert rolling past. Finally, she steeled herself and began her examination.

The pictures were in a folder labeled "Fun". Some of them made her flinch and look away to the sunlit day outside the tinted windows and the blue-fringed hills in the distance. Each shot was dated with a glowing imprint in the bottom right-hand corner. There'd be more, she knew. The metadata stored with them would hold details of exact times and locations, but even a cursory look showed at least three young women had been subject to the gang's attentions in the last nine months.

What had happened to them? How could she find out?

Had any of them filed complaints?

Probably not. They'd have been relieved to escape with their lives. She recalled Rick's words and the hint of menace they contained: "There's an awful lot of desert out there."

She knew the figures. Many victims didn't complain. Especially those subjected to gang rape. Multiple perpetrators meant multiple avenues for retribution. And that was without them claiming to be the sons of the local police chief and the mayor.

She considered sending the phone's SIM and data cards somewhere, anonymously, but the pictures on their own proved nothing. The guys would claim the sex was consensual, or that they'd paid the girls. That it was all an act. The internet was full of stuff like that. It was often difficult to tell professionals from amateurs, and amateurs from genuine victims. If there was an investigation—small chance—and complaints did result—smaller chance still—it would be the testimony of three against one, months or even years after the alleged crime. Long after bruises had healed and any physical evidence was gone.

The miles rolled past. They crossed the state line into California. When she'd boarded the bus, she thought Winnemucca, Nevada, and the three guys were behind her. But they weren't. This wasn't over.

Did you ever really leave anything behind?

She looked down and saw her right hand gripping the phone so hard her knuckles showed white. A kind of fury burned inside her. A white rage. But what could she do?

The first thing to do was control it. Angry people did dumb things, made dumb mistakes.

Revenge is a dish best served cold.

Alice closed her eyes, took three deep breaths, considered the situation as coolly as she could, and came to a decision: she'd do what she could.

She turned the phone over, slipped a nail under the cover and pried off the back. She took out the memory card, tucked it in her wallet, then replaced the back. Turning the phone over, she studied her reflection in the smooth glass front.

The bus rumbled on.

The phone was slim, shiny, looked expensive. She stared at herself as she gripped the ends and bent it till the glass cracked with a faint pop. She kept on bending. Bits came loose and dropped to the magazine in her lap, fragments of plastic, glass and trim. A thin green film of circuit board showed through the ragged tear. She twisted, turned and worked it until the two halves parted.

Taking a travel sickness bag from the seat pocket in front, she folded the magazine into a U and sluiced away the remains of the phone. Then she rolled down the top of the bag, sealed it with a series of folds, then set it on the seat beside her, ready for the trash.

No, this wasn't over.

* * *

It was a seven block walk to the Sacramento hostel, a Victorian mansion built by a Gold Rush millionaire. She took a single room with twin beds. A dorm bed would have been half the price, but dorm rooms were a lottery that Alice didn't feel like taking right now. Sometimes hell was other people.

She showered and changed, consulted a tourist map she'd picked up at the front desk, and went for a walk.

East Lawn Memorial Park was a leafy green resting place three miles from the hostel. The cemetery office was still open when she got there. She consulted a computerized register, located the man she was looking for and, with the help of a map from the counter, set off to find him.

Joseph Lewis Moncrieff had a far better resting place than he deserved. Green lawn, the shade of maple trees, a polished marble headstone that might have been erected last week, not two decades earlier. Alice considered it as she studied the words:

Joseph Lewis Moncrieff
30 May 1969–2 June 1995
Loving son of Beryl and David
Brother of Mary, Annie, and Suzanne
"A good man sorely missed."

If she'd been the spitting kind, Alice would have done so. A big fat loogie on the fat prick's shiny stone.

NINE

The collapse came suddenly. They were crossing the corner of a leafy park near the river when Solikha simply stopped in her tracks. Chatri was ahead. He turned and came back to her, his look quizzical. In reply, she closed her eyes, clasped her hands together and placed them against the side of her face.

He nodded and tapped his chest. Me too.

It was past midday. The air was warm, and the bustle of the endless city that surrounded them seemed more distant in the park. The long night, the long morning and the hours of walking hit them at a rush. It was all Chatri could do to steer her to the shelter of some long grass before they both collapsed in a wave of fatigue.

Despite her weariness, Solikha couldn't sleep at first. The aches of her body consumed her. A low throb that pulsed and pounded like a living creature somewhere deep inside. She tried to piece together what had happened, how she'd come to this, but the wounds were raw and the scars ran deep. When she finally dreamed, it wasn't of blood or murder or frenzied flight. What forced her awake with a cry, what left her tearing at the grass with grubby hands, was the face of Young One, smiling, laughing, making games with her. Coaxing and encouraging. She thought she'd found a friend.

The shadows told her it was late afternoon. She was curled on one side in the shade of a baobab. The boy, Chatri, was curled behind her, one arm resting on her shoulder, holding her as if she was a toy. He murmured something in his sleep. Twitched. Then he let out a louder cry. A stronger convulsion went through him, and she felt him shake himself awake. She closed her eyes again, listened as his ragged breathing slowed and the choking sobs subsided.

She lay quietly, recalling the old man's words: "They use you?"

They'd used him too.

She sensed him sit up, heard him sniff, counted down from twenty and began to stir herself. By the time she sat up and looked over at him, he was smiling again.

He made a sign. Two fingers to his mouth. They should eat. Solikha nodded and took out the money. He selected another green note and passed the fat wad back. She tucked it away, wondering what they would do when it was gone.

They rose carefully and looked around. It was a comfortable spot. Quiet. Worth remembering. They'd need somewhere to sleep tonight.

They made their way back towards the park gates. The market lay three blocks north and Solikha's mouth was already watering at the thought of the food stalls and fruit sellers and all the tempting treats on offer.

A guard in the uniform of a park custodian watched them pass through the stone pillars at the entrance and frowned thoughtfully. Then he rummaged in his pocket, found a few coins and walked over to the payphone on the corner.

The market was a delight to the senses. The smells, sights, sounds, and colors seemed brighter than before, enhanced by strings of clear incandescent bulbs strung from stall to stall. It lay in the shadow of tall buildings either side of a narrow road. Elsewhere, it was late afternoon. Here it was already evening.

They dined on fish in a spicy-sweet chili sauce. Chatri held out his hand, thumb up, and said, *"Dee?"* Then he flattened it, tilting it from side to side and said, *"Oh-kay?"* Then he held it thumb down and said, *"Mai-dee?"* and looked at her quizzically.

"Dee," Solikha said. *"Dee, dee, dee!"*

He laughed.

They sat on a broken curbstone in a narrow lane opposite a side entrance to the market, their feet in the gutter, licking every speck from their plastic forks and paper plates. A fresh breeze came off the alley, carrying with it the scents of herbs and flowers from the nearby stands.

A battered brown tuk-tuk went past with three men on it. It swerved, braked sharply and stopped across the road. The men got off and fanned out.

Solikha wasn't sure what alerted her to their presence. The sunglasses, perhaps. Or the clean white shirts, tan pants, and brown shoes they all wore. Like a uniform. Or perhaps it was the way they separated when they stepped off the tuk-tuk. No words passed between them. It was a practiced move.

Two images flashed across her mind: the girl with the burned arm being beaten, and the old man in the quadrangle who said they'd come looking for her. But how?

she'd wondered. How would they ever find her in a city as crowded as this, amidst these choked streets and teeming markets?

Suddenly, she knew.

They should never have stopped, never have slept. They should have kept on moving and got far away. The house men didn't know about the stolen money. They'd search the streets nearby in widening circles. Easy if you had a tuk-tuk and many men. How far could two children go on foot? They'd have to rest. Have to eat. But the real giveaway, the real betrayal, was the pretty dress with its bold floral pattern. She remembered the matronly woman in the red shawl selecting her size from a rack of identical dresses.

Uniforms.

Like tan pants, white shirts, and brown shoes.

Solikha elbowed Chatri and flicked her eyes across the road at the man in sunglasses advancing on them. He saw her expression and understood immediately.

There was a high stone wall behind them. No way out there. Two of the men had gone wide, effectively closing off the sides of the narrow lane, so Chatri and Solikha bolted straight ahead, towards the body of the market, trying to dodge the man in front.

He threw out his arms, caught Chatri's blue shirt in one hand—the fabric tore as Chatri pulled free—and Solikha's wrist in the other.

The twist and pull dragged her off her feet. She fell, grazing her knees. The man yanked her upright, yelling to his friends. Solikha saw Chatri up ahead. He stopped, turned and ran back. She seized the man's arm and sunk her teeth into his wrist as the boy shunted into him from behind, stabbing at his shoulder with the plastic fork he was still carrying. The fork broke harmlessly, but Solikha appreciated the gesture. And the distraction was enough. She managed to twist free.

They raced away, urgent cries behind them as the men regrouped. She heard the tuk-tuk roar into life and glanced back. Two of the men followed on foot while the third raced away to cut off their retreat.

Chatri was quick, dodging shoppers, leaping crates and produce scattered in the narrow, twisting path between the stalls. Solikha couldn't keep up. He was taller and his legs were longer, but it was mostly her dress. The long, hateful dress that had given them away. She hauled it up to free her legs, careless now of her lack of underthings, and held it bunched in one hand as she sprinted after him.

They made good progress. They were more nimble than their pursuers and could duck under things and dart between people. Solikha heard angry cries in her wake as one of the men shoved someone aside in his haste.

This part of the market ended at a busy intersection, pooling on the pavement before continuing on down a side street to the right. The man on the tuk-tuk appeared, riding straight up onto the sidewalk, blocking their exit. Chatri was almost on top of him and barreled into him as he stepped out of the vehicle, knocking him off balance. The man fell sideways into the stall of a vendor of metal pots, bringing down the display in a series of resounding clangs and crashes. Solikha leaped over a rolling brass planter and ran on.

Chatri disappeared, weaving through the traffic at the intersection. Six lanes. A segment of a huge circular roundabout. Cars, buses, trucks, tuk-tuks, scooters, and bicycles in a slow but steadily moving confusion of merging traffic.

Solikha hesitated. She was a village girl. Traffic unnerved her. Her parents had died beneath the wheels of a truck. She paused, wary, as footsteps thundered up behind.

That reminder was enough. She darted out recklessly, brushing past the fender of a car and drawing angry cries from a weaving cyclist. Suddenly she was in the midst of the moving throng, lost between a bus and a truck loaded with woven baskets, forced to keep pace with them and unsure of how to get past. She couldn't see the men now. Or Chatri. Or the pavement opposite.

A moment of panic. She was startled by a blaring horn. It was answered by other toots and shouts, but they weren't directed at her. Then Chatri reappeared around the front of the bus, waving her towards him.

They kept low and stayed with the traffic. It was good cover as it moved in stops and starts, and even when it did surge briefly, it didn't go at much above a jogging pace. They saw the men in sunglasses once, one lane over, visible through the open sides of a tuk-tuk, scanning left and right, but facing the wrong way.

Chatri led her back to the side of the road, the same side from which they'd entered the roundabout. Then he indicated they should go back through the market, back the way they'd come.

At first, she thought he was crazy, tried to tell him so, but he insisted, and it took her a moment to appreciate his cunning. The house men were expecting them to run away, to put as much distance as possible between themselves and their pursuers, not double back.

Keeping low, she caught a glimpse of one of them on the far side of the road, casting about, his back towards them.

The pot seller was rearranging his dented stock when they returned. Chatri slunk past in case he was recognized as the cause of the calamity, and they began retracing their steps, following the twisting path between the stalls, a stiff breeze at their backs.

Chatri nudged her and grinned. "*Dee?*"

"*Dee.*" She nudged him back.

Suddenly they were laughing. The ragged boy in the ragged blue shirt and the girl with her bunched up skirt. Laughing fit to burst.

Then a figure stepped from a shadowed recess and seized her around the waist. She struggled and squealed, then saw who it was. Flame Hair.

TEN

The port city of Laem Chabang lies sixty miles southeast of Bangkok in the heart of Chonburi province. It's Thailand's busiest port, and the twenty-third busiest port on the planet, handling around six million TEUs of freight a year.

International freight is moved in intermodal containers—reusable steel boxes typically measuring twenty or forty-foot in length by eight feet wide and eight feet high. The term "intermodal" means they can be switched between different types of transportation—truck, train or ship. TEU stands for Twenty-foot Equivalent Unit, an inexact measure of cargo capacity based on the original containers developed by the US military in the 1950s.

A battered yellow Volvo truck carrying a single forty-foot container lumbered up to the holding area of Wharf 2A where a container lift truck picked it up and added it to the top of a three-high stack near the back. The stack was part of a shipment bound for the world's twenty-second busiest port, Long Beach in California.

The container was painted light gray and sat, bland and anonymous, in a stack of a hundred and fifty others, just one of the seventeen million containers in use around the world. It's only identifying feature was the stenciled writing on a panel on the side showing its ISO 6346 designation: an eleven-digit container identification number followed by a four-digit type code. The ID number consisted of a three-digit owner code (false), a category identifier ("U" to signify freight), and a six-digit serial number, followed by a check digit. The type code showed it was a 42V2—a forty-foot container with a mechanical ventilation system, located internally.

The ventilation system had been scrupulously maintained.

* * *

Alice stopped at a downtown bar and ordered a beer. It was early. The place was nearly empty. The barman set down a bowl of complimentary pretzels with her drink. She picked at them idly, wondering what to do about dinner.

"Hey." A guy up the bar raised an eyebrow at her.

She ignored him and picked up another pretzel.

"You new round here?" He sidled over. "Only, I don't think I've seen you in here before."

Did this shit never end?

"I'm a lesbian," she said. And in case he was really dumb, added, "I like girls."

He stopped, shrugged. "Well... that's something we've got in common." He grinned as if this was the most original line in the world. Then he looked her up and down, leaned in close and said, "Maybe I could cure you."

Alice leaned in closer. "And maybe I could cut your balls

off."

"Whoa!" He held up a hand and backed away. "Play nice now."

Alice kept her eyes on him, pushing him away by cold-stare power alone. He shuffled back to his corner. Alice turned back to her beer and took another pretzel.

Same old, same old. A single guy stops at a bar; he's looking for a drink. A single girl stops at a bar; she's looking for a man. And Alice did tend to draw attention.

It was a quality impossible to pin down. It wasn't painted on or shampooed in. It went beyond the wide eyes, the curved lips, and the flawless skin. Beyond the slender, shapely body. Something that shone from every pore, like a beacon that burned inside her. A bright light that attracted moths and assorted creepy-crawlies.

Law enforcement had been a long-abiding dream and acceptance at Quantico beyond anything she'd dared hope for. She'd thrown herself into the FBI's rigorous training programs, achieving straight A's in everything from marksmanship to the assault course, but even there she'd been singled out. Her file was marked "Unsuitable for undercover work". She was simply too memorable. In the words of her boss at the time, "Unforgettable."

Besides, field work was mostly grunt work. The FBI preferred to use her intelligence. After a mandatory six months as a rookie agent attached to a bunch of no-hope investigators, she was kicked back to base and spent the next seven years behind a computer screen doing analysis and research.

She was good. She'd made some good connections. Intuitive ones linking disparate elements of the criminal underworld that mere data gathering overlooked. The timing of phone call, a high school graduation date, and the flight time between Washington and Miami led to the exposure of a drug cartel in one case. In another, the coincidence of names used at two different rental agencies four hundred miles apart led to the vehicle used to transport a dead capo's body and enough forensics to convict a rival gang boss. She'd got a commendation for that one but only took part in the bust via a live video link in a fourth-floor conference room.

Still, she'd kept up her core training. Fitness, marksmanship, weaponry, self-defense. Familiarity with the latest counter-terrorism techniques. At each annual appraisal she expressed a desire for a more active role, but as time moved on it became clear they preferred to keep her welded to a desk. She was doing great work. Why mess with that?

Three months earlier, after the sudden death of her adoptive parents, Alice found herself the beneficiary of their modest estate, shared with her half-sister. Their loss was a profound shock, one she still felt two months later when her birthday rolled around. Her twenty-ninth. Another shock. It wasn't the prospect of approaching the dreaded Three-O—Alice could pass for twenty, was still sometimes ID'd in bars —but the realization that it represented a grim sort of anniversary. A realization that there were still things in her life left undone.

At first, she considered quitting. The money from the estate gave her a degree of independence, but when she talked it over with a colleague, told him she wanted to see more of her adoptive country, maybe even the world, he suggested she take her time.

Murray Ames was Old School, a father figure to many in her department. "You've got a bit of leave built up. Why not take it first? What do they owe you? A month? Two? Use it. Try life on the outside. See how it feels."

He was right. Two months should be enough. It was a good stopgap too if she changed her mind. Or if things didn't work out. Plus, she got to keep her badge. It might be useful.

But only if she didn't bury it in the bottom of her backpack.

The bar was filling up. Two other guys had joined the creep at the end of the counter. She felt the gaze of appraising eyes as she finished her beer and heard a mumbled word: dyke. She smiled. It wasn't true, but it would do.

ELEVEN

Flame Hair snatched her off her feet and spun her around, his mouth a snarl of triumph. Solikha squirmed and struggled in his grip, but it tightened even more, making her gasp with pain. Chatri bunched his fists and struck out, but Flame Hair kicked him aside and carried on, still holding Solikha by the waist.

He was limping, she noticed, recalling the blow she'd struck him with the iron bar that morning, but it didn't seem to slow him down.

They'd been foolish. If the house men were looking for them, it was silly to suppose they'd only send three men. Especially in a city this size. She'd killed two *farang*. There was probably a reward. For all she knew, half the population was out hunting for them.

If only I'd changed this hateful dress.

Chatri came after them, shouting and calling for help, but though people looked, no one challenged Flame Hair. Not when they saw the fierce look on his face and the muscled arm that held the struggling girl. An angry father dealing with wayward children. It was none of their business.

Chatri grabbed at his clothing, threw stones and a

piece of rotten fruit, but each attack was swatted away as if he were no more than an annoying insect.

Flame Hair climbed the steps leading to the entrance of a building and looked about, catching the eye of the tuk-tuk driver at the far end of the market. He waved and gestured to the street ahead. The driver waved back and raced off to meet them.

As they plunged back into the market, Solikha remembered the money in her pocket. Anything to slow them down...

She tore open the pocket, pulled out the wads of notes and threw them into the air. The stiff breeze caught them and carried them on ahead, a swirling cloud of colorful cash.

There was a beat, a moment of disbelief, then shoppers, traders, and stallholders surged for what seemed like a windfall from the gods. A clamor of voices rose ahead of them, each one feeding off the excited cries of the one before, and their progress was suddenly blocked by a stampede.

Flame Hair stopped, puzzled by the surging crowd.

Chatri seized his chance. Seeing something frying in an iron skillet at a nearby food stall, he grabbed it and swung it at Flame Hair's injured knee. The contents spilled and sprayed across the ground. A muffled thump was followed by a yelp of pain.

Flame Hair staggered, tripped and fell, taking Solikha down with him.

Clasping the handle of the skillet in both hands, Chatri swung it like an Olympic hammer thrower. The blow struck Flame Hair on the head. The skillet chimed like a temple gong, and he pitched forward, dropping like a sack of rice.

His arm was still round her waist, but there was no strength in it now. Solikha peeled it away and dragged herself free.

Flame Hair lay between two rows of produce. No one noticed what had happened,not even the skillet's owner. People were still clamoring for the banknotes. A fight had broken out.

Chatri dropped the pan, took Solikha's hand and pushed through the surging crowd, out into the comparative quiet of the main street.

A moment later, the tuk-tuk came around the corner.

People were still being drawn to the source of the commotion, blocking its passage, but the driver had collected the other two sun-glassed men, and they leaped off in pursuit.

Solikha and Chatri ran. On and on, weaving and dodging, their pursuers steadily closing the gap between them.

They turned a corner and found themselves in a street filled with bars and clubs and garish neon signs. Scantily clad women beckoned to passers-by from doorways, and for one sickening moment Solikha thought they'd come full circle, back to the place they'd escaped from earlier that day.

Glancing back over his shoulder, Chatri ran into someone and stopped dead. Solikha, her hand still in his, did likewise, then looked up at who they'd collided with.

Farang. A man and a woman. Middle-aged. Dressed identically in khaki.

More uniforms.

Behind them, their pursuers stopped dead too.

Who were they? Solikha wondered. Police?

The *farang* man—tall, broad, snowy-haired—glanced down at them, then back at their pursuers. He snapped something at them. Sharp, commanding words.

The leading sun-glassed man held up a hand and took a step backward.

More words were exchanged, words Solikha didn't understand, then the woman crouched and beckoned to her, indicating her brightly patterned dress.

The wretched dress. Again!

But Chatri was speaking now, earnest and serious, addressing both of the foreigners. He squeezed her hand reassuringly.

The man shouted something above their heads. Solikha turned in time to see the sun-glassed men take another backward step and melt into the crowd.

She turned back to find Chatri looking relieved.

The woman pressed her palms together and gave each of them a slight bow. *"Sawatdee-kah."*

He returned the gestured. Solikha mimicked him, still mystified at this sudden change.

It was her first introduction to Glenn and Mary Kwann from Pennsylvania.

* * *

Alice saw him waiting as the bus swung into the depot. Just a glimpse, but she recognized him at once. Despite the smart suit and open-necked shirt, there was still something of the ragged boy about him. The unkempt hair, perhaps, or that impish grin.

The bus hissed to a halt. He was right by her window. He smiled up and waved his free hand. His other was held by a girl of five or six in a pale pink dress, one finger in her mouth. Alice felt something tear at her heart, but smiled and waved back.

She took her travel pack from the rack, checked the seat pocket in front, ran her free hand through her hair, and waited for the passengers in the aisle to disembark. For the first time in a fortnight, she was truly apprehensive. Now, at the end of the journey, that was, in many ways, really a beginning.

He stood, one arm, out, beaming as she took the lower step.

Alice beamed back.

"Solikha!"

"Hello, Chatri."

"It's been a long time. Too long."

Alice Solikha Kwann nodded, dropped her travel bag and embraced her oldest friend, smiling hard, fighting to remember that village girls never cried.

II

TWELVE

They headed south on I-280, leaving the lights of downtown San Francisco behind.

"We're about twenty minutes out," Chatri said.

"It's very kind of you to collect me. I could've got the train, you know. Doesn't the BART go all the way to Daly City?"

"Yes, and nonsense. I haven't seen you for so long, I couldn't wait a minute longer."

Alice smiled. Chatri smiled back. Then his eyes strayed to the rear-view mirror and the little girl strapped in the car seat in back. Rosa was dozing.

A couple of miles passed in silence, and Alice felt the weight of time. Years had gone by since they'd last seen each other. A logjam of history that would take a while to clear.

He spoke again, his voice catching slightly. "I was so sorry when I heard about Mary and Glenn. I... we... owe them so much."

Alice said nothing.

"Do you know what happened?"

"A truck at an intersection, apparently. Didn't give way. Early morning, a clear road. The driver should have seen them. They were hit side-on. Their Jeep went off a cliff."

"Oh god. Where did it happen?"

"Chonburi, near Pattaya."

"What were they doing down there?"

"Working, as usual. Something big. They said so in their last letter."

"Do you know what it was?"

She shook her head.

"Letters. Still. They used to write me every Christmas and birthday. Started sending cards to Rosa too."

Glenn had never trusted email, saying it took effort and a certain commitment to steam open an envelope. "But any idiot can intercept your email."

"Those roads." Chatri shook his head. "You know that Thailand has the second-highest traffic fatality rate in the world?"

After another mile, he said, "I did try to get away for the funeral, but Annabel was still sick and..." He left the sentence unfinished.

"You did the right thing, Chatri. They'd have understood."

His face clouded. She could see the lines of loss etched in it. A double loss for her, triple for him.

"Will you and Annabel try again?"

He shrugged. "Maybe. The last few months have not been the best." His eyes strayed to the rear-view mirror and the sleeping girl.

Alice nodded, her eyes fixed on the road ahead.

* * *

Late in the evening, one last container was delivered to the holding area of Wharf 2A at Port Laem Chabang. Same driver, same truck, similar type code on the big steel box. It, too, was a 42V2—a forty-footer with a mechanical ventilation system, located internally—but this ventilation system wasn't so scrupulously maintained.

The container was colored blue. It was dented and scraped and had spots of rust, evidence of a long life and many crossings. It was set to the side of the main stack so that when the *Pacific Ram* docked it would be one of the first loaded. It went in first because it was headed for the ship's second port of call. First on, last off, that was the rule. When you play with boxes weighing upwards of 68,000 pounds each, you can't shuffle them around like Lego blocks.

Early next day, the gantry crane lifted the blue container into the hold of the *Pacific Ram*. Three-and-a-half hours after that, the ship now almost fully laden, the gray container was lowered to a slot on the deck and clamped in place.

The vessel was Liberian-flagged and made the eight thousand, eight hundred and fifty-mile trip six times a year. Typical transit time was twenty-two days, but the *Pacific Ram* was a fast ship. In a good sea under full power, she could make twenty-five knots with an average of close to twenty. She'd been known to make the crossing in as little as eighteen days. As always, time was money to her owners and her crew, so they pushed the ship as hard as they could.

* * *

Chatri took the Sullivan Avenue exit. "Welcome to Westlake," he said as the car passed over the brow of a hill and the suburb opened out before them. A sea of not-quite-identical houses, closely packed, sat behind short rectangles of mowed lawn. They were square, angular, double-storied, painted in suburban colors of beige, gray, fawn, and white.

"The suburb was built in the 1950s. It was the inspiration for that song *Little Boxes*. Do you know it?"

She gave him a skeptical look.

"No, really."

"How long have you been here?"

"Four years. The schools are very good."

They swung up a driveway and stopped in front of a garage door. Rosa, woken by the bump over the sidewalk, insisted on carrying Alice's travel pack. Chatri took the larger one.

Annabel greeted them in the hall and the two women shared a formal embrace. They hadn't met since the wedding.

"I can't believe it's been seven years," Alice said.

"You're in the spare room," Annabel replied, leading the way.

Annabel Young—she'd kept her maiden name—was in her late thirties, compact, tidy, with angular cheekbones and a squarish jaw. Her shoulder-length yellow-blond hair was tied back in a ponytail, and she wore a check shirt, jeans, and open-toed sandals. A cowgirl look, but crisp and neat. Alice sensed something less than casual in her casual appearance. A deliberation in her dressing and the light make-up she was wearing.

The spare room was small and bright with a folding

bed set against the far wall. It was painted in a light wash of pale blue and had a stick-on frieze of Beatrix Potter rabbits running round the walls. One of the folding closet doors was open and Alice saw spare hangers on an empty rail above a dismantled bassinet.

"This is lovely," she said.

"The bed's not much to look at, but it's very comfortable," Annabel said.

"It looks fine. Besides, after three thousand miles on buses, I can just about sleep anywhere."

"I can't believe you did that? What's wrong with flying?"

Alice shrugged. "I'm on vacation. I wanted the trip to be part of the adventure."

Annabel shook her head.

"Come down to the kitchen when you've freshened up," Chatri called, pointing out the bathroom down the hall. "Would you like coffee?"

"Or something stronger?" Annabel added.

A look passed between her and Chatri. Something private.

"Coffee would be great," Alice said.

* * *

The kitchen and dining room were paneled wood. Sliding doors along one side opened on to a wooden deck, a covered barbecue, and an expanse of neatly trimmed lawn dotted with neatly trimmed shrubs. Rosa was playing in a sandbox near the rear fence.

"You're so lucky to have a garden," Alice said.

"We get a man in," Annabel said. "Once a fortnight."

The espresso machine on the breakfast bar bubbled and hissed. There were nozzles and pipes and gauges. It looked something concocted by a steam-punk plumber. Chatri worked it with practiced efficiency and set down two steaming cups.

"Black, right?"

"Like my soul. Thanks."

Annabel raised her wine glass in a toast.

"Sol was saying she hitchhiked some of the way," Chatri said. He still used her old name.

"Hitchhiked? On your own? Are you kidding me?"

"Most people are fine," Alice said. "If someone seems a bit shady, I don't get in. It's a great way to meet people and see the country."

"And your conclusions, now you've seen the country coast to coast?"

"There's a whole lot of emptiness out there."

Chatri said nothing. Sipped his coffee.

"I guess working for the FBI gives you a bit more... I dunno... confidence than the average hitcher," Annabel said.

"The training, maybe, but I'm not in the field. I'm an analyst. I sit behind a desk all day. I don't even get a gun."

"Who'd have thought we'd turn into a couple of desk jocks," Chatri said.

"How's the computer business?"

"Long hours. Companies are cutting back all over. They claim they can't find qualified people here, so they need to import cheap coders on contract. Either that or move the whole operation offshore. But there's a lot of good people here, they just don't want to pay them decent rates. Many of my friends are unemployed. Sometimes I wonder if I wouldn't be better off back home."

Annabel raised an eyebrow. Apparently this was news to her.

Home. Alice thought about the word. Chatri still considered himself a foreigner. Even his accent set him apart. A hint of his adoptive parents' Indian lilt. She thought about her village, now a memory so distant it might have been a dream. Was that home? Or the Kwann's house in Pennsylvania? But she'd left there years before, for college, then her job. It was sold now anyway. The only home she had now was a small rented apartment.

"But you're OK, aren't you? Your job, I mean?"

"Oh yes. Systems always need testing and integration. Especially high-security ones."

"And you, Annabel?"

"Marketing never goes out of fashion. I get to work school hours, plus they let me work from home."

"A real bonus," Chatri said. "She can work all weekend if she wants. It's most kind of them."

Annabel pursed her lips and looked towards the yard where Rosa was calling for attention. She set down her glass and excused herself. They watched her go, then Chatri said, "So why are you really here, Sol?"

"Vacation, like I said."

"Now? After all this time? I've been out here eight years and the best you've ever managed was a weekend for my wedding. Do you even take vacations?"

"I spent a few days in the Caribbean last year."

"Sounds romantic."

"It was work. But I did go sightseeing on the way to the

airport."

"I rest my case. And now, suddenly, it's three months leave of absence. Just like that."

She sipped her coffee, thought of all the answers she could give, weighing each one against the other. Finally, she said, "It was Glenn and Mary. Their passing got me thinking."

"What about?"

"Life. The universe. Everything."

"Next you'll be telling me you've found the answer and it's forty-two."

She smiled.

Rosa called from the yard. "Daddy, Daddy, come and see what I've made!"

Chatri put down his cup and followed Annabel out.

THIRTEEN

The doorbell rang three times in quick succession, but at first Tony Ferriera thought he was dreaming. He rolled over and looked at the illuminated bedside clock. 4:30am. He'd only switched his computer off two hours ago.

He stared at the digits and let his mind drift, waves of fatigue luring him back to sleep.

The doorbell rang again, three more times.

"What the fuck?"

A little moonlight filtered through the blinds, adding to the perpetual nighttime glow of downtown LA. Enough light to see by without the bedside lamp. Ferriera drew back the sheets, slipped on a pair of slippers and walked naked to the bedroom door. He took a silk robe from a hanger on the back and pulled it on as he shuffled out into the living area.

The doorbell rang again.

The apartment's automation system detected his movements, its biometric system recognized its owner and made the appropriate adjustments. Based on the time of day, the ambient light and his known habits, it brought up the apartment's concealed lighting to its lowest level.

The glow filled an open-plan living area measuring

sixty feet by thirty. A decorator had themed the place, opting for warm, rich colors to offset the stark lines and harsh faces on the antique tribal masks that lined the walls. Ferriera still wasn't sure about the pale orange sofa, but the guy had fucked like a trooper.

The lighting stepped up a notch as he reached the door console and turned on the video feed. His heart rate kicked up a notch to match.

Three guys stood in the hall. Two uniforms behind an older guy in a rumpled looking suit that looked like it had been slept in. One of the uniforms was carrying a battering ram.

The rumpled guy was holding out his ID. Ferriera read the name beneath the badge. It meant nothing to him, but the guy's divisional listing seemed to leap right off the card. ICAC, the Internet Crimes Against Children task force.

"Fuck, fuck, fuck, fuck, fuck!" Ferriera muttered, fumbling for the door release as the rumpled guy signaled to the cop with the battering ram.

* * *

"Fuck!" Thomas Hartley muttered. "How bad is it?"

Hans Reisinger sipped his coffee. "Bad, but not so bad. He's been charged with possession of child pornography, but there's no intent to supply. One occasion and only three images. He'll say it's a personal sexual problem for which he's been undergoing treatment. A good lawyer, his lack of record, a word from the governor—he might only get four years."

"I don't mean Ferriera. I don't give a fuck about Ferriera. I mean us. What's our exposure?"

"Taken care of."

"You've had a word?"

"Six, actually." Reisinger counted them off on his fingers. "Four years is less than forty."

"And he understands that?"

"He's no fool."

"He was stupid enough to download that shit in the first place."

"An aberration. A moment of weakness. Even alcoholics fall off the wagon sometimes."

"Yeah? Tell that to the judge." Hartley gestured to the waiter for more mineral water. "This could get big *and* public. A governor's aide up on a charge like that? We don't want the press sniffing around."

"Relax Thomas, there's nothing to find."

"Damn ICAC."

"ICAC, my pants."

Hartley grinned. "I bet Ferriera did when he saw them. So what about our merchandise? Nothing in his apartment? Nothing in a locked drawer at work?"

"I said he's no fool. He has a self-storage unit in Koreatown in the name of Randolf Smith."

"A self-storage unit?" Hartley scowled. "That suggests a padlock. A padlock needs a key. And a key is something for the cops to find."

"Actually, it's a combination lock."

"You have the number?"

"He was keen to give it up. I've sent Russo to deal with it."

"Nothing spectacular this time. No fires. Keep it low-key. Just a clean out."

"Of course. And Ferriera said to pass on his appreciation for all we're doing for him."

"You mean he appreciates we still have video of his antics."

"*And* appreciates it won't get out."

"What about his contact in the harbor department?"

"Old pals network. Secure, but we can't use it. And it would be foolish to try to do so now."

The waiter returned, topped up Hartley's Perrier, and set the bottle down.

"Which brings me back to my original statement," Hartley said, watching the waiter go. "*Fuck!* This couldn't have come at worse time. Tak's just dispatched a shipment. We need someone down there to guide it through."

Reisinger nodded. "I'll see what Nancy's got."

FOURTEEN

The physical examination was almost as frightening as the original assault. White coats, white masks, bright lights. The air of deliberation. The instruments and the photographs and the assistant with the clipboard recording observations. Solikha had only ever seen a doctor twice in her life. Once when she was very small, and once for a routine examination at her school where the children were lined up side by side to have their chests listened to and their throats inspected.

There was no one to explain things to her. No one spoke Khmer. No one could be found at that hour. Later she understood, but then, in spite of the nods and smiles and kind-sounding words, her mind—freed to its imaginings—imagined the worst. She lay on the bed, gripping the metal frame, her eyes scrunched up tight, fearful that when she opened them again she'd find Young One standing over her.

Mary Kwann saw the fear and the child's grim resilience. The screwed-up face, the fierce determination to endure whatever was to come. Her heart ached for the girl, especially when she read the medical report. Nine years old. The brutes. A lingering death was too good for some people.

The boy was not much better. He'd been brutalized too.

Several men by the looks of it, but he too refused to speak of what had happened. It was common enough amongst victims, especially the young. They were still fearful. Re-establishing trust could take a long time.

There were two curious aspects to this case. At first, the Kwann's thought Chatri and Solikha must be brother and sister because of their obvious attachment. They were surprised to discover the boy was Thai and the girl Cambodian, and that they'd known each other for only one day.

The second was the girl's odd attachment to her dress and her desperation to retrieve it once the medical examination was complete. The pattern was a pattern they knew well. A uniform of debauchery. One of Kulap's houses, well known for his willingness to cater to extreme tastes. Usually, the girls were happy never to see those dresses again, but Solikha begged to have hers back. Mary Kwann relented, guessing the value a peasant girl might place on such a garment, especially one that she had yet to make associations with, but almost immediately after retrieving it, Solikha changed her mind, cast it aside and wanted nothing more to do with it, wrapping herself in the plain smock the Kwann Institute provided.

The days that followed were full of fear and wonder for Solikha. The metal-framed bed and mattress they gave her felt uncomfortable and had unsettling connotations. She couldn't sleep on it like the other girls in her dormitory. She would wait till after lights-out, till the others settled, then slip off it as quietly as she could. Mornings would find her with her blanket, curled on the concrete floor.

Late the following day an interpreter arrived. The

woman spoke Khmer and it was good to hear her mother tongue again and once more have a voice.

They sat together in a quiet, shaded room, Solikha, the interpreter and Mary Kwann. Words of encouragement were spoken, of her enterprise, endurance, and courage. But how had she got there? Where were her family?

Solikha told of her village and the fate of her parents, but not of the uncle and aunt who had sold her. In part because she didn't want to get them into trouble, but mostly because she feared she might be sent back to them.

"So you're an orphan?"

Solikha nodded and dropped her eyes.

"How did the truck men find you?"

"I was living on the street," she said simply.

The questions grew more difficult. Did she know where she had been taken? Would she recognize the place? What had happened when she first arrived? And then? And then? And then?

Her hand gripped the fabric of the smock, screwing it into a ball. "Three men," was all she would say. "Three men... *Farang*..." The tears started of their own accord. Even the village girl couldn't stop them.

Now they would find out what she'd done. Perhaps they knew already. The interpreter's opening words about her being safe here were meaningless in the light of her crime. They'd send her back. Or call the police. She'd go to prison.

She began to shake.

"And then, Solikha?"

She stared back, wide-eyed, fighting the honesty her mother and father had always insisted upon. The words, "And then I stabbed them," were half a breath away.

"How did you escape?"

At first, she couldn't believe the question and looked back in wonder, feeling dazed. As if time had shifted somehow.

"They left you alone, yes? But how did you get away?".

It was like a ray of light in the black pit of her darkest fears. A lifeline to a drowning girl. She didn't have to lie after all. She didn't have to tell them.

The interpreter was right, the *farang* had left her alone. They were far, far away by then.

So she told of the fire escape and her perilous descent. Of helping Chatri and their flight. Of the old men and the pursuit through the market. She didn't mention the money or the skillet—felt certain Chatri wouldn't either—and concluded with the chance meeting with their saviors.

Mary Kwann reached over and squeezed her hand. The interpreter repeated her words. "It's all right, child. We understand."

It was over.

* * *

They gave her a toy. A fat yellow bear. A thing of fabric and stuffing and glass-bead eyes. Some of the younger children carried things like it—elephants, donkeys, cows—but it was little use to Solikha, except that its fat belly made a comfortable headrest when she curled up on the floor. She'd had a rag doll when she was little, but put it aside when she began to work in the fields.

She treated the new toy casually until she discovered

the stitching around the back was loose. Curious to see what was inside, she investigated and found thick white wads of foamy filling and realized it was the perfect hiding place for the small cassette and the identity card she'd retrieved from the pocket of the hateful dress.

There were sewing classes at the institute, but she already knew all she needed. Her mother had taught her. It was an essential skill for a village girl. She borrowed a needle and some thread and repaired the broken seam. After that, Solikha and the fat yellow bear were practically inseparable.

Fifteen

"Ah, Mr Tubble. You still have him?" Chatri said, picking the faded yellow bear from the top of Alice's backpack. "It's good to see him. It's been a long time."

"He's become a sort of talisman," Alice said. "He always travels with me."

"A fine companion." Chatri set the bear back. "But you should have a proper companion by now, you know."

Alice pursed her lips.

He gave her a quizzical look.

"It's my work."

"Back home, you'd practically be a grandmother by now."

Home. That word again. Alice said nothing.

"I remember you all through college. The prettiest girl on campus, but they called you the Ice Queen."

"Amongst other things."

"So is there anyone?"

"Not really."

"Has there ever been?"

She couldn't answer for a moment, couldn't look at him., drew a long breath before she replied. "There was once. A long time ago. Ancient history."

Chatri said nothing.

Alice picked up the fat faded bear and studied its beaded eyes. Eventually she said, "We need to talk, Chatri. There're things I need to do."

"You mean on your vacation?"

"Yes."

"I'm guessing you're not after tourist information."

Alice said nothing.

He glanced over his shoulder. "Tomorrow. Lunch?"

She nodded and put the bear back down. "Good night, Chatri."

"Good night, Solikha."

* * *

The *Pacific Ram* had been at sea for six days. She was making good progress. Almost three thousand nautical miles lay in her wake.

The gray container was clamped to the deck with two others were stacked on top. The ones either side gave it some shelter from the equatorial sun, but it was still hot inside. The internal ventilation system was working overtime.

It was almost impossible to tell the passage of time inside the container. A little light filtered through gaps around the edge of the ventilator grille, but it was so heavily shaded by the surrounding stacks that it seemed more like a memory of light. Kanya Kajornchaiyakul marked the passage of time by the digital watch her husband had given her before they left. Arthit had a matching watch with the same purple plastic band. He was somewhere nearby with the other men. Maybe even right next door. It was comforting to think he was close.

If the passage of days was hard to measure, their passage through space was not. The steady rumble of the ship's engines, deep and constant, was now so much a part of the background that it went unnoticed. There was gentle swaying too. A side to side motion that had to be allowed for when moving about. Several of the children had been sick in the first few days, one of them prodigiously, but although now all had acclimatized, the smell—mingled with the smell of the chemical toilet—still lingered in the brackish air. But smells like that were nothing to a former slum dweller.

A string of LEDs crisscrossed the first two-thirds of the container, giving off a cold blue glow. They were powered by a truck battery attached to a hand-cranked generator. Each of the adults took turns to keep the battery charged. It was the only exercise they got.

Inactivity was the thing Kanya struggled with most. All her life she'd been busy. Enforced idleness felt unnatural, so twice each day she would pace the length of the container, going to and fro twenty times, twenty-six steps each way. In the beginning, the others joked and laughed—"Look, she thinks she's an American already. Soon she will be jogging." Now they joined her, even the children, weaving backwards and forwards in a long line, laughing when an unexpected roll of the ship caught them off guard.

They'd also come to regulate their days by the digits on Kanya's watch, giving themselves sixteen hours of daylight and eight hours of night. Then they would unfurl the hammocks, attach them to metal pegs either side of the container, and lie in swaying darkness, trying to sleep.

Each morning, Apinya—at twenty-five the oldest of the group and therefore their nominal leader—would solemnly mark another day off with a chalk mark on the steel wall of the container.

Mealtimes were regulated by Kanya's watch too, though they took on a certain monotony once the fresh fruit and vegetables ran out. Nothing would keep in this heat but dry biscuits and water. There was plenty of both. Cartons of biscuits occupied the far corner of the container, stacked to the ceiling, while plastic water barrels ran along both sides and doubled as seats. When the barrels were empty, they'd been instructed to refill them rather than risk overtaxing the chemical toilet. A funnel was provided. Kanya didn't like to think whether the barrels had made this trip before.

When mealtimes were over and the children had been attended to, there was little else to do but talk. Apinya taught them a little of her fractured English, but mostly they talked about where they'd come from, and about their hopes and dreams. Kanya's was to work in a garden or on a farm, side by side with Arthit, out in the sunshine and fresh air. The others looked forward to the cooking, cleaning and domestic jobs they'd been promised.

It would take years to pay off the debt for this trip, which Mr Tak told them was twenty thousand dollars apiece. They'd paid a deposit. All their savings, plus loans from relatives. Five hundred dollars each. Which left nineteen thousand five hundred dollars to pay. A vast amount of money, at least back home. But in America, you could earn in one day more than you might make in a month back home. And as Arthit said, they were young. Even if it took ten years to pay their debts, they would still be under thirty.

That was Arthit. Always thinking of the future. Always planning ahead.

And when it was paid, they would become proper citizens, Mr Tak said. Then they could send for their families—brothers, sisters, mothers, fathers—and make new lives for them all. So it was worth three weeks in this hot, cramped, smelly box. What was a few weeks discomfort compared to the prospect of a whole new life?

* * *

Alice spent the morning playing tourist, doing the things any first-timer to San Francisco might do. The cable cars, Fisherman's Wharf, Golden Gate Park. The day was mild and the sky an endless blue. She took a few photographs, but her heart wasn't in it. Her mind was elsewhere. In a sense, San Francisco marked the end of her vacation. Now she had a job to do.

Two jobs, she reminded herself.

She bought a souvenir memory stick from a street vendor. It had a red heart on one side between the words "I" and "SF", and a capacity of eight gigabytes. More than enough. At a nearby internet cafe, she copied three carefully selected photographs on to it from the memory card she'd taken from Rick's phone, each one cropped to just a face.

At a secondhand camera store on Kearny Street, she bought a Sony Handycam Camcorder with a two-inch fold-out screen. It cost fifty bucks.

"Real classic, that," the guy in the store said. "I remember when they first came out. Must be twenty years ago now. No one believed you'd get anything decent on them little cassettes. Couple of years later, even the pros were using them. I can throw you in a ten-pack of blank tapes for an extra twenty."

"No thanks," Alice said. "I've already got some."

The transaction made her late for her meeting with Chatri. He was waiting on the corner of Mission and 4th and waved out to her as she crossed over. He worked nearby, for a defense contractor on a project he couldn't even talk about. Alice knew what that was like, working for the FBI. Secrets. Walled-off places in your head. Places you couldn't let friends or loved ones see. But secrets took their toll.

They bought coffee in polystyrene cups and bagels wrapped in clingfilm, then wandered through Yerba Buena Gardens till they found a vacant patch of leafy shade and settled on the grass.

Chatri asked about her morning.

"Usual tourist stuff. But that's not what I wanted to talk to you about. How's the system testing going?"

"You know I can't talk about that."

NGI, isn't it? The FBI's Next Generation Identification system?"

He pursed his lips.

"The contract's a matter of public record, Chatri. And you work for Aerodyne. I put two and two together. I'm an analyst. It's what I do. We are on the same side here, you know. Playing for the same team."

"NGI-II actually," he said. "Still in early alpha. The next, next generation. It'll be a couple of years yet."

"Facial recognition on steroids, they tell me. The current system's already pretty good. We use it all the time."

"Wait till you see this. Imagine the names and profiles of everyone on that street corner over there," he pointed and snapped his fingers, "just like that. Real time. All the time."

"Impressive."

"And scary."

"Could you do a little testing for me?"

"What do you mean?"

She took out the memory stick and dropped it on the grass.

"What's that?"

"Three friends I've lost touch with."

"Why do you need NGI? They can't be hard to track down in this interconnected age. Or do you not yet have search engines on the East Coast?"

Alice smiled. "That's just it. My memory's getting bad. I've forgotten their names."

"Or where you first met them, or how you even know them?"

"I knew you'd understand."

"Who are they really?"

"Three young women who were raped by a gang of thugs in a small town in northern Nevada. The pictures come from the cellphone I took from of one of the gang. The victims were released—at least as far as I know—though I suspect the perpetrators made threats. I don't believe any of them filed complaints, but I'd like to check."

"On your vacation?"

"I only came across this a couple of days ago."

"Why not simply send it to your office?"

"*Because* I'm on vacation."

"So you've found a holiday job. Private detective."

"I keep telling them I want to work in the field."

Chatri studied the memory stick. "I need to know exactly what's on here before I go plugging it into a work computer."

"Three photographs. JPGs. Head and shoulders. Nothing else."

"Not the contents of the phone card?"

"God no, I wouldn't compromise you, Chatri. The stick's brand new. I cropped and cut the photographs directly to it."

"And the machine you used to do this?"

"In an internet cafe."

He groaned and shook his head.

"I'm not a complete novice, you know." Alice took another memory stick from her backpack. Tossed it to him. "Just before I used it, the machine had an outage and accidentally booted that instead."

He read the label on the side. Handwritten. It said TAILS. The latest version.

"Ah, The Amnesiac Incognito Live System."

Alice smiled. "Only you would know what that acronym meant."

TAILS was a complete, discreet operating system that ran from a memory stick and left no trace of its presence or activities in the host computer's memory, or on its hard drive.

"Very well. I'll see what I can do." He tossed the TAILS

stick back to her and slipped the first into the pocket of his shirt. "But there's something else, isn't there Detective Kwann?"

"What makes you say that?"

"Only everything. From your claim to be on vacation, to this," he patted his shirt pocket, "right down to the way you said those last words. We know each other too well, Solikha. I know when there's something you're not telling me.

"Do you?" Alice prized the lid off her coffee and looked down at the dark liquid. "We don't know everything about each other, Chatri."

"Tell me something you don't know about me. I'm an open book."

"All right. What happened to you the night before we met? When I found you huddled by that window?"

His face clouded. He looked away. "That's ancient history."

"Is it? I still have nightmares. Don't you?"

His face showed she'd struck a chord. Part of the program at the Kwann Institute had been some rudimentary therapy. It helped, but the scars remained. Bodies healed. Minds rarely did.

"I've never told anyone," he said. "And you and I... we didn't have the language, not at first. Later, when we did... well, who would want to revisit that?"

Alice took up her travel pack, unzipped an internal pocket, and took out a small cassette. It measured two-and-a-half inches long, by two inches wide, by a half-inch thick. She set it on the grass between them.

"Know what that is? A MiniDV cassette. Digital video. State-of-the-art back in "95. Holds thirteen gigabytes of data. One hour of recording. On there is what happened to me."

"What? They filmed you?"

Alice nodded.

He shook his head. Reached out to pick it up.

"That's the original."

His hand froze.

"The original? What do you mean? Where did you get it? How?"

"The night before we first met. I took it from the camera of the men who raped me."

SIXTEEN

Solikha and Chatri spent nine months at the Kwann Institute in Bangkok. Conditions were basic, the food plain, and all residents were expected to help in running the place, but it was safe, secure and vastly better than trying to eke out a living on the streets.

The population varied. People came and went, mostly the older ones. The vast majority were teenage girls. Some were reconciled and reunited with their families, some used the training they received at the institute to find proper work in the city, and some were too broken to help. So inured to their way of life by the age of thirteen or fourteen that they could imagine no other.

The younger children were more of a problem. If parents or relatives could be located, they were sometimes returned. But although promises were made, there was no guarantee they wouldn't be resold and end up back on the streets. Many families owed crippling debts to unscrupulous money lenders, and their children were indentured to repay them. If they absconded, the debts returned, often with added penalties. Besides, many of the children were deeply scared by their experiences and exhibited a wide range of problems, principally withdrawal, distrust and a lack of communication.

Solikha suffered from communication problems too, not because of any unwillingness on her part, but because of her language. She spoke Khmer, the world around her spoke Thai, so she had to learn it. She did so in remarkable time, picking up the rudiments of both the spoken language and Thai script in a matter of weeks with only Chatri as her guide. The two were inseparable, spent hours together each day, miming and gesturing at first, then, as time went on, talking quietly together.

Her aptitude for languages was reinforced by inclusion in more formal classes at a nearby school. There she excelled, and as was soon at a level comparable with children her own age. She also picked up a smattering of English.

At first, the Kwann's were puzzled. Where was she learning it? There weren't any English classes at the institute. Then they discovered Solikha had found an old Thai/English phrase book and, in practicing her recognition of Thai script, had picked up English almost subconsciously.

More books and more intensive classes followed. The girl consumed both and soon began to outstrip her tutors. It was Glenn Kwann who first raised the possibility of taking her to the States.

The problems in doing so were immense. The bureaucracy on both sides was fearsome. Adoption would be the only way.

They pursued the matter quietly, not wishing to get the child's hopes up.

The Kwann's were closely examined, by Thai authorities and US embassy officials. They already had a grown-up daughter. Why would they want to take on a ten-year-old, especially in their early fifties?

But their credentials were impeccable. The institute had been founded by Glenn's sister, a pious and preachy woman. When her health declined, Mary and Glenn had stepped in, their energy and enthusiasm greatly expanding its reach. Bankrolled by wealthy benefactors back home, they'd become feared in certain districts of the city for their willingness to stand up to the gangs that ran the child prostitution trade, sometimes publicly snatching kids from the hands of prospective clients.

Solikha's statelessness helped, as did the medical reports of her abuse.

Finally, with the adoption approved and all hurdles overcome, the idea of returning to the States with them was put to Solikha.

Without a moment's consideration, she declined. "Not without my brother."

"Chatri's not you brother, Solikha."

"No, he is better."

Mary looked at her husband. He shook his head. They couldn't take another child.

"I'm afraid that's not possible."

Solikha bowed and thanked them for all they'd done. She was very grateful, grateful beyond words, but she had not left Chatri behind that first morning and would not do so now.

They tried reasoning with her, but she wouldn't budge. For the first time, Solikha revealed a stubborn streak. A fierce, unwavering determination. Chatri was the closest thing to a family she had left.

Glenn and Mary blamed themselves for letting the children grow too close in the intervening months. But what else could they have done?

They appealed to Chatri. He understood the nature of the opportunity and told her so. He would be sad to see her go, but really, it would be the best thing for her. They could keep in touch. They could still be friends.

His words fell on deaf ears. Solikha crossed her arms and shook her head. Her mind was made up.

They could have taken her anyway, unwilling though she was. They were now her legal guardians. But Mary Kwann opposed the plan, drawing parallels with the original crime: a powerless child in the play of a system in which she had no say.

The impasse continued for several days and was finally resolved with an offer. Would Solikha agree to go if they could find a family for Chatri?

Of course she would! It was what she'd hoped for all along.

Once more, wheels were set in motion. The foothills of another mountain of paperwork were approached. But Chatri's case wasn't so clear cut. He was a street kid from Udon Thani. An urchin, the leader of a gang of small boys who supplemented their meager diet by stealing from market stalls and shops. There was a drug-addled mother and a number of possible fathers, all of whom disowned the boy when he was finally caught by the police. But when a corrupt captain sold him to traffickers, they all claimed a share of the money.

The Kwann's approach was oblique, through a local intermediary. Any hint of the possibility of foreign adoption would have seen the child—abandoned to the streets at the age of five—suddenly become a treasured son and a valued family member.

The boy had been found in Bangkok, relatives were told. They would like to return him. Who would care for him?

Silence.

The other possibility was a foster family. In the city perhaps. But papers would have to be signed. Legal documents.

The only question then was how much such a signature was worth.

The other hurdle was finding a family for him. Older children, boys especially, were difficult to place, but the Kwann's network of contacts and benefactors was extensive, and Chatri proved himself a star in the video of adoptive children they sent back to the States. As soon as the camera began rolling, he turned on his engaging smile, widened his dark, endearing eyes and expressed—in Solikha-coached, but still slightly broken English—his great desire to find a family to replace the one that had abandoned him.

Charming and engaging, he sold himself.

On March 18, 1996, Chatri Juntasa and Solikha Duong, in the company of Mary and Glenn Kwann and two other Americans from the Kwann Institute, boarded a Thai Airways Boeing 747 bound for New York.

SEVENTEEN

C hatri stared at her in disbelief. "You took it?" he repeated. "You've had that tape all these years?"

"I should have given it up, I know. Handed it in. But it's personal. Very personal. Besides, I was scared."

"But how did you get it in the first place?"

"The men left the room," she said simply. "I stole it."

"Stole it?"

"Remember that money I had? How we sorted it into piles and bought *Khao Kha Moo*? I stole that too. At the same time. From one of their wallets."

"And they didn't notice you'd cleaned them out when they came back?"

"They... didn't come back," she said evasively.

"I thought you were a pickpocket. I never guessed you were so audacious."

"You'd be surprised."

He shook his head. "You're a wonder to me, Solikha. Still!"

"You never asked me where I got the money from at the time. I couldn't have told you anyway. And when I did have the words, it was like you said; who'd want to revisit that place?"

His smile faded. He looked down at the cassette. "You've watched this?"

"No."

"Then what...?"

"I want you to.

"*What?*"

"Just the first bit. The first few minutes. There's a man on there. His face... Your software... That's all I want. I want to know who he is. Or was."

He opened the clear plastic box and took out the cassette.

"But only the first few minutes, Chatri. Promise me."

"What about the others?"

"Others?"

"You said you took it from the camera of the *men* who raped you. You said the *men* left the room."

"I... don't care about them. Just the first guy. He set it up. He was in charge."

He looked at her, sensed there was something she wasn't saying, but didn't press the point.

"You never told the Kwann's of this?"

"You're the first person I've ever told."

"They could have used it, you know. Evidence."

"I know. But they'd want to know how I got it."

"You stole it. You just told me."

"I was worried there might be implications. What with them being foreigners."

He looked doubtful.

"I was a child. I was frightened. I didn't know what to do. Besides, the longer it went on, the harder it was to come out with it. Easier too, in a way. I *wanted* to forget." She bit her lip and swallowed. "That's me on there. That's about as personal as you can ever get."

Chatri looked at the cassette. "You know this thing is twenty years old? Tapes deteriorate. It may not even be playable. I don't suppose I can take it into one of those conversion shops and have them put it on a DVD for me."

She stared at him in horror.

"I'm joking. But where am I going to find a MiniDV player these days?

"I've got one." She opened her travel pack and held it out. "It seems to work OK, but I haven't tried that in it."

"I absolutely will *not* take this back to work with me, no matter how sweetly you ask."

"God no! I wouldn't expect you to."

"What do you want then?"

"A mugshot. A picture of the man who's haunted me for twenty years."

Chatri examined the camera, studying its output sockets. "I'll need to get it on to a computer first. To get a printout."

"His face still comes to me at night, you know," Alice said. "He's like the face of all the men Mary and Glenn spent their lives fighting. Died fighting.

"After their accident, I had a sort of breakdown. Nothing major. Nothing dramatic. More a crisis of conscience, I suppose. That animals like him still prowled the earth. That he might still be out there, preying on the innocent. If so, that's down to me. I've let him get away with it for twenty years.

"How many other children has he raped in that time? I should have handed this over the day they rescued us.

Maybe something could have been done. Maybe he could have been stopped. Maybe a few kids could have been spared.

"I have tried to put it behind me, tried to forget like they told us in therapy. But I realized I'd been carrying this burden all those years. The guilt. And the fear. He terrified me, Chatri. Still does. But I have to find out who he is—or was. Alive or dead, it's time to lay his ghost."

"And if he is not a ghost, Solikha? What if he still lives?"

Alice said nothing for a long time, then slowly shook her head. "I don't know, Chatri. Really, I don't."

* * *

Namthip was a serious girl, quiet and studious, always the last to speak when the question circle began, always the one to give a considered answer, even though the questions were often frivolous. Who is your favorite movie actor? What is your favorite song? She was four years older than Kanya and had a five-year-old daughter. Kanya admired her maturity and quiet reserve, even envied her a little. The child, Eri, was as lovely as her mother.

One day, after their afternoon walk—twenty times, back and forth along the length of the container—they found themselves together in a corner.

Kanya checked the chalk marks on the wall. "Two weeks already. Not long now till we see our husbands again."

Namthip said nothing.

"Are you not looking forward to seeing your man?"

120

"I have no man." Namthip spoke in a whisper, barely louder the thrum of the ship's engines.

"But in the circle you told us his name was Akara. Like Akara Amarttayakul, the actor. I remember. Apinya asked if he looked like him and you said, 'Better'."

"His name is... *was* Akara. But he is not my husband."

The thrum of the engines continued. Namthip kept her eyes fixed on the floor of the container. "He was the father of my child, but I have not seen him since I discovered I was pregnant. He ran off. Made me my family's shame. I cannot redeem myself in their eyes, but one day perhaps, when my debt is paid, they will forgive little Eri for who she is and where she came from."

Kanya said nothing.

Namthip looked at her imploringly. "Please, don't tell the others."

"No, of course not. Your secret's safe with me."

Namthip smiled ruefully. "That's what he said too. After our one time together."

"One time only?"

She nodded.

Kanya thought of Arthit and the weeks and months after they were married. Suddenly she didn't envy Namthip so much.

The ship rolled unexpectedly, catching them off guard. Namthip gasped and clutched her side.

"What's the matter? Are you all right?"

"Yes, yes. It's nothing."

But Kanya could see the sheen on Namthip's brow. For the first time, she noticed the tremble in her hands.

"You have pain. What is it? Another child?"

Namthip gave a bitter laugh. "Not so soon, I think."

"What do you mean?"

Namthip looked away. "What did Mr Tak tell you when you paid your money?"

"He wished us a successful trip."

"You went together? You and Arthit?"

"Of course. Why?"

"And he said nothing about taking photographs for your documents?"

Kanya's heart skipped a beat. For a moment she thought they'd missed some important part of the process. Then she saw the look on Namthip's face.

"No. Why? What sort of photographs? ... Namthip?"

The older girl buried her face in her hands. "He said to make myself look pretty for them and gave me an address. There were four men there, waiting. *Farang*. They hurt me." She clutched her side. "Something is broken. I still bleed."

Kanya was horrified. "Did you tell Mr Tak?"

"No need. He was there. He took the photographs."

Kanya stared, not sure whether to believe her. Surely not the friendly middle-aged man she and Arthit had dealt with...?

"Are you certain it was him?"

Namthip nodded, then gave another little gasp at the pain.

"We must bathe you and clean you at least."

"No, you mustn't tell the others."

"But we must. We have no medicines."

Namthip gripped her hand. "Promise me, Kanya. Promise you will keep my secrets and my shame. Promise me you will tell no one."

Kanya's instinct was to help, to do all she could, but the other woman stared at her, desperate, imploring, her ashen faced filled with anxious tears. Finally, she reached out, clasped Namthip's hand and nodded reluctantly.

Eighteen

Alice took a BART train from Embarcadero to Daly City then walked the mile and a half to Chatri and Annabel's house in Westlake. She had a key to the back door, but Annabel was home ahead of her.

"Hi," Alice called, finding her in the kitchen.

Annabel held up a bottle of Napa Valley chardonnay. Alice nodded. Annabel poured her a glass. The bottle was already half empty.

"Good day?" Annabel asked.

"Great, thanks. Seems a fun town."

Alice raised the drink. They toasted each other without touching glasses, then Alice reeled off the checklist of sights and activities she'd accumulated.

"You covered a lot of ground," Annabel said. "But then, I guessed you would."

Alice gave her a quizzical look.

"Well, you seem pretty fit. I guess you work out."

""Running mostly. And a bit of sanshou."

"What's that?"

"A martial art. Like a combination of kung-fu and kick-boxing."

Annabel raised an eyebrow. "Remind me not to mess

with you!"

Alice smiled. "How was your day?"

"Another in a long line of them."

"You sound bored."

"I am bored. Still, I don't suppose we can all be FBI agents."

"I'm really just a desk jock."

"Despite the kung-fu kick-boxing?"

Annabel sipped her drink and led the way into the lounge. She stood by the picture window, looking out at the street. "You know, I don't even know your real name. You call yourself Alice, but Chatri calls you Sol. What is that? A nickname?"

"My birth name. Solikha. It's Khmer. When the Kwann's adopted me and brought me to the States, they thought I should have a more conventional name. To help me fit in. To signify a break with the past."

"They didn't change Chatri's name."

"They didn't adopt Chatri. Friends of theirs did. The Devarajah's lived about a hundred miles away in upstate New York."

"But the pair of you grew up together on the streets of Bangkok?"

Alice wondered how much Annabel knew of Chatri's background, how much he'd told her. She said simply, "We found each other on the streets. Then the Kwann's found us and brought us here."

"Then you found each other again at college. Despite the age difference."

"It's only a few years. I was lucky. I got a scholarship. I was good at languages, and they encouraged me."

"I heard you were something of a prodigy. Not just languages. Pretty much everything."

"I was lucky," Alice said again.

"So what does your birth name mean? Solikha?"

"Literally? 'Flower of death'."

Annabel raised an eyebrow.

"But it's also supposed to be the flower of salvation. There's an old Sanskrit legend about a black flower with a beautiful scent growing on top of a mountain of corpses. Men trek to it because it's supposed to grant them wishes, but it actually reveals their true intentions. If a man goes to it with a false heart, the scent poisons him, and he becomes part of the mountain. But if his heart is true, it reveals the path to enlightenment."

Annabel sipped her wine. "I think my name just means 'joy'."

"In Latin, it means 'loving' or 'lovable'."

Annabel regarded her a moment, then grunted.

Chatri's car swung up the drive. He came in carrying a plastic bag and another bottle of wine. "Ah," he said, "you've started without me."

He kissed his wife on the lips and Alice on the cheek, then went in search of his daughter. Annabel opened the new bottle and poured him a glass. He returned bouncing Rosa in his arms.

"What's in there?" The little girl pointed to the other bag.

"Treasures, look." He tipped it up, scattering a collection of cables and leads across the benchtop. "Surplus from work."

Rosa reached over and picked one up. It had a black

box-like connector on the end.

"There, you see. That's a SCART plug. For old European televisions. With this lot, I can plug anything into anything."

"But why would you want to, Daddy?".

"Oh, you never know." He glanced at Alice. "One day they might come in handy."

* * *

It was like falling asleep and finding yourself in a fairytale. For the first few weeks, Solikha was terrified she might wake up and discover she was back in the bare concrete dormitory in Bangkok.

Clean, wide streets, ordered and orderly. Not the chaos and noise she'd lived in for the last nine months. Blue skies, uncluttered roads, houses so big they seemed like palaces. A room of her own. A whole room!

A new sister too, June, Mary and Glenn's real daughter. A plain, pleasant girl with a fierce intelligence and a passion for astronomy. There was a telescope in an upstairs window, and she was partway through a degree in physics and math. Solikha was in awe of her. And of her books. So many books! So much to know!

The gave her money too, each week, just for being there. An allowance, they called it. So she could buy things for herself. But what? She didn't need anything. She already had too much. It came as a shock to realize they gave her more money each week than her parents would have earned in a month.

There was a new school, new classmates, new teachers. Everything was sparkling and new. Even a new name.

That was Mary's suggestion. She was a proper American girl now, she said. Perhaps she'd like to choose a new name to go with her new life?

At first, Solikha was dismayed, though she was careful to hide it. It wasn't what she wanted. She'd always been Solikha. But the Kwann's had done so much for her already, it seemed such a small thing to let them have. And Solikha had been there when the forms were filled out, spelling the unfamiliar name to strangers, hearing it mispronounced and mangled.

So she chose the name of the girl who fell down the rabbit hole and found herself in Wonderland. It seemed appropriate.

Mary bit her lip and hugged her when she told her of her choice. There were even tears. Only then did she learn that Mary's mother, who'd passed away the year before, had also been called Alice.

* * *

There was a tap at the door. Alice finished changing into her pajamas and opened it to find Chatri in a dressing gown, holding a glass of water. He glanced over his shoulder and said quietly, "I didn't have a chance to give you this earlier."

He took a piece of paper from the pocket of his gown. "Two out of three. No match on the dark girl. Might have been a tourist. The alpha system isn't hooked up to the international databases yet. I could try it on the live system, but all inquiries are logged and questions might be asked."

"No, no, don't do that." Alice opened out the note and saw Chatri's familiar cursive handwriting. "This is perfect. Thanks."

"Do you have the camera and the tape?"

"You want them now?"

"Might as well. I'm on a roll." Another glance over his shoulder. "I'll take a quick look in the morning before work. There's an old computer in my workshop. I'll try connecting it to that."

Alice went to her pack and took out the small vinyl pouch that contained the camera. She found the cassette and slipped it into a side pocket.

"Keep it afterwards." She handed it to him. "I have no use for it. But I'd like the tape back."

"Of course."

"And don't watch it, Chatri. Please? Just the first few minutes. Just enough to get a usable picture. Promise me."

He held it to his heart. "I promise."

Annabel appeared from the bathroom and glanced down the hall. At Alice in her night things still holding a note in Chatri's handwriting. At Chatri with his hand on his heart. She walked on and closed the bedroom door behind her. Not loudly, but not softly either.

NINETEEN

The first address on Chatri's list was in town. The second was in Fresno, three hours' drive away. Amelia May Kilcorn, age 27. Alice called ahead from her mobile.

Kilcorn was reserved but professional, at least until Alice said she was with the FBI and thought they shared a common interest."

"What do you mean?"

"We've both been to Winnemucca, Nevada."

The line went quiet. For a moment, Alice wondered if she'd hung up.

"Where are you calling from?" Kilcorn's voice suddenly sounded smaller.

"San Francisco. But I can drive out and meet you. I can be there this afternoon. Your workplace perhaps? Or your home?"

"No." The response was too quick. She relented. "Can you get here by three o'clock?"

Alice checked her watch. "Sure."

"I'll be at Old Clarke's Coffee Shop near the corner of Fulton and Ventura. How will I know you?"

"I'll find you," Alice said. "I've seen your picture."

"Oh god," Kilcorn breathed and hung up.

* * *

Alice hired a car downtown and took the I-80 across Bay Bridge to Oakland, the I-580 east, then the I-205 heading south. She arrived just after one o'clock, ate a leisurely lunch, and took a stroll around Fulton Mall and Chinatown. At 2:45, she pulled up opposite Old Clarke's Coffee Shop and found a table at the back.

The place had a western theme. Gnarled wood, gingham tablecloths, old Wanted posters on the walls. Alice ordered coffee and a donut, then spent ten minutes looking through the local paper.

Amelia May Kilcorn arrived on the dot of three. She was tall, slim and dressed in a light gray business suit. She wore heels and carried a leather briefcase. NGI listed her occupation as a legal executive, and she looked the part— right down to her stern expression. Blond hair, smooth complexion. An all-American girl except for a downturned mouth that gave her a somewhat spoiled look.

Alice raised a hand and caught her attention.

"Ms Kilcorn?"

She nodded. Alice could see caution in her eyes. The way she took in her jeans, T-shirt and nylon jacket.

"You said you're with the FBI."

"I am." Alice showed her ID. "But I'm currently on vacation."

"So this is not official?"

"No."

"Then what...?"

"Please." Alice gestured to the seat opposite. "Can I get you anything?" Kilcorn shook her head. "Then let me explain.

"As I said, I'm on vacation. On my way here, I passed through Winnemucca. It seems we have some mutual acquaintances."

"What's that supposed to mean?"

"Big Jim, Davy, Rick."

"Who are they?"

"You've never heard of them before?"

Kilcorn said nothing.

"But you have been to Winnemucca?"

"I may have passed through there sometime."

"You don't remember? Only, I took a cell phone off the one called Rick. It had some pictures of you on it."

"What sort of pictures?"

"Either consensual group sex or gang rape. My guess is the latter."

Kilcorn closed her eyes and let out a breath.

"Do you want to tell me what happened?"

She opened her eyes again. "Do you want to tell me how you got those pictures?"

"I had a similar experience. But I got a lucky break. I escaped and stole the phone."

"They raped you too?"

"Tried to."

"And? Please tell me they're all in jail."

"They're not, but they could be. If you're willing to make a complaint."

Kilcorn shook her head and looked away.

"Why not?"

"Because of what they said they'd do."

"Which is what, precisely?"

She twirled the gold ring on her left hand. "You've seen the pictures. They took a video too. Said they'd put it on a porn site and send links to all my friends if I ever said anything. I've just got engaged, Ms Kwann. To a hard-working, decent guy. Donny doesn't know anything about this. No one does. But once something like that's out there, you can never get it back."

"It's already out there," Alice said. "*They* have it. They could release it any time."

"But you said—"

"I took a phone off one of them. It had some pictures on it. Stills. You say there's a video too? If you help me, we can get the lot. *Before* they do anything with it."

"There's no guarantee of that. I know how these things work, Ms Kwann. They could have made a hundred copies already."

"They raped you."

"Not... all of them."

"What do you mean?"

She stared down at her hand. Twirled the ring. "The sandy-haired guy, Davy. We met in a bar. I thought he was OK. Kind of cute. We had a few drinks, a few laughs. Went out the back and had a smoke. He said he fancied some fun. I did too. I just... didn't expect he'd invite his friends."

"It didn't look fun."

"It wasn't."

"So it was rape."

"Look, it was almost a year ago. I just want to forget it. I was a bit drunk, a bit stoned, and I was stupid to have got into that situation in the first place."

"You're not the only one, you know. There have been others."

"*I'm* the only one sitting here right now," she said with sudden vehemence.

Alice said nothing.

The waitress came over. Kilcorn waved her away.

"How did you find me anyway?"

"From your picture. Government agencies use facial recognition software. We get data from social media sites. Millions of photographs, all tagged with people's names. We can pick you out in a crowd."

"There you are then! I know the way high-tech advances. Everyone'll have that soon. If they let those pictures out, my kids could find them in twenty years' time and see it was their mom!"

"That's very unlikely."

"Oh yeah? Ten years ago, who'd have believed you could carry a computer round in your pocket? Ten years ago, who'd have believed the government and corporations would track you everywhere you went? Spy on every call you make and every message you send?" She shook her head. "No, I'm sorry. I know you mean well, but I won't risk it. I can't."

"You'd rather risk those guys keeping their word?"

"They have so far."

Alice said nothing.

"Besides, you said they tried it on you. Why don't you make your own complaint?"

Alice said nothing.

"Is it because you don't want to take the flak personally? Because one of them's the police chief's son and one of them's the mayor's?"

"Neither of those things are true. They say that to intimidate their victims. And I don't want to file a complaint because it would draw a counter complaint that could see them walk away scot-free."

"What's that supposed to mean?"

"Let's just say that when I left town I left some walking wounded behind. And some property damage."

Kilcorn twisted the ring again and chewed her lip. "I'm sorry, I really can't help you. I don't want to get involved. I just want to forget it ever happened."

"Can you really do that?"

Kilcorn regarded her coolly. "Yeah, actually I think I can. If I'm allowed to."

With that, she got up and walked away.

Alice sat a while, thinking. She could understand Kilcorn's perspective. How she'd come to rationalize it to herself; the drink, the dope, the dumb mistake. No long-term damage done. Learn the lesson, pick yourself up and move on. She had a career, a fiancée, things to look forward to. A whole life ahead. Why look back?

Because sometimes your past won't let you go.

* * *

Alice stopped halfway back and called ahead, told Annabel she'd run into an old friend, and they were planning to eat uptown.

"Fine. You have a key, right?"

"Yes, the back door."

"We'll leave the light on. See you tomorrow."

She sat for a long time, thinking, then drove back slowly, barely noticing the trip. It was late by the time she dropped the car off. The rental agency was closed, so she left the keys in the after-hours deposit box and walked to the nearest BART station.

The encounter with Amelia Kilcorn had unsettled her. Maybe Kilcorn was right. Maybe she should let sleeping dogs lie.

The past is another country. They do things differently there.

Another country *and* another world.

Twenty years. A night that had defined her. A night that had brought her here. Shouldn't she be grateful? Not for what had been done to her, but for the consequences. Could she, in her remote village in the time before her parents died, ever have imagined she'd end up here?

Something else Kilcorn had said resonated too. When Alice told her she wasn't the only one who'd been raped, she'd replied, "*I'm* the only one sitting here right now."

Alice thought of the others on the truck. She was the only one walking these quiet streets. One of a handful who'd got a lucky break. By pure chance, she'd hit the jackpot.

But was that any reason for complacency? She couldn't forget those who hadn't been so lucky. The other girls and boys who'd traveled with her. The hundreds, the thousands of other children subjected every day to what she'd been through.

Yet for twenty years she had forgotten them. Or tried to.

The porch light was on when she got home. And the hall light. She locked the back door behind her and threw the security bolt, only realizing as she padded through the kitchen that she hadn't eaten. It was too late now. She helped herself to a glass of milk and some cookies, noticing two fresh wine bottles in the recycling basket.

She tried to read, couldn't concentrate, so turned out the light. Still, her disquiet didn't fade. She tossed and turned and rearranged her pillow. There was something underneath it.

She sat up and switched on the lamp. The video cassette. Chatri had returned it, along with a note.

A sheet of letter paper folded in half. Heavy stock, the output of a color printer. In the top left-hand corner was a photograph of a smiling man looking directly at the camera, one arm outstretched, pointing. Alice felt something catch in her chest. It was him. The face of her nightmares. Beside it, written in Chatri's cursive scrawl, were two words: "Long Tom". There was nothing else.

TWENTY

Hans Reisinger shook his head and watched the ball fly up the fairway from a near-perfect drive. Three hundred yards at least. Dead straight. It bounced twice then landed on a corner of the green.

"Like I keep telling you," Thomas Hartley said, "Stance and shoulders,"

"My stance and shoulders keep landing me in the rough."

"As in golf, so in life," Hartley grinned. "See you on the green. Eventually."

At the end of the round, Hartley was five strokes off the course record. Reisinger wasn't even close.

The clubhouse was a single-story sprawl of tinted glass and stained timber. The back bar spread over an open deck dotted with tables shaded by umbrellas. It overlooked the water hazard on the fifth, an S-shaped pond that was long and deceptively steep sided. It caught out so many unwary players that it had to be dredged twice a year.

Hartley and Reisinger took a spot in the corner, away from the occupied tables, and watched as another ball dropped into the pond. A ragged cheer went up from further round the deck. Another addition to the club's secondhand ball collection.

A waiter brought their drinks. Whisky for Reisinger, club soda for Hartley.

"I can't believe you drink that stuff." Reisinger shook his head. After more than thirty years in the States, he still had a hint of his German accent.

"Alcohol impairs your performance."

"It also deadens the pain."

"You should know, I saw your scorecard."

Reisinger saluted him and drank deeply. "So what's our situation?"

"Couldn't be better."

"Despite our recent loss?"

"Sometimes it seems like things are meant to be."

"Explain."

"You know how we always have a problem with the... unwanted extras?"

"Not my department, but I've heard you mention the disposal problem before."

"The second shipment goes to a cartel frontman down in Mexico. Guy named Salgado. Complete shit. He's been beating us down on price for years. We barely break even on that part of the deal. It'd almost be cheaper to have the damn thing pushed off the boat."

"Why don't we?"

"Containers float. Surprising, huh? Just below the surface, apparently. Makes them a shipping hazard. They send out boats to pick them up."

"Ah."

"So, Salgado's had us over a barrel. Till now. I've been working on another deal through a Chinese contact. Cost plus ten percent. As many as we can bring in. They're working up a distribution network as we speak. They're also interested in a first look at our main product."

"Sounds good."

"Except they won't be ready for another month. And we have a shipment on the way." Hartley sipped his club soda. "So this one goes to Salgado, one last time. With a bonus. I had Tak add a little extra to this consignment. A sort of parting gift. Like, 'Thanks for all the business, motherfucker.'"

"What do you mean?"

"In the past, he's just paid off Mexican authorities and walked away with the goods. This time, we set something up. Something to excite a little interest on our side of the border, before the shipment even reaches him. And it just so happens that the tip-off will help embed our new guy, Ferriera's replacement."

"You've found someone already?"

"Nancy lined him up. And get this, he's only an intel officer in Customs and Border Protection."

"You're kidding?"

"Nancy's checked him out. Been on the database for years. Lives in Culver City but uses a box number in Rossmoor. Drives sixty miles return just to pick up our packages. That shows a certain commitment. And caution."

"Clearly not enough if Nancy tumbled him. What's his history?"

"The usual. A steady tendency towards the more extreme."

"How much does he want?"

"Five hundred."

"*Thousand?*"

"Bucks."

"What?"

"He wants five hundred bucks up front."

"That's it?"

"It's pin money to pay off some clerk he knows. A nephew or something down at the port."

"What else?"

"A little career boost wouldn't go amiss. I said we can guarantee him that with our parting gift to Salgado."

"What else?"

"Merchandise. You know what these guys are like. Years of watching but not touching."

"Returnable?"

"Does it matter?"

"Can we afford it? Depending on breakages, we might be a little tight this time. Don't forget the back orders."

"Tak's got a second full shipment lined up for next month. Anyway, we should consider this an investment. We got four good years out of Ferriera, and he's still as tight as a clam."

"I've seen the footage we've got of him. He can't afford to be anything else."

"Same will go for the new guy once we reel him in. Intel from inside the CBP, for fuck's sake. That's gold dust!"

"I hope you're dealing with this personally."

"Of course. We don't want Nancy freaking him out, right?"

Reisinger nodded and sipped his drink. "You're smiling, Thomas. I think there must be more."

"Oh yeah, I almost forgot the best part. Now we're

officially informers, we get protected status. The CBP look after its own."

Another golf ball landed in the S-shaped pond beyond the balcony. There was another ragged cheer from further round the deck.

Hartley raised his glass. "Stance and shoulders, my friend. It's all in the stance and shoulders."

* * *

Alice woke to the sound of giggles and a curious face at her door. Daylight streamed through the blue curtains giving the room a vaguely underwater feel.

"Hello," Alice said.

Rosa swung on the door handle, her dark eyes gleaming. "Daddy said do you want a cup of tea?" A low voice murmured from the hall. "Or caw-fee?" she added.

"Caw-fee would be great," Alice said.

"OK." Small footsteps pounded away.

A minute later there were murmurings outside and an insistent, "I can do it!"

Rosa reappeared, moving carefully, her concentration focused on the mug and the small tray she was holding.

"Why thank you," Alice said, sitting up. "Great service round here."

She took the cup as Rosa looked around the room.

"Is he yours?" She pointed to the stuffed bear on her backpack.

"That's Mr Tubble."

"I got a bear too. He's called Bruin. He's bigger than

that."

"Newer too, I expect."

Chatri's face appeared around the door, beaming. "Good morning."

"Morning. I was just complimenting Rosa on the service." Alice raised the mug.

"She's very good with guests, aren't you poppet?" Rosa ran over and hugged his knees. He glanced at the folded paper on the bedside table adding, "I'm going in a little later this morning if you want a ride. Just after eight?"

"Perfect," Alice said.

She finished her coffee, showered, dressed and straightened the bed. The video cassette was still under the pillow. She tucked it back in the belly of the bear where it had lain for the last twenty years.

"Daddy says breakfast," Rosa called from the hallway.

"Coming."

It was just the three of them at first. Annabel surfaced when they were almost done. She was wearing a housecoat, her hair was still bed-rumpled, and without make-up her face looked sallow and drawn. She sat at the breakfast bar quietly sipping coffee.

"Solikha's coming in with me."

She nodded.

"We'll drop Rosa off at school. You'll pick her up?"

Annabel nodded again.

Rosa waved as they reversed down the drive. Annabel was visible in the lounge picture window, still in her housecoat, one arm around her waist, the other clenched to the coffee cup. She didn't return the wave.

Rosa's elementary school was a mile away. She gave her

daddy a kiss, said goodbye to Alice, and joined the mass of kids inside the gate. No time to turn and wave. She was already swamped by friends.

"So, 'Long Tom'," Alice said. "What does that mean?"

"I don't know. That's all I got."

"Complete with quote marks?"

He nodded, swung out into a break in the traffic and accelerated away.

"Could it be a nickname? Or did someone just miss out a comma out and it's really Tom Long?"

"Honestly, I have no idea. I got one hit and that's all it said."

"It is an old photograph. He will have changed."

"Not that much. The system creates a faceprint from more than a hundred nodal points. Things that don't change, like the distance between the eyes, the shape of cheekbones and the length of the jawline. Even if he's had plastic surgery, even if he's bald and bearded now, the system should find him."

"Does that mean he's dead?" Alice felt a flicker of something as she spoke the words. Disappointment or relief? She wasn't sure.

"That's what I thought at first. But dead people take a while. The system digs deeper and deeper. It can take hours sometimes. This came back promptly. Too promptly in the circumstances. So I looked at the metadata. It appears someone put a security trigger on his file."

"When?"

"Last week."

"What? You mean I've missed him by a week?"

"Looks that way."

"Who the hell is he that he qualifies for a security trigger? A senator or something?"

"Not necessarily. Just someone of interest. Or someone with influence. You think anyone can look up a VIP's home address without tripping an alarm?"

"Where does this particular alarm go? Do you know who set it?"

"I don't know who, but I do know the where: the DHS."

"Homeland Security?"

"Customs and Border Protection division."

"Shit!"

Alice mulled over his words. Someone of interest, or someone with influence. The latter seemed unlikely, so it had to be the former. Maybe his past was about to catch up with him after all.

"It's a heck of a coincidence," Chatri said.

It was. An almost unnerving one. But coincidences happened. They were the lifeblood of data analysis.

"He's clearly still alive then."

Chatri said nothing.

They merged with northbound traffic on the I-280.

"So how come you got what you got?" Alice said. "Long Tom and nothing else? Why didn't you get a security lock on the whole record?"

"Maybe someone slipped up and didn't associate that link with his real name. Or it may just be the alpha system. Some of our older databases only get refreshed once a month. It's only test data, after all. Next month, he may disappear completely."

"So the name Long Tom is old data?"

"Most likely."

Alice said nothing.

"Look, if you want me to, I can always click the unlock and make up an excuse. Say I hit the wrong key by mistake. Testing the road blocks is all part of system testing."

"What would the consequences be? For you, I mean?"

"Depends on how important he is. Anything from a mild reprimand to a full-scale SWAT call-out."

She looked at him.

"OK, maybe not that bad. But you know what I mean."

"You know what they say: don't mess with the DHS. They can make your life miserable. Especially as you're not US-born. You know how paranoid those bastards are."

"And five percent of the Thai population are Muslim. Yes, yes, I know all that, but I'm not a Muslim or a Buddhist. I'm an atheist."

"That would make you even more suspicious in some peoples' eyes. Better not to rattle that cage."

"What will you do now then?" Chatri asked.

"I don't know. Just hearing he's still out there makes me feel kind of weird. I need to think about it."

She was lying. She didn't need to think about it at all. She'd just decided. Right then. She knew exactly what she was going to do. But it couldn't involve Chatri. He worked for a defense contractor and would, at the very least, be liable to regular security checks. Which would include all known associates, and that included her.

They drove on. The traffic was getting heavier. They slowed for a tailback near Exit 52.

"You were late back last night," Chatri said.

"I... caught up with a friend."

"So Annabel said. Good evening?"

Alice gave her head a so-so shake.

"Male or female?"

"Who's asking?"

"I'm taking a professional interest. Now you've turned me into an FBI agent."

"Female," Alice said.

He nodded. Said nothing.

"There's no need to look like that, Chatri."

"Look like what? I don't look like anything."

"I know you too well. And you know me."

He drove on for a half a minute. "Sometimes I wonder if we really ever know anyone. Even ourselves."

"Why do you say that?"

He stared straight ahead at the traffic. Eased to a stop behind the car in front. "No reason."

There was, she could tell. But she could also tell from the slope of his shoulders and the set of his mouth that it was something he didn't want to talk about. That if she began to probe, he'd clam up entirely. Best to let it surface of its own accord.

"Would it bother you if I was?" she said.

"Was what?"

"What you suspected."

"I suspect nothing!"

"You'll make a lousy agent then. You have to suspect everyone, of everything, all the time. Discount no possibilities."

"None at all?"

"Well, maybe that one."

He smiled. "Meet me for lunch?"

"Same time, same place?"

* * *

The main branch of the San Francisco Public Library was located in a fortress-like gray slab on Larkin Street. Alice scoped it out before inquiring about using the free internet.

"Are you a cardholder?" the young man behind the counter asked.

"No, I'm from out of town."

"Visitors and non-card holders only get thirty minutes."

"I see." Alice gave him a wistful look.

"But it's early, and we're not too busy right now." He looked around. "Maybe I can give you a one-time guest pass. That'll give you two hours."

"That would be very kind of you."

"If I could just have your name?"

"Sure. Lee, Jane Lee."

"And your email address?"

She made one up on the spot.

He tapped some keys on his computer then handed her a card. "There you go. Ms Lee. Terminal 116. Over there. Just input that number."

Alice settled behind the computer and logged in. Chatri's mention of a security lock made her cautious. Depending on his level of importance, every search for Long Tom might be scooped up by the NSA and checks run on the source of the inquiry, so she searched using StartPage instead of Google. The European site redirected searches back to the local search giant, but unlike Google, no record was kept of what was being searched or where the search

148

requests were coming from.

Her caution proved unnecessary. Long Tom turned out to be the name of a field gun used in World War II. There were hundreds of references. Thousands. She refined her search to ignore them and got links to a gold sluice, a rocket, a golf club, and a river in west Oregon instead. Once those were eliminated, once she'd refined the terms all she could, it was a matter of scrolling through what was left. Page after page, checking every reference. About 30,000 of them, the screen told her.

After an hour, she stretched and yawned and eyed a new arrival's takeaway coffee. Then she cupped her chin in one hand and continued the search.

Towards the end of the second hour, a possible hit appeared. Her pulse quickened as she stared at the screen. A long-forgotten directory of porn. Someone's pet project, by the looks of it. It hadn't been updated in a decade but, as Amelia Kilcorn had observed, once something was out there, it never went away.

Long Tom had been the name of a third-rate ninety's porn star. Or rather, co-star. Women got top billing—not surprising considering the audience—with their fellow performers getting only a passing mention, if any at all. He was credited with a handful of films with jokey titles based on then-current movie releases: *Pump Fiction*, *Jurassic Prick*, and *The Even Bigger Lebowski*. But there was nothing later than the millennium.

The same guy? It was possible. The timing was right. But there was no way of knowing who he was in real life. Porn stars often took on names as silly as the film titles, and even if the movies were still about, she didn't want to watch him in action, she wanted to know who he really was.

A warning popped up saying she had only five minutes left. It was now late morning. All the terminals were occupied and there was a queue waiting their turn. The guy behind the counter and gave her a helpless shrug. She waved her thanks and shut down the browser. She needed coffee anyway.

* * *

Chatri beckoned her over. "Have a good morning?"

"So-so." Alice settled on the grass beside him and unbagged the Cobb salad she'd brought. She told him about the library. "All I got was guns. Apparently the Long Tom was a World War II artillery piece. I tried Tom Long, but that gave me about seven hundred million hits. They might take a while to work through."

"At least half the afternoon." He smiled, then grew serious. "Does that mean you've decided to track him down?"

"I've been thinking about that. What I'd do if I find him? If he was sitting on that bench over there, I know what I'd like to do, but I'm not sure I could. It seems the closer I get..." She shrugged and left the sentence unfinished.

"What looks large from a distance, close up ain't never that big."

"What?"

"Bob Dylan. *Tight Connection To My Heart.*"

Alice laughed. "I'd forgotten about your Dylan phase."

"Dylan is not a phase. He is a way of life."

150

"Oh, very Zen! And isn't there a double negative in that lyric? Still, I take your point."

"Does that mean you're giving up this foolishness?"

"What foolishness?"

"Whatever foolishness you had in mind when you asked me to look him up in the first place."

"You don't think he should pay for what he did?"

"How? You can't take back twenty years. And in a way, without him, you—we—would not be sitting here right now."

"Are you suggesting he should go unpunished because a couple of his victims hit the jackpot?"

"No, but I am saying that if you find him, you should think carefully about what to do next. A case like this will be bound to attract publicity. You have your career to think about, to say nothing of your future."

She nodded. Chatri was a good man. She was right not to involve him any further, especially as the last thing she'd been thinking about was a court case.

They ate in silence for a full minute. Without looking up he said, "You probably noticed things are not so good at home. We had a row last night. Another one."

"About me?"

"Only peripherally. Mainly about Annabel's drinking."

"Look, if my staying is making things awkward—"

"No, no, don't even think that. The wheels came off our relationship months ago. We've been skidding across the tarmac ever since, trying to avoid the crash." He stared into the middle distance. "After we lost the child, Annabel had an affair. A work colleague. It only lasted a few weeks and ended badly, but she blames me. Thinks I told the wife of the other man. I didn't, but once suspicion has been raised..." He gestured helplessly. "Now she finds fault with everything I do.

"She always drank a little more than she should, but lately it's got worse. I don't like Rosa seeing her mother like that. *I* don't like seeing her like that. But of course, I can't say anything. It's a fine thing when you find yourself dreading the weekends and looking forward to Monday so you can get away to work."

Alice didn't know what to say. People's lives were almost too complicated sometimes.

"How much does Annabel know about us?"

He looked at her. "What do you mean?"

"Where we came from. How we met."

"Only that we were street kids in Bangkok before the Kwanns found us."

"You've never told her what we were doing there?"

He looked out across the park to the city beyond. "People don't understand about that sort of thing, Solikha. Not here. Not in America."

"What sort of thing?"

"Selling children. They think that such a society must be barbarous or primitive. They think of poverty as some sort of personal failure. They can't imagine how whole communities—whole countries—can be born into it. How mothers, fathers, entire families have to work ten, twelve, fourteen hours every day just to survive. How children are the only asset you can ever have because, as they grow, they can share the burden. How sometimes they're superfluous, or sometimes indentured to pay off debts.

"There was a woman in our office who came back from

a holiday in Bali. She told how one day she and her husband strayed beyond the comfortable hotels and restaurants around Kuta beach. They didn't get far. Ran back to their hotel double-quick. I remember her words: 'There were people with children living in bits of shit at the side of the road!' She was outraged. When I pointed out that this is how one-third of the world live, do you know what she said? 'Well I don't want to see it.'"

Alice thought about his words. Who was she to talk of secrets?

She took a bite of salad then said, "Do you regret it? Your marriage, I mean?"

"I don't regret Rosa. But the rest? I don't know." He stared down at his untouched lunch. "Don't you sometimes wonder about the world we grew up in? Don't you wonder what happened to those people we used to be when the future seemed so full of promise?"

TWENTY-ONE

A lice took an early train back to Daly City, bought groceries along the way and arrived at the house on Wildwood Avenue a little after 5:00pm. She figured Rosa would have been collected from elementary school after it finished at 3:00 or maybe 3:30. Chatri wasn't due home till after 6:00.

Annabel's car was in the garage. The back door was open. Alice set the grocery bags on the kitchen counter and went through to the lounge.

"Hi Alice," Rosa called. She was sprawled on the floor watching television. Annabel was standing behind her, watching too. She was still dressed in work clothes; a smart pantsuit in pale blue with a crème colored blouse. She hadn't even taken off her jacket. But she had poured herself a glass of wine.

"I brought some things for dinner," Alice said. "I thought I'd cook tonight, if that's all right?"

"Oh. Sure. But there's really no need. I was going to call Chatri. Tell him to stop for something on his way home."

"It's the least I can do. For your hospitality."

Alice returned to the kitchen and began unbagging things. Annabel followed her through and stood in the doorway, watching. "You cook too?"

"I try to. Every night if I can. It's too easy to not bother, living alone. I thought I'd cook something for Chatri. A dish we ate the first day we met in Bangkok. But I'm sure you've heard that story."

Alice turned away and continued her preparations.

"Probably. But remind me."

"It's not the sort of thing you'd forget."

Annabel gave her a quizzical look, put down her glass, picked up a fresh one and gestured at the bottle.

"Sure," Alice said. "Thanks."

Annabel poured. "So, tell me the story. Or remind me."

"What exactly has Chatri told you?"

"That you were a couple of street kids running wild in Bangkok. That you got lucky. Were picked up and taken to that place the Kwanns ran."

"But he hasn't told you how we got there in the first place? How we came to be on the streets of Bangkok?"

"No."

"Did it never strike you strange that he was originally from Udon Thanai, four hundred miles north? And that I came from a remote village in Cambodia and didn't even speak the language?"

"I never really thought about it."

Alice said nothing.

"Is it a big secret then?"

Alice's eyes flicked to Rosa, sprawled on the lounge floor, then back again. "Perhaps not in the way you imagine."

Annabel took the hint and closed the intervening door. She returned and leaned on the breakfast bar.

Alice set a shoulder of pork on the bench along with garlic, coriander, soy sauce and chili peppers. "It's a dish called *Khao Kha Moo*. Stewed pork with rice. Does Rosa mind spicy food?"

"Not with a Thai father who was brought up by a family from India."

Alice smiled. "I won't make it too fierce."

She found a saucepan, part filled it with water, added the crushed peppers, coriander, garlic and a little sugar, then set it over a medium heat and added the pork. When it began to boil, she turned down the heat, covered it and left it simmering.

She turned back. Annabel was watching her.

"So what is it Chatri's never told me? Don't worry, I can keep a secret. Besides, how big a deal can it be? You were kids."

"We were sex slaves."

It took a moment for her words to register. Annabel frowned. "What?"

"Do you have a blender? I'd like to make a dressing for the side salad."

Annabel pointed to a cupboard. "Did you just say what I thought you said?"

"Yes."

"I... don't understand."

"Chatri was a proper street kid, pretty much from birth. His mother was a drug addict who basically abandoned him. My parents died in a traffic accident, and I was sent to an uncle and aunt who couldn't afford to keep me. They sold me to the same gang that picked Chatri up. We ended up on the same truck and were transported to Bangkok, though we didn't meet properly till a few days later."

"Sold you?" Annabel repeated.

"Children can be an asset or a burden to the very poor. Girls particularly. Depending on customs and religion, marrying them off may require a sizable dowry. An added burden. The demands of just finding adequate food for a family can be immense, and there aren't any safety nets like health care or unemployment insurance. And there are people who prey on that insecurity and exploit those at risk and those in need. They clean up the waifs and strays—for a profit.

"Trucks go round the villages at regular intervals, picking up the abandoned and unwanted, or promising the girls work as maids and nannies in the cities or overseas. Whatever it takes. Girls often go willingly to help support their families, not really knowing what the *work* will entail. Sometimes money changes hands.

"The sex trade is the third-largest criminal business in the world, right up there behind illegal weapons and illegal drugs. But no one ever talks about it. Customers come from wealthy countries and pay big money for things they can't get or dare not seek at home. Like children."

Annabel's face was a mask of horror.

"And that's how we came to be in Bangkok."

Alice measured canola oil into the blender and added peeled garlic, soy sauce, sesame oil, honey and lime juice.

"But you got away before anything happened, right?"

"No."

She let the word sink in. Gave the blender a short burst to combine the ingredients then dipped a teaspoon in to taste it.

"I got away after the first night by climbing down a fire escape. I found Chatri at a window two floors down. He was locked in. Crying. I don't know why, but I felt sorry for him. He seemed to personify all that had happened to me. All the stuff I didn't want to think about. So I found a metal bar, pried the window open, and we escaped together. That was how we met."

Annabel said nothing.

"The men came after us, but we managed to avoid them. I stole some money, and we bought *Khao Kha Moo* from a roadside vendor. We ate it sitting in the gutter. A little later, Glenn and Mary Kwann found us and took us in."

Alice added some water and a little lemon grass paste and powered on the blender again.

Eventually, Annabel said, "Chatri was what, eleven, twelve?"

Alice nodded.

"And you?"

"I was nine."

"My god." Her words were almost a sigh. "He's never ever said anything about... being abused."

"It's not something either of us likes talking about."

Annabel found a stool and sat down heavily. "I had no idea."

"There's no reason you should. Chatri's adjusted very well."

"And you?"

Alice shrugged. "Yeah."

"When I was nine I went away to summer camp. That was my big adventure. Kind of pales in comparison, huh?"

Alice looked up and caught her eye. Annabel's gaze was

searching.

"Sorry. Looks like I trumped you again."

Annabel laughed. "Fuck that. You can win that hand, girl. You can win the lot." She picked up her glass and raised it.

Alice accepted the toast, clinked her glass and sipped. The wine was cool and crisp.

"So... you and Chatri are just friends?" Annabel said.

"More like brother and sister."

"That's what he said. I've never been close to my brothers."

"When you've been through something like that, you form a bond. I guess it's like war buddies. Men who've been through battle together. Something you can't fully explain." She looked up. "But that's all we've ever been, like brother and sister."

Chatri arrived home to a kitchen filled with rich, spicy smells and the two women chatting like old friends. He looked surprised and a little relieved. More surprised still when Annabel welcomed him with open arms and a kiss on the cheek. He glanced at the wine bottle. It was still half-full.

Later, while Annabel was setting the table, he handed Alice a note.

"What's this?" she said.

"Metadata. The CBP agent who requested the lock on Long Tom."

She looked at the name: Markham, Ronald P. It meant nothing to her.

"I thought perhaps with your FBI contacts..."

"Thanks. It might be useful." She folded the note and slipped it in her pocket.

TWENTY-TWO

For the second time this trip Alice was pleased she'd brought her ID. She worked a hunch, dressed up a little so she looked the part, and showed it at the main desk of UCSF's Mission Bay campus. It got her immediate attention.

Carla Ahearn was small and nervous. The lush auburn hair Alice had seen in Rick's cellphone pictures was gone, now cropped so closely that patches of her scalp were visible. She was pale, wore no make-up, and dressed in a plain, lumpish garment that might have been a cross between a poncho and a shawl. It was dark brown, faded in patches, accentuating the whiteness of her skin. She'd lost weight too. Her cheekbones showed. Her neck was thin. The girl in the photographs had been fresh and full of life. The girl approaching Alice looked drained of it.

"Hi. Carla, is it? I'm Agent Kwann." She held out her ID.

The girl looked at it and scratched one arm nervously. "I've never met anyone from the FBI before." She had a light, slightly nasal voice. Like a little girl lost.

"Call me Alice."

Alice had decided on a different approach this time. Carla Ahearn's online presence was almost the opposite of

Amelia Kilcorn's. A locked-down Facebook page—friends only, no updates for weeks at a time—and a forgotten travel blog with a day-by-day account of her summer vacation. A girl, a dog, a beat up Toyota, heading back to college. The entries stopped two days before the date on the photographs.

"Shall we find somewhere to sit?" Alice said. "Outside maybe? Seems a shame to waste a day like this."

"Oh. OK. I thought there'd be an office or something. Shall we go to Koret Quad?"

"Sure."

Carla led the way to a grassy area surrounded by slab-sided monoliths. The whole place appeared to have been built to a corporate agenda, leaving this one patch of begrudged greenery as a consolation to the drones who worked and studied there. Students were scattered around the lawns. A few were reading books. Most were studying phones or laptops. Carla found a vacant spot under some pines.

"This all right?"

"Fine."

Alice settled. Carla settled opposite in a smooth scissor movement, spreading the poncho over her legs and crossing her arms.

"First, I should tell you this is off the record. Forget the badge. It was just a way to get to see you. This is *not* Bureau business. It's just us, girl to girl. OK?"

"OK."

"You're probably wondering why I've come to see you."

"I guess." The girl didn't look directly at her but plucked at the grass with one hand.

"Do you have any idea what it might be?"

"No. Why should I?"

"Ever met a guy called Big Jim?"

The girl said nothing, but her plucking hand went still.

"From northern Nevada. A town called Winnemucca. Know it?"

"No."

"Never been there?"

"No."

"Not even passing through?"

"No."

"Are you sure?"

"Yes."

"That's strange. Your summer vacation blog shows you in Boise National Forest on your way down here. You were traveling Route 95, right? So you must have passed right through the place. It's not much of a town, but there's not much of anything up there. The kind of place you'd stop for gas, maybe a meal, maybe even for the night. It's still three hundred miles to Sacramento."

The girl said nothing, sat still and stiff as a board, but tears started down her cheeks.

Alice reached out a hand and took her shoulder. The girl's eyes were unfocused, her face impassive. The tears might have been coming from someone else entirely.

"I understand, Carla. I know what happened."

The girl said nothing. The tears continued. Finally, she focused, her eyes fearful. "How? How do you know?"

"I passed through there myself a week ago. Traveling on my own."

The girl stared at her. The irises of her dark eyes were

speckled with green flecks.

"What happened?" she said very quietly.

"I met Big Jim and his buddies."

The girl's breathing stopped, but the pulse at her neck fluttered wildly.

"Rick and Davy, wasn't it?"

The girl said nothing.

"I'd like to put a stop to what they've been doing."

"Did they...? Are you OK?"

"I'm fine. But I got lucky. I don't think everyone they met did."

The tears started again.

"Do you want to tell me what happened?"

The girl shook her head.

"I checked your record while I was waiting. That badge of mine gets me places. You've been a good student. Biology and biomechanics, isn't it? Impressive. Only, your grades have slipped a little since summer vacation."

"They're making me see a counselor. I don't like her."

"Have you told her?"

"No."

"Have you told anyone?"

"No."

"Want to tell me?"

"No." She looked fearful. "They said they'd get me if I did. Get my mom and dad. Put pictures of me everywhere so the whole world would know, and say they'd say they paid me to do those things."

"And did they?"

"No! They made me hold a wad of money, took a picture, then took the money back. They said it was insurance." Her face crumpled, she buried her it in her hands, and the sobs began in earnest.

Alice put her arms around the girl and comforted her, feeling the bony shoulder blades beneath the shawl. The crying continued for a long time.

Finally, Carla sat back, wiping her face with a free end of the poncho. Her eyes were red and raw, her lips puffy, but somehow she looked better than she had.

Alice held her by the shoulders, looked into her eyes. "You want to tell me what happened now?"

The girl bit her lip and drew a breath. "They had Benji."

"Your dog?"

She nodded. "I got gas and takeaways. We stopped at an out-of-town rest stop, so he could get out and run around. These guys stopped nearby in a truck. They were friendly at first. Asked about Benji and stuff. Where I was heading, what I did. Then one of them said, 'I know all about you college girls, so how about it?' Just like that."

The tears started again. She looked away.

"They had Benji. One of them stubbed a cigarette out on his back. He was howling. They said they'd kill him. I didn't have a choice."

She broke down again. Alice held her.

Some students went past, chatting gaily. One of them carried a Frisbee, using it like a fan.

"How's Benji now?" Alice asked, sensing the dog was the key to this walled-off memory.

"He's OK." Her voice was squeaky. Bird-like. "They locked him in the car. He didn't see."

She took a breath. Steadier now.

"They made me wash-up afterwards. In the restroom.

Filmed that too. Said I had to smile, or they'd go back and stab him. Said they had my registration. Got my name from my license. Would find out where I lived. If I ever made them trouble, if I ever told another soul, I'd come home one day and find my dog gutted and my pictures on every porn site in the country."

Alice studied her, thinking what a trial would do to this fragile girl already torn apart by the memory of that fateful afternoon. The witness statements and interviews. Testimony and cross-examination. Facing those brutes again across a courtroom. Listening to their lies. She couldn't, wouldn't ask for that.

Carla sat forward, hugging her knees, rocking slightly. Eventually, she said, "What happens now?"

Alice took out a notebook. "I'd just like a few more details. When. Where. Anything you can remember."

"Then what?"

"Then nothing. I just want to... build my case. Get an idea of how these guys operate."

"But you'll stop them, won't you?"

"Oh yes," Alice said. "I promise you that."

* * *

With Carla's permission, Alice spoke to the head of student services, an overworked woman in her early fifties. Norma Natros had heard of every student calamity imaginable. Still, she was shocked to learn the real reason for Carla Ahearn's sudden performance downturn.

"We could see she was having problems, but I had no

idea something like that was behind it. She's been so withdrawn. So hard to reach."

"Perhaps you can reach her now," Alice said.

"I'm sure we can. There's a whole range of social services for women who've been through something traumatic like that. If she's willing, I can certainly find someone to refer her to."

With that assurance, with Carla's email address, and a promise to keep in touch, Alice left the Mission Bay campus and headed downtown.

She stopped at the first rental agency she came across, hired a car and drove. Found the I-80, headed east.

She guessed Carla had a reasonable chance of a reasonable recovery. Better now the wall she'd built around it had been breached. But there was no objective measure. Rape affected different people in different ways. Women like Amelia Kilcorn—tough, forward-thinking, sexually liberated—might be able to put it behind them, bury it and move on, but people like Carla were undone by it. The happy, carefree girl of the blog postings was gone forever. If she was lucky, some semblance of her old self might return. But she'd never again step out to walk her dog without a flicker of uncertainty and a glance over her shoulder.

A road sign up ahead said the Nevada state line was two hundred miles away. Alice kept on driving.

Twenty-three

Nancy Templar was dressed like an executive in a business suit of olive green with a simple, sheath-like skirt that ended just above the knee. She wore a plain white blouse, buttoned to the neck, and her shoulder-length auburn hair was combed in perfect furrows and secured with a gold clasp. Her bearing and crisp manner suggested a military background, which she had. The business suit looked much like the uniform she'd worn to her court-martial.

"Let's go through this again," Hartley said. "Make sure we've got the right guy."

Templar sighed, gesturing at the file. "It's all there."

"Not everything. Do we know what he does with our packages after he collects them?"

"For fuck's sake Thomas, what do they normally do?"

"I don't mean that. I mean where he takes them."

"Well, if he's driving thirty miles to pick them up, he's hardly going to carry them home and watch them on the lounge TV."

"Can we get Russo on it?"

"And do what? We're busy shipping the latest disks. Plus we've got a new batch due next week, remember?"

"You think it's safe to risk it? Till we get a proper hold on him?"

"You do those assessments, Thomas. All I can tell you is he's been with us seven years. If he is an undercover cop, that's one hell of a commitment."

"It's the CBP angle that bothers me."

"Oh yeah, I was forgetting. Those Customs and Border Protection guys are all as pure as driven snow."

"I'm just saying—"

"Look, I've checked his record and I know the type. A mid-forties desk jock, career going nowhere, an ugly wife in an ugly suburb. Our stuff's probably the only thing that keeps him going. Now you've offered him a little real-life excitement, he'll be whacking off at the thought of that alone."

"That was my gut feeling."

"Then go with your gut."

"OK, I'll meet with him. Set it up." Hartley pushed back the file. "How are we at this end? Ready for a fresh intake?"

"Reisinger's taking out the last of them this afternoon."

"The fat one? The one we couldn't place?"

"She slimmed down OK."

"You should market that No Food diet of yours, Nancy." Templar didn't smile. "What's Hans got planned?"

"A gang of bikers." She sneered. "They make a fucking mess, Thomas. There'll be nothing left for me."

"You surprise me, Nancy. You can usually do something. But if you don't want her I'll send her straight to Benny."

Templar sighed. "I guess if she's still got a pulse."

Hartley smiled, despite the fact that Templar's

predilections sickened him. But this business took all sorts. It was what made their cooperative venture so successful.

"That's the attitude," he said.

* * *

Alice stopped at a Walmart in Sacramento and called Chatri.

"San Jose?" he said. "I thought you were on vacation."

"The office tracked me down. An emergency. An East Coast-West Coast liaison thing. I happened to be around. It'll save them flying someone out."

"All your things are back at the house."

"It's on expenses, and I'll only be a couple of days." She hated lying to him, but it was for his own good. The less he knew, the better. "I'll be back for the weekend."

"You sure?"

She recalled his words about spending his weekends looking forward to getting back to work. "Definitely. I promise."

She went into the store and cruised the aisles, picking out a costume wig, some cheap clothes, lipstick and a padded bra. In Hardware, she added a can of matte black spray paint and a length of rope to her basket. In the toy department, she chose a water pistol modeled on a Glock, and at the checkout she added a cheap pair of sunglasses.

The total bill came to $29.99. Alice paid cash. If things worked out the way she was hoping, ten bucks a head represented great value.

* * *

It was nearly midnight when she pulled into the motel lot. The place was two blocks back from the highway, but the roar of the occasional eighteen-wheeler was still audible. It was a cheap place. A little rundown, a little frayed at the edges. The windows were grimy. The paintwork was chipped. She disturbed the clerk, a young guy half-asleep at his computer in reception, registered in the name of Susan Wong, paid cash, and took a room on the end of a block of five.

She closed the door, took off the sunglasses and wig, and threw them on the bed. Then she ruffled her short dark hair. The wig was a cheap synthetic thing that prickled her scalp. Shoulder-length, auburn. The same color of Carla Ahearn's before she'd hacked it off.

The room was basic, the fittings old, but it was clean. After seven hours on the road, she was pretty beat. The bed looked appealing, but she had to do some preparation first.

The rope was forty foot long. She cut it into six equal lengths and put them to one side. Then she spread the pages of a tourist newspaper over the floor and took up the toy gun. It had an orange squirt nozzle at the end of the yellow plastic barrel. She pried the nozzle out and picked up the spray can. Several light coats would be best.

Once it was done, she undressed, showered, dropped into bed and closed her eyes. She could still half-see the fall of her headlights on the patch of road ahead and the vast empty blackness all around. She wondered vaguely what the hell she was thinking of, then mercifully sleep overtook her.

TWENTY-FOUR

A lice parked the rental in the lot behind The Little Ray of Sunshine then walked to the entrance feeling self-conscious in the wig, lipstick, and sunglasses. The T-shirt over the padded bra was too short to tuck in, but the skirt she'd chosen was flared. Like the flat-soled sandals, it was comfortable and gave her legs plenty of room to move. Be OK for running too, though she hoped she wouldn't be doing much of that.

Carla Ahearn's travel blog said she'd spent the night before her rape in McDermitt, about an hour north on the Nevada–Oregon border. She'd been attacked late morning, around eleven o'clock. On a weekday. Alice had been attacked around nine in the evening. Less than twelve hours later they'd been cruising the streets, looking for her. Also on a weekday.

The times suggested they were unemployed, or part-timers at best, and definitely not late shift, so Alice figured a ten o'clock start might be their more usual routine.

It was ten minutes after ten when she entered the diner.

She was good with accents as well as languages. She put on a Southern drawl. Doreen, the sharp-faced waitress

—still no ray of sunshine—took her order without a hint of recognition. The place would get a lot of passing traffic.

She took out a magazine—movie stars and gossip—and flicked through it while keeping an eye on the entrance. Seven minutes later, a yellow pickup drew up out front. Davy and Rick got out.

The swelling around Davy's cheeks had gone down. Apart from the nose splint and a shadow of bruising under one eye, he looked pretty normal. Rick was walking funny. Wide-legged. Like he'd just got off a horse after a hard gallop. There was no sign of Big Jim.

Davy walked with a swagger, two thumbs hooked in his belt. He wore a string vest and glanced around the diner like he owned the place.

Alice put down her magazine, sat back, stretched her legs and arched her back, looking out the window straight ahead. She was sitting on the end of one of the U-shaped booths near the front. There was plenty of room for company.

The stretch pushed her short skirt even higher, and her movements drew Davy's attention. From the corner of her eye, she saw him nudge his friend.

Rick muttered something. Davy shrugged and ambled over on his own.

"Mornin'," he said.

"Mornin'."

"Great day out there."

"Sure is."

"You passing through?"

"I guess. Don't seem like there's nothin' else to do round here."

"Oh, I don't know about that." He grinned and helped himself to the seat opposite. "Depends what you've got a mind to do."

He had short-cropped hair and big hands. Not a bad looking guy. Fairly trim, except his waistline, which was starting to show a few too many of the diner's breakfasts.

Alice saw his eyes linger on her padded breasts.

"Sorry, you don't mind, do you?" He gestured at the seat he was already occupying.

"Long as you don't mind watchin' me eat."

The waitress delivered her pancakes. Alice added maple syrup from a squeeze bottle, ran her finger around the top to catch the last drop, then slowly licked it clean.

Davy moistened his lips.

"I guess you live round here," she said.

"Uh-huh."

"What happened to your face?"

"You should see the other guy."

"Must've hurt."

"A little." He shrugged

"What happened?"

"Bikers. Came round here trying to mess us round. Me and my buddies saw 'em off."

"You took on bikers?"

"Six of them, three of us. They won't be coming back. See, they forgot the rule."

"The rule?"

"This is *our* town."

Alice smiled and pushed out her chest. "I guess I better remember that too."

He grinned, held out a hand. "Davy," he said.

Alice put down her fork. Took it. "Lou-ise," she said, drawing out the syllables. "My friends just call me Lou."

"Nice to meet you, Lou. So, where you from?"

"Pensacola."

"I don't know Pensacola, but I do know Coca-Cola."

Alice laughed.

"Where are you heading?"

"LA."

"You an actress or something?"

"How d'you know that?"

"I dunno. You just look like you might be." He took the opportunity to look her up and down again.

"I've done a bit of actressing and stuff, and I hear there's a lot of opportunities for girls like me out in LA. Actressing."

"Hell, I reckon there're opportunities for girls like you anywhere."

"Except round here." Alice took a forkful of pancake. Chewed it slowly. Licked her lips. "My motel room was awful quiet last night."

"We could go back and noisy it up a bit now if you want."

He grinned. A joke. Except it wasn't really.

"I already checked out. Besides, I guess you gotta get to work. I wouldn't want to make you late. You might get fired."

"I don't gotta get anywhere. Me and my buddy over there work part-time at the auto parts store. Ain't on shift till this afternoon. And Rick's daddy runs the place, so we ain't ever gonna get fired."

"So... what do you have in mind, Davy?"

"Whatever you like, Lou. A little weed, maybe. A little relaxing. A little fun. You can show me your actressing and stuff."

"You got a place to go?"

"I got my truck out front. Big cab."

"I don't like trucks. I'm an open air kinda gal. Back home, I just like walking round," she flexed her shoulders, "in the open air. You know what I mean?"

He grinned. "I reckon I do. Well, if you like fresh air, there's a real quiet rest stop off Mackenzie Road. Pretty view, but no one hardly ever goes there. It's got trees and grass and shade and stuff. I even got some blankets in the truck. We could make ourselves a picnic."

"Sounds like my kinda place. But what about your buddy?"

"We could let him watch. Don't you actresses like an audience?" He grinned. Another joke that really wasn't.

Alice shrugged. Made a show of checking his friend out. "I don't mind," she said.

Davy laughed. "Ain't you a wild one!"

He waved to Rick. "Hey, get over here. Come meet my new friend. This here's Lou-ise, but we can call her Lou."

Rick sidled over.

Alice gave him a big red lipstick smile. "You a cowboy?"

Davy guffawed. Rick glared at him.

"That fight with the bikers I was telling you about. Rick got kicked in the guts. Busted something. I dunno. Liver or something, weren't it?"

"Yeah," Rick muttered, scowling.

"Well, that ain't so bad. I hear the liver heals real quick."

"Lou here's looking for a party. I said we could maybe

go out Mackenzie Road. Want to come along?"

"I guess."

"What happened to your other buddy?" Alice asked. "He get kicked in the guts too?"

Rick looked from Alice to Davy.

"The bikers," she added. "You said it was three against six, right?"

"Oh. Right. No... he got cut. Switchblade. Got an infection. He's laid up right now."

"In the hospital?"

"No, back home."

Alice shook her head. "You boys got cut up, a kicked-in liver and a busted nose, and you still saw them bikers off. I am im-pressed. You sound like you got a lotta spunk."

"Oh, we got plenty of that. Ain't we, Rick?"

"Sure have." Rick brightened.

"Well, when I finish my coffee, maybe you can show me..."

* * *

The rest stop was a mile from town. It lay in a shallow depression between two parched hills. A space fifty yards long by twenty wide. One edge dropped into a barren gully with a dried-up stream bed far below. There were a few gnarled trees, some low brush and tough, patchy grass. A wooden picnic table anchored in cement sat at one end, overlooking the gully. The interstate was half a mile off. The place was deserted but strangely familiar. Alice recognized it as the backdrop to the photographs of Carla Ahearn.

The yellow truck bounced across the grass and stopped behind an outcrop of rock, out of sight of passing traffic. Not that there was any. Alice followed, nudging the fender of her rental into a patch of sagebrush.

Davy leaped from the truck and watched her park, grinning, hands on hips.

Alice got out, smiled, then turned back to her open driver's door and bent low to pop the trunk release. The short skirt rode up, and she heard a low, appreciative whistle.

"I got some party things myself back here."

"Oh yeah? What sort of things?"

He followed her to the back of the car where she took out two lengths of rope and tossed them to him.

"You any good at tying up?"

He grinned. "Sure am."

Alice dropped the accent, took the painted pistol from the wheel well, and jammed it in his face. "Then tie your friend up. And do a proper job, or I'll be *very* disappointed."

She nudged his nose splint with the barrel. Davy twitched reflexively and backed away, hands raised, still holding the lengths of rope.

"What the fuck?" Rick emerged from behind the truck.

"Undress," she told him.

"What?"

"Recognize this?" She tilted the gun. "It's a Glock 19, semi-automatic, fully loaded, fifteen rounds in the clip. It's carrying NATO standard nine-millimeter parabellums. Muzzle velocity, thirteen hundred feet per second. Projectile weight, eight grams. At this range, the bullet will pass through your buddy's thick skull without breaking a sweat.

Probably won't come down to earth for a mile or more. Davy here'll hit the dirt before it does. But before either of them do, the second round will be in your balls.

"Are you reading me now, Rick? Get your clothes off!"

"What the hell is this?" he said, unbuttoning his shirt.

Alice pulled the wig off with her free hand and raised the sunglasses. "Remember me?"

"What the fuck...?"

"You're a little slow, Rick. How about I shoot your buddy's kneecap off to hurry you up." Alice lowered the gun, aimed it.

"No, no, no!" Davy howled, holding out the palms of his hands as if they'd deflect a bullet. "Do what she says, man. Do what she says."

Rick threw his shirt aside. Started on his belt.

"Shoes, socks, shorts, everything. Hurry it up."

When he lowered his pants, Alice grinned. "That still hurt?"

He covered himself with his hands and muttered, "Bitch."

"Go over there and hug that tree," she told him. "You, tie his hands together."

She checked the knots when Davy was done. Nodded her satisfaction.

"Now spread your legs." She jabbed the gun in Rick's side. "Tie his ankles too. Good and tight. I'll be checking."

Davy did as he was told. She could see his hands shaking.

"Look, if you want money..." he said, looking up to see she had her phone out and was taking pictures. Rick looked too, then jerked his face away.

"What the fuck?"

"Your turn, Davy. Clothes off, throw them over here then stand behind your buddy. Real close now."

"Huh?"

Alice gestured with the gun.

"No way!"

"Then you both die here," she said coolly, raising the gun.

"What... what... what is this?" Davy stammered.

"You raped some friends of mine. Took their pictures. Threatened to release them if they ever told. This is payback. Their pictures for your pictures. If any of theirs get released, so do yours."

"You already got the damn pictures," Rick said.

"I want the videos too. And all the backups."

"There ain't no back—"

"Shut up, you dumb fuck," Davy hissed.

"Huh?"

"Well, that's good to know. So, who's got the videos?"

Davy said nothing.

"You heard the question."

Still Davy said nothing.

"Aw fuck it, I don't really care. You terrified my friends, but there's nothing to tie them to me. Easier to just finish you now." She raised the gun again.

"No, no, no! Don't, don't! It's Big Jim. He's got the camera."

"Guess I better pay him a visit then. Right after I finish with you two. Cuddle up close now."

TWENTY-FIVE

Tying Davy up on her own was trickier. After taking two more lengths of rope from the trunk, she made him tie his own ankles, loosely, around the tree, right behind Rick. His hands shook, the knots weren't great, but it would slow him down if he got any ideas.

Then Alice knelt in the grass and tied a slip knot in the other length of rope. She held it out to him, gun in one hand, looped it over his wrist and jerked it tight. It closed around his wrist like a snare.

"Free arm around your buddy now. Nice and close."

He did what she said.

Keeping her weight on the knotted end, she moved to the other side of the tree, set the gun down briefly, caught his free hand and lashed it tight.

"Well now, don't y'all look cozy." She stepped back to admire her handiwork, picking up the Southern drawl again as she took more pictures.

Two naked men, tied to a tree, one behind the other. It made an interesting subject.

"Rick seems to be enjoying that," she told Davy as she took another picture. "He's got a boner."

"The fuck I have!"

"Aw Jesus, man." Davy squirmed, trying to pull away.

"Good job I didn't tie y'all the other way about. You wouldn't be sitting down for a month."

"Aw Christ—"

"She's making it up, man. It's not true!"

"You keep believing that, Davy." She took some more shots. "Just don't drop the soap when your buddy's around."

Alice kicked their clothes into a pile and took Davy's keys and cellphone from his pants pocket.

"Mind if I borrow your truck? You don't look like you're going anywhere right now."

She double-checked the knots, retied a couple, then picked up the wig and sunglasses.

"Y'all have fun while I'm away."

* * *

Big Jim's place was an easy find. The address was in Davy's phone, and the truck's GPS did the rest.

The house was plain and boxy. A step up from a trailer, but not a big one. There was a Ford pickup and a battered Nissan sedan in the drive. Alice parked in front of both, tucked the gun in the passenger-side door pocket, and got out, pausing to fluff her wig and straighten her skirt.

A middle-aged woman in a greasy apron came to the door, eyed her suspiciously and glanced behind her at the familiar vehicle. Alice had found a fresh pack of gum in the truck and chewed as she spoke. "I'm a friend of Davy's. Is Big Jim around, please ma'am?"

"He ain't s'posed to go out," the woman said, showing

her inside.

The house looked like a storm had swept through it and its inhabitants hadn't yet had time to set things straight. There were old newspapers and junk mail flyers scattered up the hallway. A broken table sat propped up by a chair. The walls looked like they were covered in brownish grime. A dust storm, maybe.

Big Jim was in the lounge, reclining on a battered leather sofa, a remote control in one hand, a beer in the other. He looked up as they entered.

"Friend of Davy's," the woman said, and left them.

Big Jim muted the TV, swung into a sitting position and rose awkwardly.

"Well lookee here." He looked her up and down. "Where'd you spring from?"

"That your mama?" Alice gestured. "She's a right charmin' lady."

Big Jim's eyes narrowed.

Alice grinned.

He grunted. "Yeah, ain't she."

The dressing over his left eye was gone, but it still looked bloodshot.

"The bikers do that?"

"Huh?"

"Rick and Davy said you took on bikers."

"Oh, yeah. Where are they?"

"They said I should collect you cos they're kinda *occupied* at the moment." She underlined the word with a couple of hip thrusts.

"Oh yeah?"

"The rest stop off Mackenzie Road. They got a party

going down with some friends of mine."

"I... ain't s'posed to be going out. On account of having a fever."

"Yeah, Davy told me you got problems." She glanced at his crotch. "Said you prob'ly couldn't make it."

"He said what?"

Alice chewed. Said nothing.

"I can make that all right!"

"Don't matter if you can't. You could make a video. Enjoy it later."

He looked at her. Hesitated.

"You want I should ask your mama if you can come?"

"Fuck that. And fuck Davy. Let me get my stuff."

She followed him to his bedroom. It looked like the storm had swept through there too. He took a camera from a table and a six-pack from under a pile of bedding.

"Fridge's broke," he said by way of explanation.

"Your computer too, by the looks of things."

The remains of an Acer laptop were scattered over a desk in the corner. The layout of the pieces suggested someone had started a careful disassembly, then lost patience with the process.

"Fucking hard drive," he said. "Everything's fucking broke in this house."

"Hope your camera's not."

"That works just fine."

"So where'd you put your movies?"

"Nowhere at the moment. They're all on cards." He gestured at a plastic wallet containing half a dozen SD memory cards. "But once I get me a new computer, I can do a proper edit job. Put 'em all together. Make proper movies, you know?"

"Uh-huh. Hey, is that gonna be enough beer?"

He looked at the six-pack in his hand. "Maybe not." As he reached for another, Alice slipped the plastic wallet up the back of her too-tight T-shirt.

Outside, the screen door banged shut behind them and Alice saw the middle-aged woman hovering in the shadows, scowling. She gave her a wave.

"Best you drive. Figure you know the way better than I do."

Big Jim took the wheel, pulled a cigarette from a packet in the pocket of his shirt, and leaned across to push in the lighter, taking a close-up look at Alice as he did so.

"So... where you from?"

"Pensacola."

"Florida way?"

"Uh-huh."

It took five minutes to reach the rest stop. Alice dropped her hand to the door pocket.

"Park up there by the edge of the gully."

Big Jim swung the wheel and stopped, bringing the two men tied to the tree into view. They'd worked at it, but hadn't made much progress freeing themselves.

"What the fuck?"

"I told you they were occupied." Alice raised the gun.

Big Jim exhaled a stream of cigarette smoke and stared at her, then reached for the ashtray. He was quicker than she expected. He stubbed out the butt with a resigned air then slammed his elbow back into her forearm, jamming the gun against the seat. He reached around to grab her with his free hand.

If it hadn't been a toy, the gun would have fired harmlessly through the seat back. More importantly, Alice was right-handed. Big Jim's move twisted her sideways and wedged both her arms against the seat.

He turned and seized her by the neck with his left hand, jamming his thumb in the base of her throat, right over the windpipe. But Alice was more flexible than he expected. She swivelled with the turn inflicted by his slamming elbow, brought her right foot up and kicked back at his chest, pitching him back against the driver's door. It broke his grip, but some mad instinct—preservation, maybe —made him scramble for the gun. He seized it by the barrel, tried to snatch it from her hand, then realized what he was fighting for.

"Huh?" he muttered, his expression halfway between puzzlement and surprise at the heft of the plastic toy.

The momentary pause gave Alice time to recover. She released the gun and lunged at him, clawing at his face, and he made a snap decision to run for it. Better the open air than trapped inside a cab with a wildcat. He popped the door and half-lurched, half-fell to the ground outside.

Alice dived after him.

He was a big guy, knew his way around, knew how to handle himself. He rolled, came to his feet quickly, and faced her, braced in a low crouch.

Then he charged, thinking bulk must give him some advantage, but Alice leaped back lithely and tripped him as he passed.

He was quick, got to his feet again, but Alice was quicker, and there was one place he was vulnerable—even more so than other men right now. She kicked him, hard, and he went down, doubled-up and howling.

After that, she could lead him around like a puppy. His mind was elsewhere, locked on his pain. He hardly seemed to register his surroundings. Even when she dragged him by the neck and rammed his face against Davy's ass.

She tied him to the tree like the others, but only by the hands. Poor guy could barely stand.

Figuring she had more than enough incriminating shots, she took the wallet from his back pocket and rifled through the pile of clothes, extracting the other two. All three guys had licenses. She laid them on the grass and photographed them. Nice clear shots giving full names, addresses, dates of birth, height and mug shots. "To go with the other pictures. So folks know who you really are," she told them.

Rick and Davy watched sullenly as she left the wallets and bundled their clothes, heaping them on the floor of the truck. She plucked out Rick's T-shirt and used it to wipe both exterior door handles. Then she popped the hatch on the gas tank, unscrewed the filler cap, twisted the shirt into a fat rope and fed it down inside.

There's an old Hollywood myth about rags in gas tanks. Strike a light, touch it to the cloth, and seconds later, *Boom!* Truck, car or bus explodes. But that only happens in Hollywood.

Alice knew that combustion required the correct mix of combustible substance and oxygen. No oxygen, no burn. Light a puddle of gasoline and you'll get a wild blaze, but light the top of a full can and only the area exposed to air will burn.

At Quantico, they were taught the flammability of a

liquid is measured by its Lower Explosive Limit and its Upper Explosive Limit—LEL and UEL for short—with the numbers expressed as a percentage. Gasoline has an LEL of 1.4 and a UEL of 7.6 percent. Anything lower and it won't ignite. Anything higher and the mixture is "too rich" to burn properly.

Gas sloshing about in a sealed tank saturates the surrounding air, pushing the fumes way over the UEL. You don't want to go dropping a lighted match in there, but chances are that if you do, it'll just go out.

Alice hauled the dampened shirt out again. Davy watched her, wide-eyed, as she threw it in the cab with the other clothes, added the filler cap, then turned on the truck's ignition and pushed in the cigarette lighter.

Big Jim's cigarettes were on the dash. She helped herself, went to the tree and offered them round. Rick and Davy shook their heads.

"Big Jim the only smoker?"

Davy nodded.

She went back to the truck, lit the cigarette, took a puff and returned.

"I guess this is for you then." Big Jim blinked at her glassily. "For Benji."

She stubbed it out on the side of his neck. He bucked and writhed and howled again.

Back at the truck, she added the camera and the wallet of memory cards to the pile of clothes, relit the butt of the mangled cigarette, took another puff and discarded it.

Davy saw her. "No, no, no! Fuck no. Not my truck!"

It landed in the pile of clothing, catching the gas fumes somewhere between their LEL and their UEL. The clothes

ignited. Alice checked the windows were partway down—
essential for good air flow—held her foot on the brake,
pushed the shift into neutral, then released the parking
break. The truck, already on an incline, inched forward as
she backed out the cab and slammed the door.

By the time it reached the lip of the gully it was moving
at maybe five miles an hour. The interior was already
boiling with orange flames. Davy wailed. The truck bumped
over the edge and disappeared.

It stayed upright for almost twenty yards, still
gathering speed, then it came to a steeper face, dropped,
flipped end-for-end three times before skidding to a halt on
its battered roof. There was no explosion. No fireball. This
wasn't Hollywood. But there was a good hearty blaze.

Alice took off the wig and sunglasses and threw them
in her car, then settled in beside them and drove away.

TWENTY-SIX

Three blocks away, still buzzing with adrenaline and nervous energy, Alice pulled over. A good time to review the situation.

Would the guys complain? Not about her specifically because that would mean they'd have to admit having their asses whipped for the second time in a week. By a girl. If they told the truth about this incident, they'd have to tell some shadow of the truth about who she was and why she came back and how they'd lied in the first place. That was unlikely. If they were smart, they'd blame the mythical bikers and keep it to themselves.

But the fabric of the friendship was broken now. It would only take one of them to step out of line. The most aggrieved, most likely. Davy. He'd lost two vehicles now and would be wearing that nose splint for another month.

On the other hand, Big Jim would blame him and Rick for being taken in in the first place. Two against one in such a remote spot? With a toy gun? Hell, he'd taken her on himself, and he was half crippled.

Rick would say how it had been Davy's approach, Davy's idea. He'd just been riding shotgun.

Maybe Davy would mention Rick's reaction to him

being tied up behind him. Maybe he wouldn't. Either way, the suspicion would remain.

Which left the crime scene.

It *was* a crime scene. Whatever reason they came up with for being tied to a tree, the police *would* investigate. And that was where most criminals came unstuck. The elation of a successful job, the victory moment when escape was certain. That was the moment vital clues got left behind.

Davy's phone and Big Jim's camera were in the truck cab. Gone. Likewise, the box of memory cards and the cigarette butt. They wouldn't get any saliva or DNA off that.

What about her own stuff?

Wig, sunglasses, toy gun. Check.

The rope? Just rope. Maybe it had picked up a few fibers from her clothes, but she'd dispose of them later. Besides, it wouldn't likely get examined anyway. She hadn't killed anyone.

Footprints? Tire tracks? The ground was dry and hard.

Fingerprints? Only in the interior of the truck, and that was now a burned out shell. She'd touched nothing at Big Jim's mama's house. There was the coffee cup and cutlery in the diner, but they would have been in the dishwasher right after she left. As for the motel room, if the cleaner was sloppy, there'd still be a few prints around. But if the cleaner was that sloppy, there'd be a few hundred other prints besides.

That just left the rental and its registration plates. She'd nudged the front of the car into brush deliberately. And the way she'd tied them up, the car was right behind them. Hard to see. They might have memorized the plates from the parking lot or on the drive over, but that was unlikely.

All in all, she was pretty clean. All they had was a memory of her face. And guys like that weren't big on faces.

* * *

Alice had four hours to kill before she reached Sacramento. She was still riding a high, so she decided to use it. After swinging into a rest stop, she took out her phone and called her office.

It was lunchtime in Quantico, but Murray Ames was still at his desk. He ate there, sandwiches brought in from home, prepared fresh each day by his wife. He was Old School. A creature of habit. He'd been a desk jockey for twenty-five years.

"Hey, Murray."

"Kwann! How's the vacation?" Ames called everyone by their surnames, men and women alike. Another Old School thing.

"Can never quite get away from the job, you know how it is."

Ames chuckled.

"I've got a friend of a friend here who's looking to jump ship. He's currently with CBP and was wondering if he might be better off with us. I said I'd scope it out under the radar. See if it'd be worth bothering to apply."

"This guy got a name?"

Alice read from Chatri's note. "Markham, Ronald P."

She heard the clack of keys then Ames' voice as he read

from the screen. "Markham, Ronald Peter. CBP Field Office, Long Beach, California.... Former Import Specialist now with Monitoring and Intel.... Fifteen years in. Steady record. No big scores, but no black marks either. Only on GS-9 though, so we're not looking at a rocket scientist. Or a go-getter. There's a chance, I guess, but I gotta say it's less than fifty-fifty."

"I'm hearing 'Don't call us,'" Alice said.

"I'd say 'Stick with what you know.'"

"Thanks, Murray. I'll pass it down the line."

"And if you want a quiet vacation Kwann, don't mention the firm. Just say you work for the government. People will think you're with the IRS and leave you alone."

"Good tip. I'll keep it in mind."

She googled the number of the Long Beach office of the Customs and Border Protection agency then dialed the number.

"Markham," Markham said.

Alice identified herself as FBI and gave her ID number.

"How can I help you, Agent Kwann?" he said.

She heard the sound of a keyboard as he checked her out.

"Call me Alice."

"Sure, Alice." His tone eased, from businesslike to friendly. Maybe he was studying her mugshot. Zooming in. "So, how's the weather back East?" He had a gravelly voice and a Midwest accent. A big man's voice.

"What's weather? Hardly ever get out to see stuff like that round here."

"Ride you pretty hard, huh?" There was something insinuating in his tone. "The bosses, I mean."

"Tell me about it."

"Bet you can take it though."

What the hell is this? Phone sex?

"Listen Ron—OK if I call you Ron?"

"Call me anything you like, Alice."

How about "creep"?

"NGI's picked up a facial recog off a surveillance tape. Got a guy who may or may not have witnessed a bank heist. Or rather, he may have seen the possible getaway car."

"Where was this?"

Oh-oh.

She had no idea where Long Tom was based. Could have been anywhere. But Markham worked in Long Beach, it was his lock on the file, so the West Coast seemed likely. A tenth of the country's population lived in California, which whittled it down further, and almost half of them lived in the greater Los Angeles area. So she took a guess.

"LA."

"It's a big place."

"So I hear." She kept her tone light. "But I don't have any more details. You know what the bosses are like. Mushrooms, right?"

"Keep us in the dark and feed us shit," he chuckled. "So what's your angle, Alice?"

"The system's pulled up that guy you tagged last week." She felt her pulse quicken.

Say his name, dammit. Say his name.

"Oh yeah?" was all Markham said.

"So... just a courtesy call really. To see if you'd mind a couple of our locals paying him a visit."

"What, for the possible sighting of a possible getaway

car? Fuck no! This guy's a source of foreign intel. I don't want him hassled. That's why I tagged him in the first place."

Just say his name, damn you!

"That's what I figured. That's why I called. No harm asking, right?"

"Yeah, I guess. Thanks for taking the time, Alice. A lot of people wouldn't."

"So this guy's one of yours, huh?"

"Why d'you say that?"

"I'm getting a sense of 'proprietary' here." Alice put a smile in her voice. "Hell, I don't blame you. Good intel's like gold. When you strike a seam, you don't want someone else jumping your claim."

"You're a smart woman, Alice."

There was a brief silence. Alice tried another angle.

"What's with the Long Tom business?" she said, pretending to be reading from a screen. "Is the guy hung like an artillery piece or something?"

Markham guffawed. "You sound like you know about that stuff."

"What, you mean the military hardware?"

He guffawed again. "Yeah, that too."

"My ex was into war gaming. Second World War simulations."

"Your ex?"

"If I recall rightly, the Long Tom was a field gun, right?"

"You do know your stuff. I'm impressed."

"Thank you."

"But in this case, it's a golfing nickname. As you'll see if you read down a little further."

Alice paused, pretending to read. "Ah, got it."

Still no name. Bastard!

She couldn't think of anything else to say or any other way to work it.

"Well, thanks for your help Ron."

"Thanks for your call, Alice. If you ever get out this way, look me up."

"That's very neighborly of you, Ron. I might just do that."

* * *

The girl didn't moan much when she was brought in. She had the glazed look of the beaten and badly abused. They often looked like that. Shock, mostly. The mind shutting down. Not surprising, seeing what they'd done to her.

She was a mess. Bruises and lacerations. Cigarette burns. Covered in dirt and congealed blood. Benny brought her in, chained her up and left promptly. He didn't need to be told to close the door.

Nancy Templar liked her victims fresh, or at least conscious and fully cognizant of what was happening to them, so she took her time, washing the girl down with warm water, using detergent and a soft brush, the sort you might use on a car. Then she turned the water temperature down and sluiced her off.

The girl shuddered and her eyelids flickered open. Templar checked the cameras. Her videos were more niche as Reisinger's. Gang rape was a perennial favorite, but her videos commanded a better price from a more discerning clientele.

The girl was about nineteen. Her flesh still firm in spite of the beating. She pulled on her restraints, finding her arms and legs tethered to the cinder block wall behind her.

Templar took off her shoes one by one and placed them on the top shelf of a locker, replacing them with a pair of green rubber clogs. She took off her jacket, hung it on a peg and closed the locker door. Then she put on a long rubberized work apron. The sort you'd find in a chemical lab to protect yourself from splashes of acid.

The girl watched, wide-eyed, as Templar pulled on a pair of latex gloves and unrolled the canvas bag containing her operating kit. A collection of knives and scalpels, pliers and pincers. Some of the tools came from medical supply stores, some from hardware stores. All were quality instruments. Sharp, clean and meticulously maintained.

The girl's eyes grew wider as she saw the glint of chrome and polished steel reflected in the bright lights. She stared at Templar and whimpered.

Templar picked up a wooden box, carried it over to her and opened the lid. It was the size of a cigar box, finely made, with dovetailed corners and brass hinges. The inside was lined with green felt. On the felt lay what looked like a crudely-made belt, stitched together from a lot of little somethings. Templar took it out and held it up so the girl could see it more clearly.

The girl opened her mouth and screamed.

Templar placed the belt carefully back in the box, closed the lid, started the videos, and got to work.

Those screams were only the beginning...

TWENTY-SEVEN

Alice drove towards a late lunch in Sacramento, smiling, tapping the steering wheel in time to the ridiculous beat of a pop song the radio had dragged in. She'd achieved something this morning, she thought. Something worthwhile. A feeling she'd never had in all her seven years behind a desk. It was heady, intense, almost like a drug. But also a distraction.

The radio crackled, lost the signal briefly, and her mind turned back to the real reason for her visit.

Markham had given her almost nothing. Long Tom, LA, and golf might narrow down the search a little, but it would still leave a mountain of data to sift. Perhaps she should get Chatri to test the security lock on his file? Or Murray Ames? Problem was, both links implicated friends and led directly back to her.

If he was still alive, of course.

As she passed another sign for Sacramento, it suddenly occurred to her there was an angle she'd never considered. One lying in a peaceful grave in East Lawn Memorial Park. Joseph Lewis Moncrieff. Fat One. The guy whose wallet she'd plundered all those years ago.

Time to pay him another visit.

Alice stood looking down at the grave, wondering why she'd made the pilgrimage in the first place. It certainly hadn't been to pay her respects. But his name had stayed with her since she'd first been able to read the details on the California driver's license she'd taken. She'd even looked him up and discovered where the body had been taken. And here he lay, physical proof of a what otherwise might have been a childhood nightmare. The only proof she had.

Proof, and a reminder.

Besides, Sacramento was a natural stop-off on her way west. How could she not visit?

Moncrieff's loving parents were still alive. David and Beryl. She found them listed in the white pages and called from the graveside before she could have second thoughts.

"Good afternoon. My name is Jane Lee. I'm with the Sacramento Observer. Am I speaking with Mrs Beryl Moncrieff?"

"Yes."

"I'm sorry to bother you, ma'am, but may I ask if you lost a son twenty years ago?"

"Yes, I did."

"And that would be Joseph Lewis Moncrieff?"

"Joe, yes."

"I've been going back through our archives. We're doing a series on unsolved murders and I wonder if I might have five minutes of your time?"

The details were still fresh for the old woman and spilled out with little prompting. Joe had been working in

LA, in the movie business, one of the smaller studios, and had traveled east with two friends on vacation. According to her they were innocents abroad, yet had somehow become involved in a dispute between two rival gangs.

"The embassy did all they could. They were very helpful. But things over there... well, they're not like they are here."

"Can you remember the names of the friends he traveled with?" Alice asked, her pulse skipping up a notch.

"Well, there was Aldo Simpson. He died too. But their other friend had just stepped out. Ever such a nice young man. He came to the funeral, you know. Oh, what was his name? Heart-something, or something-heart... No, Hart*ley*. Big heart Hartley, my husband called him."

"And his first name?"

"Oh, I can't—"

"It wasn't Tom, was it?"

"Thomas! Yes, that was it. Thomas Hartley."

* * *

After that it was easy. All it took was a half-hour at an internet cafe.

An image search on "Thomas Hartley, Long Tom, golf" brought up a tiny black and white picture—maybe a hundred by two hundred pixels—but one that leaped off the screen at her. Those eyes, that smile, the teeth.

She moved the cursor, clicked the link, her heart in her mouth.

The image came from the scanned front page of the *Terra Nova Country Club Quarterly* dated four years previously. The headline read: LONG TOM DOES IT AGAIN!

The story concerned an amazing three-hundred-and-fifty-yard drive on the seventeenth that secured the club trophy for the third year running for Thomas "Long Tom" Hartley.

She stared at the picture, mesmerized. Young One approaching middle age. The hair was going at the temples. The jawline was softer and the neck had lost its tautness, but there was no mistaking him. He still had it—she could see it in the eyes of the joyful crowd around him. That certain something. Charm. Charisma.

Asshole!

She let out a breath she didn't realize she'd been holding.

Thomas Wilton Hartley was owner and chief executive of Hartley Imports, a registered company specializing in the distribution of Asian antiquities and period furniture, based in Simi Valley, thirty miles northwest of downtown LA. The company website said they were strictly wholesale. There was a form for dealers to sign-up for an account, but no contact address or 1-800 number. Still, within minutes, thanks to public records and his company registration, Alice had a street address and the names of his associate directors: Thaksin Prasert Metharom, Hans Reisinger, and Nancy Elizabeth Templar.

Seconds later she was cruising Reeve Road outside Hartley Imports, courtesy of Street View. The pictures showed a nondescript warehouse, a prefabricated office building, and a parking lot in front of that. There were six painted slots. All six slots were filled. Four for the directors, which left two for staff or clients. Alice pulled out a pad and started making notes.

* * *

She was back in San Francisco in time to meet Chatri after work and caught a ride home with him. It was Friday afternoon.

"Told you I'd be back for the weekend."

"Successful trip?"

"Very."

A pause. "Want to tell me what it was really about?"

"What do you mean?"

"You're three weeks into a three-month leave of absence, Solikha. A leave of absence that you suggest may become permanent. The only way your bosses could know you were anywhere near San Jose was if you regularly called in your location. Are you seriously telling me this is what you do?"

Alice said nothing.

"And your call came from Sacramento, not San Jose. You were heading in the wrong direction."

"How do you know that?"

"Oh please, Solikha. My line of work?"

She pursed her lips.

"Another thing: translators. This is California, the most heterogeneous state in the union. Are you saying that an agency like the FBI couldn't find another Khmer speaker here, out of forty million people? That they'd fly someone in from the East Coast?"

"I didn't want to involve you, Chatri."

"Ah, that old story."

"What's that supposed to mean?"

"You never have, Sol. You never would. All the time we were growing up. All that time at college. People would ask me, what is wrong with her? And I would tell them: she's a loner, she'll speak when she's ready. But you never have. Not to me, at least."

She looked at him, surprised.

"Tell me truthfully, have you ever really confided in another person?"

Alice said nothing.

"Because I'm starting to suspect you may be the world's oldest, prettiest virgin."

"I haven't been that since I was a child."

"You know what I mean."

Alice looked out the side window. Parking lots and strip malls. Where was the grass, the greenery? She wanted to see trees.

"There was Perry," she said after a time.

"Ah yes, Perry O'Reagan. Two years, wasn't it? He told me about your arrangement."

"What?"

"The arrangement you came to. How dangling him on your arm kept the jocks at bay, and how visits to his parents kept them off the scent of his real preferences."

"He told you that?"

"He told me everything. About the trust fund to pay for his education. The military family heritage. The pressure of a gung-ho father. The need to keep up appearances. He confided in me, Solikha. And I kept his confidence. Would have done so to this day if I hadn't run into him by chance a few months back. He lives here now, in San Francisco. His father is dead, the world has moved on. He can be open about his sexuality now."

Alice swallowed the unspoken rebuke. "So, how is he?"

"Very well. Has a place in Haight-Ashbury. Runs an HIV clinic. He asked after you. Said did I ever hear?"

"What did you tell him?"

"I told him yes, and I told him no. I told him I only ever heard what you wanted me to hear. Still."

Another long silence. The Daly City exit sign showed up ahead. Chatri eased into the correct lane.

"All right," she said at last. "I'll tell you what I've been doing. But it's a long story. Can we pull over somewhere?"

He drove to a headland overlooking Thornton Beach. They got out and walked down a narrow track, past soft dunes where wind whipped sand around their ankles, out to the hard pack of the receding tide. The sun was lowering towards a misty horizon. Alice picked up a driftwood stick, trailed it in one hand as they walked, and told him everything. About the bus breakdown, her sprained ankle, the diner, and the toothpicks. About meeting with Amelia Kilcorn and Carla Ahearn. About going back. About what she'd done.

He listened in silence till the very end, asking only the occasional clarifying question.

She finished up, her eyes fixed on the horizon, waiting for his rebuke.

He stared at her, his face unreadable. "You did all that?"

She nodded.

He shook his head then broke into a joyous grin. "You bloody beauty!" He took her hands and shook them, grinning. "You avenging angel! You champion of the oppressed!"

"I'm a vigilante, Chatri. A criminal."

"A bloody blasted marvelous crook is what you are!"

She'd never heard him swear so much.

"I can't believe it. That you would do such a thing." He hugged her. "I have been harboring a Robin Hood in my house and did not know it."

"It was wrong, Chatri."

"Yes, but it was also right. So, so right. You must tell Annabel."

"No, please, I can't tell anyone. Jesus, I might be a desk jockey, but I'm still a Federal agent."

"And I bet you are not the first to apply a little summary justice. Two cars! I can't believe it. You torched two cars. And left them tied up to a tree. Naked!" He laughed again. "Oh Solikha, what fun. What justice!"

She felt herself to relax a little, realising she'd hoped for this; his approval. As they turned and headed back towards the car she said, "You know, I'm glad it was a toy gun. There were moments there where I could easily have pulled the trigger. What would you have thought of me then?"

"I would have thought no different. I would have thought they got what they deserved. Not only were you vengeful, you were merciful too. A veritable King Solomon."

She snorted.

"I don't know whether you were very brave or very foolish," he continued. "This time I will give you the benefit of the doubt. But if you ever do something like that again, you must promise me one thing."

"What's that?"

"If I can help in any way, any way at all, you only have to ask."

"Thanks, Chatri. I'll keep that in mind. Not that I plan to do anything like that ever again. "

He gave her a rueful smile. "No, of course not."

III

TWENTY-EIGHT

Tim Clayborne took a slip of rice paper from his wallet, settled at his desk in the Long Beach Harbor Department control center, and signed in.

The beige keyboard was smudged with grubby finger marks, the screen smeared from people pointing things out or running their fingers across to adjacent columns. His job required a kind of dumb accuracy. Every day he'd input or cross-check hundreds of eleven-digit container codes, reassigning them, changing their designations or destinations with four-, six- or eight-digit codes. It didn't require much thought, just following instructions forwarded by his supervisor or the sheets handed to him by comptrollers and clerks. And it wasn't the kind of job that would lead anywhere, except maybe unemployment when some automated system finally replaced him.

Which was what made this afternoon special.

He could feel the wad of notes in his back pocket as he leaned forward and glanced around the office. People were at work, heads bowed. He got to work himself, tapping out the eleven-digit number from the slip of paper in front of him. Then he tabbed to the CSI field, entered the eight-digit code that followed it, and double-checked everything.

The Container Security Initiative had been launched by Customs and Border Protection shortly after 9/11. The idea was to extend the US security zone out to exporting ports so that American borders became the last line of defense, not the first. Containers could be pre-inspected and pre-approved before they were loaded on a ship.

Clayborne paused. The moment of truth. CSI was a field you didn't meddle with. He took a breath and hit Enter.

The status line at the bottom of the screen flashed a message:

> *Homeland Security inspected. Customs cleared.*
> *Priority dispatch.*
> *Input next container number.*

He breathed out.

That was it. Dumb accuracy. He didn't know or care what was in the container. But he did know what five hundred bucks would buy, and that he'd just earned that much for ten seconds work. A total of nineteen keystrokes. Twenty counting the Enter key. Twenty-five bucks a keypress. Now *that* was easy money.

Then he did what his uncle had told him to do with the rice paper. He put it in his mouth and swallowed it, following it down with the cold dregs of the morning's coffee.

He belched. Job done. Easy money.

* * *

Finding an empty motel in Chatsworth seemed impossible. The "No" on every Vacancy sign Alice passed was illuminated, and she briefly considered carrying on to Canoga Park or Woodland Hills, but it had been a long drive from San Francisco and she was sick of the endless freeway that seemed to constitute Los Angeles. Eventually, she found a place in a rundown part of town called Stiler's Motor Hotel and Backpacker Lodge.

"Motel's full, but we got room in the dorm round back," the guy at the front desk told her. He was short, fat and greasy. "You here for the thing?"

"The thing?"

"You know, the quarterlies?"

Alice didn't know, but she didn't like the guy's look or the way he licked his dry lips. It was about as close as a look could get to being sexual assault.

"Round back?" she repeated.

"You're a day late. Going to have to work it extra hard now." His wheezy chuckle followed her out.

The dorm was separated from the motel by a parking lot. It was a long timber structure with cheap joinery and metal-framed windows, and it seemed to be staffed by travelers. Alice was signed in by a girl in minuscule shorts and a halter top fresh from a volleyball game on the back lawn. She was maybe nineteen with honey-blond hair and a Hollywood tan.

Alice took her room key and carried her backpack through the lobby and down a passage, passing a communal kitchen, a TV lounge, bathrooms, and lockers. The four-bunk room she'd been assigned had one free bed, the upper right. A young woman sat on the lower bunk opposite, sorting through her stuff, but before they could exchange greetings, a second woman breezed in behind her, steaming from the shower, wearing nothing but a towel. She took it off and stood naked, drying her peroxide hair, her breasts bouncing in time to the vigorous toweling. She had a full, shapely figure, but Nature's endowments had been enhanced to an almost ridiculous degree.

"I'm Cora-Jane," she called. "Pleased to meet you."

"Alice," Alice said.

Cora-Jane gave her an assessing look, taking her in from top to toe as if she was some kind of human body scanner. "And that's Violet," she added, gesturing to the seated girl with a wave of her elbow.

"Hi."

"Hi," the girl said.

She was plain but pretty in a homely sort of way. Straight dark hair and a smattering of freckles. She looked very young.

Cora-Jane had the bunk below and made it clear Alice was in the way. The room was small and felt smaller still in the face of Cora-Jane's unnatural chest, so she dumped her stuff, took her travel pack and headed out.

The reception goddess was back playing volleyball. A bunch of guys passed by carrying six-packs. They all had gym physiques and wore nothing but shorts.

California, Alice thought as she stepped into the low heat of the parking lot.

The rinsed blue of the sky had faded to a mottled gray. Alice set the car's GPS to the corner of Mawney Street and Reeve Road and headed out to look over Hartley Imports.

She cruised past, taking in details of the cement slab

warehouse and the timber office building in front of it. It was early evening. There were lights on inside and two cars in the lot. An old blue Toyota at one end, a new green Porsche Cayenne at the other. She stopped half a block away, adjusted the rear-view mirror so she could keep them both in sight, and settled down to wait.

Forty minutes later, two figures emerged from the office. The light was fading and it was too far to make out features, but one wore a suit while the other was dressed in a T-shirt and jeans. Employer and employee, she guessed.

Suit guy went to the Porsche. Alice started her engine.

The blue Toyota passed her first, heading for the freeway, followed by the bigger four-wheel drive. Alice gave it a hundred yards then dropped in behind.

Tailing a subject with a single vehicle was tricky. The best way was with a team in constant radio contact, assigning the job to different vehicles at different stages. With only one vehicle, the rule was to keep well back, two or three car lengths at least. Let other vehicles slot between you and the target. Which works fine unless those other vehicles are vans or a semis.

Alice had no such problems. Traffic was light, the back of the Porsche was high, and its tail lights distinctive. Besides, the guy had no reason to suspect he was being followed. She dropped back further.

After four miles, the Porsche indicated for an exit lane. Alice did the same, closed the gap a little, and followed it down an off-ramp into an up-market residential area. The streets were wide and neat and lined with trees. Houses hid behind high fences. The Porsche swung left up a hill. Alice read the sign as she did the same; Presley Drive. Up here, the lots were even bigger. Like miniature estates.

Ahead, the Porsche indicated another left then swung across the road to a pair of wrought iron gates, pausing on the sidewalk while they opened fully. Alice continued past, watching its tail lights disappear in her rear-view mirror.

She stopped fifty yards further on, took her running gear from her travel pack, and changed in the cramped space of the driver's seat. She got out, flexed and stretched, then headed off, testing her ankle as she went. There was still a little weakness there, but it was coming on. She'd just have to take it easy.

Sticking to the grass verge, she headed down at a gentle jog and glanced across at the number on the stone pillar beside the wrought iron gates as she passed. Big brass digits glowed under a streetlight: 1064.

The house was up a gentle rise and obscured by trees, but she made a mental note of the front fence; stone pillars every twenty feet with eight-foot-high spiked iron railings set between them.

At the bottom of the hill she crossed over and headed back, this time pausing right outside, resting one foot on the crossbar of the gate while she retied her shoelace. A security light came on. She was wearing a baseball cap and kept her head down, but glimpsed the casing of a camera in a nearby tree. The whole rig was activated by motion sensors. She tightened the lace and carried on back to her car.

If, as she suspected, the Porsche driver was Hartley, she now had his home address.

Massaging her ankle, she considered the situation.

Perhaps he really was a respectable businessman these

days. Perhaps right now he was greeting a wife and a family overjoyed to see him. Two teenage kids, a dog... Or perhaps not. Something about Hartley Imports didn't seem right.

She started her car and headed back to the intersection of Mawney and Reeve.

TWENTY-NINE

The sidewalk outside Hartley Imports was narrow and little used. Tufts of grass pushed up between the cement slabs. Alice jogged slowly past, carefully noting all she saw.

The lot occupied the southeastern corner of a block of four. There was a machine shop on the southwest corner, a battery warehouse on the northwest, and a signwriter advertising laser cut signs on the northeast. Across the road sat a while-you-wait muffler franchise.

The warehouse covered the width of the lot and half its depth. It had a truck-sized roller door on the western end, and a human-sized door beside it leading to what looked like a workshop. There was a barred window beside the door and a large extractor fan in the wall above.

On the eastern side was a single-story office block with a corrugated iron roof. A stepped entrance led to a pair of doors, and a sign on one of them read "Registered Office of Hartley Imports Limited". The rear of the block was connected to the warehouse by a short passage.

The parking lot and yard out front were surrounded by an eight-foot high mesh fence. The tops of the support poles were split, and the Y-shaped cavity filled with strings of razor wire. There were lamps on poles in each corner of the lot—currently off—and she saw a security camera mounted high on the front of the warehouse, angled down at the yard. Whatever it was that needed such measures wasn't there right now because the entrance gate on Reeve Road was open and latched back.

Alice continued past, heading around the block, trying to figure out what didn't feel quite right.

The proportions for a start. According to their website, Hartley Imports dealt in antiques. Exclusive one-off pieces, not furniture kits. They had a few larger pieces like tables and dressers, but did they need a warehouse that size to store them? It looked more like a small factory. Besides, antiques required careful handling and proper environmental controls, not cavernous spaces like that.

Maybe they didn't use it. Maybe everything went on in the office building.

So why have a warehouse?

The numbers didn't add up either. The lot held six cars. Four directors plus two staff, which made the company was top-heavy. If the other directors lived as well as Hartley, the business must have quite a turnover. In which case you'd expect more staff.

Maybe the others parked out in the street.

The location also bothered her. An industrial park? It didn't seem the spot for an antique business, even a wholesale one. Wouldn't they operate out of a downtown showroom?

Maybe they had one.

It wasn't mentioned on the website.

She'd checked the advertising indexes of antiques

magazines and trade fair catalogs in the San Francisco Public Library before she left, but found no mention of Hartley Imports.

Maybe they didn't need to advertise.

The fence bothered her too. It looked more like a prison yard. No other businesses in the neighborhood had anything like it.

Maybe it came from a former tenant. The gate is open after all.

Maybe...

Still uneasy, she returned to Stiler's

The lobby was empty, but the lounge and kitchen were crowded with people, talking, laughing, chugging beers. It looked like a frat party. She saw the reception goddess talking to one of the gym guys and suddenly felt old.

Slipping past to her room, she got some things, showered, brushed her teeth, then tiptoed back, hauling out her sleeping bag by the light of her torch. Violet was curled up on the lower bunk opposite, her back to the room.

Alice got comfortable, zipped the sleeping bag up partway, and listened to the hum of the air conditioner and the distant sounds of the night. She was woken a couple of hours later by the room light and Cora-Jane stomping around, stripping naked, wandering out and back carrying a towel and toothbrush, before finally crashing into the bunk below and falling into a broken, snore-laden sleep.

Alice curled away from the light, took ear plugs from a pocket in the hood of her sleeping bag and drifted back to sleep.

* * *

Benny Benedict got in early, unlocked the workshop, took a crowbar from the workbench and went through to Templar's bunker. He checked on the chained, mutilated figure, giving her a prod with the curved end of the crowbar then kept it raised. No movement, no response. The girl was dead. He grunted and lowered the weapon. He wouldn't be needing it after all.

Returning with a pallet truck carrying a large semi-transparent plastic barrel, he unclipped the ankle cuffs, lifted her legs into the barrel then got a step-stool and released her wrists one by one. Gravity did the rest.

There were a few other bits lying around. Skin. Tissue. Blood, of course. Templar must have done the girl's nails. Torn them out. He got a hose and sluiced the place down. The miscellaneous bits were caught by a mesh trap set over a drain in the floor. He upended it over the barrel to clear it out, but some bits stuck to the grating.

Fuck that, Mad Nan can pick those bits out.

Back in the workshop, he lowered the deck of the pallet truck and rolled the barrel off, keeping it upright, setting it beside a fifty-five-gallon plastic drum with a triangular yellow hazard sign on the side. He took a heavy apron, breathing mask and industrial-strength protective gloves from a locker by the door, then flicked on the extractor fan. Using a wrench, he removed the bung from the top of the drum, inserted a hand pump and began transferring liquid from one barrel to the other. The liquid splashed over the girl's body, turning a pale coffee color and giving off fumes.

Pumping was hard physical work. He was sweating by the time he finished. He screwed a stout plastic lid down on the top of the barrel, then took off the mask and cleaned up, letting the draft of the extractor fan cool him down.

Coffee, he thought, glancing at the color of the liquid through the side of the semi-transparent barrel. And donuts. Hard work always made him hungry.

THIRTY

Alice had always been an early riser. More of that country-girl upbringing. It had its advantages, especially in accommodation like this. You got to use the shared facilities before sharing led to queues.

She left Cora-Jane snoring. Violet's bunk was empty—another early riser—and there was an unknown shape in the other bunk. Someone with long reddish hair was all Alice could see in the half-light filtering through the window blind.

She showered, dressed and headed down the hall. A ghostly glow came from the TV lounge. Picture only. The sound was off. Alice recalled a coin operated coffee machine in the corner. It wouldn't be up to much, but she needed something to kickstart her day.

The plug on the coffee machine was out. Some asshole had pulled it to charge their cell phone.

"Fancy a tea?" Violet called through the serving hatch. The kitchen was full of steam from a boiling kettle.

"Sure," Alice said.

"It's chamomile." Violet set a second cup on an old wooden table as Alice walked through. "I find it's good for my nerves."

She was barefoot, wore track pants and a black T-shirt emblazoned with the name of a heavy metal band.

Alice took a stool opposite and sniffed. "Mmm, I haven't had this in years."

"The freight train keep you awake?"

"You mean Cora-Jane? No, I've got earplugs. But what's up with her strutting around like that?"

Violet shook her head and blew on her tea. "Mind if I ask you something?" She put down the cup. "I mean, we don't know each other at all, right? You can be perfectly honest." She reached down and pulled up her T-shirt. She was wearing nothing underneath. "Are these OK?"

Alice scalded her tongue on too-hot tea.

"I know I'm being over-sensitive. It's just... well... Cora-Jane with those *constructions* of hers. The way she's always shoving them in your face. We're in a different market anyway, but you start to wonder, you know? And I've always felt my right was a little bigger. A little unbalanced. What do you think?"

"They look fine."

"Really?" She jiggled a bit.

"Just fine."

Violet lowered the T-shirt and took up her tea. "So what are you up for? Any specialty?"

"I'm sorry?"

"You know, market. What market are you in?"

"Market?"

"I'm trying out for Schoolgirl. I think I can still get away with it." She reached up, separated her hair into bangs and gave Alice a wide-eyed coquettish look.

"You're... auditioning for something?"

Violet gave her an odd look. "You mean you're not here for the quarterlies?"

"The quarterlies?"

"Vixen Pics' quarterly casting?"

Alice shook her head.

"Oh shit! You must think we're a bunch of crazies. Cora-Jane with her breasts. And me just now..." She tugged at the bottom of her T-shirt and laughed. "I'm sorry, but that's really funny!"

"What's the quarterly casting?" Alice said.

"You really don't know? You know where you are, right?"

"Chatsworth."

"Uh-huh." Violet said it like she was coaxing a small child. "And where is Chatsworth?"

"San Fernando Valley."

"Do you know what the valley's most famous for?"

Alice shook her head.

"Ever heard of Silicone Valley? San Pornando?" Violet laughed again at Alice's blank expression. "It's only the Hollywood of the porn industry!"

Alice thought of the buffed, muscle guys and the goddess at reception.

"Santa Clara got the high-tech companies, San Fernando got the porn. Or rather *adult entertainment.*"

"Oh."

"No need to look like that. It's a respectable business. Disney even once had a share in it. Vixen Pics are one of the largest studios. They make two or three movies a day."

"*A day?*"

"So they're always on the lookout for new talent."

"And that's what the quarterlies are for?"

Violet nodded and sipped her tea. "It's tough though, and getting tougher. Competition's fierce. I came along last time, but my car broke down and I missed my medical. That's it. No rescheduling, no second chances. Come back next quarter.

"I'm prepared this time though. Not just my car. I've been doing my research. Ten years ago, the industry made twenty movies a day. Now it's less than half that. You know porn used to be worth more than the music, sports, and regular movie businesses combined?"

"What's changed?"

"The internet. Who wants to go out and rent a dirty movie when you can download one for a couple of bucks? Why go to a store and buy a magazine when you can get thousands of pictures online for free? Why pay actors a decent wage when girls in Eastern Europe or Asia will work for a pittance?

"Not a long-term career then?"

"Never was. It's all looks and age-based, like it's always has been. Get in, make a pile and get out, that's my plan.

"Besides, the culture's changed, you know? It used to be this great taboo. Secrets. Stuff you couldn't talk about in public. Stuff you couldn't show on TV. But cable and streaming changed all that. Every big series has nudity and sex these days. Porn stars can become celebrities nowadays. College girls take naked selfies and post them online."

Two more people filed into the lounge and scowled at the coffee machine.

"Who's fucking phone is that?"

"Sorry, sorry," the reception goddess hurried in

wearing a skimpy negligee. Her hair was matted, her face unmade, but she still looked stunning.

She pulled the charger and gathered up her phone. The coffee machine bleeped and came to life. A scrolling LCD display read "Please wait..."

"Give it ten minutes." She hurried out again.

"That's Tina," Violet said. "She's screwing the manager. Gets free accommodation and a little paid counter work. I guess when you're auditioning for Extreme, letting an old fat guy fuck you is nothing."

"Extreme?"

"You know, public humiliation. Ropes and chains and stuff."

"She's into that?" It seemed incongruous. Such a pretty girl.

"Who knows?" Violet shrugged. "But if she's smart, it'll be the opposite."

"What do you mean?"

"Work-life balance. This business can fuck you up for relationships—no pun intended. If you're screwing all day, who wants to go home and do it again? But if you've been tied up and whipped, well, that's gotta seem like work, right?

"They really hurt the girls?"

"Nah, not really. A few smacks and slaps maybe. Most movies get shot in a few hours so there's not much time for special effects, but they ham it up and use a bit of make-up.

"I thought about it myself if the schoolgirl thing doesn't work out, but maybe I'll try for lesbian instead. Guys don't mind if you've been going down on girls all day."

Alice blew on her tea. "What's the appeal?"

"A job, for a start. I've got a college degree—Business Admin—but there's nothing out there for anyone with less than five years' experience. But how do you get five years' experience if no one will give you a break?

"Then there's the money. You can make a thousand bucks in an afternoon. More. That's better than a fortnight flipping burgers. And if you make it, it's like being a regular movie star. Some of the big names make millions, have their own websites and fan clubs and merchandise.

"It's clean too. Everybody's tested. You don't get near a set unless the docs say you're OK, so it's safer than whoring. A *lot* safer.

"The way I figure it, I can do a year or two of the schoolgirl thing, then maybe two or three more after that, tops. Work it while you've got it, you know? Then quit while you're ahead. Or you end up like Cora-Jane, some plastic surgeon's meal ticket." She leaned in confidentially and added. "You know, I heard she's almost thirty."

"No, really?" Alice smiled.

"Wild, huh?"

THIRTY-ONE

The changes started hours before. Everyone noticed, but no one spoke of them, as if doing so might bring bad luck. But eyes kept straying to the chalk marks on the container wall, counting and re-counting. Twenty-two days now...

The first change was in the motion of the ship. The roll of the open ocean eased as if they were in sheltered waters. Then the thrum of the engine—their constant companion day and night—dropped one note, then another, then finally fell silent.

Still no one mentioned it.

They were all exhausted. Everyone felt they were courting madness. Three weeks in a metal box forty foot long by eight feet wide by eight feet high. Three weeks in the close company of nineteen others, with the stink of sweat and the smell of excrement, and nothing to do but sit and talk. Three weeks in semi-darkness. Three weeks of water and dry biscuits. It had been so long, so numbing, so monotonous, that it was hard now to recall any other way of life.

They sat in the talk circle, listening to the sounds outside. Bangs and crashes, the whine of winches, shrill whistles, the crackle of radios, and once even the sound of a voice. Apinya doused the lights and they sat in silence. Pinpricks of daylight showed through gaps in the rubber seals around the steel doors and through the slats of the humming ventilator.

Namthip moaned and cried out in her fever. Apinya glared at Kanya. "Silence her. She endangers us all."

Kanya went to her friend, exiled to the far corner beside the latrines where the stench was worst. The others feared her sickness. Only Kanya tended her.

Namthip looked like the ghost Krasue from late night tales. A beautiful face atop a gaunt, shriveled body. For days, she hadn't been able to keep anything down but sips of water, and now lay doubled-up, racked with pain and violent tremors.

Kanya bathed her brow. Whispered the good news in her ear. They'd arrived. They'd open the container. There would be doctors. Soon Namthip's troubles would be over.

Namthip gave a little cry at the news. Apinya hissed for silence.

When Kanya looked back at her friend, she saw from her stillness and the fading light in her glassy eyes that Namthip's troubles were already over.

* * *

Alice headed back to the warehouse. It was still early and the traffic was about as light at LA ever got. She figured the boss would keep boss hours, so maybe a nine o'clock start. That meant she should be in position by eight.

She made good time. Stopped at a convenience store three blocks away and loaded up with cakes and coffee and a copy of *Antiques Today*. As she was leaving, a tubby guy in a floral print shirt came in, pushing past her at the door

On Reeve Road, she stopped across from the southeast corner of Hartley Imports. The spot gave her a clear view of the front of the lot. She eased her seat back a notch to put most of her outline behind the door pillar, then took a small hunting scope from her travel pack. It was less conspicuous than binoculars—she could conceal it in her closed fingers —but it was almost as powerful.

After a quick scan of the building, she settled in to watch and wait.

Seven minutes later, the blue Toyota from last night swung into the park furthest from the office door. It was the tubby guy from the store. She recognized the floral print shirt. Mid-thirties, cargo pants, sneakers, and a weight problem he wasn't addressing, judging by the box of donuts he carried.

He punched a code into a panel beside the front door and went inside. First in, she guessed.

The next arrival came eighteen minutes later. An old Chevy Impala. Big, boxy, soft on its springs. It swung in beside the Toyota and a guy in his mid-fifties got out. Chiseled features, slicked-back hair. He looked pretty smart. Polished shoes, black and gray striped pants with gray pearl snaps on the front pockets. A white shirt and check jacket. But the clothes looked like the car. Like they'd driven in together from another era. He looked like the kind of guy who straightened his collar and snapped his cuffs when he got out of a vehicle. Alice wasn't disappointed when he did just that.

He was followed a few minutes later by a dark blue Audi. Its driver was tall and slim, wore a gray business suit and an open-necked shirt. He, too, was in his fifties, with a tan face and thick, steel gray hair swept back from a high forehead. Hans Reisinger, Alice guessed. He looked hard and muscled and moved like a panther.

The parking lot suggested a pecking order. The guy in the floral shirt had taken the spot furthest from the office door, which meant he was the junior of the two hired hands. Check jacket outranked him. Reisinger took the spot second-nearest to the door. That made him second in command, although thirty seconds later that seemed to be in dispute.

A red Fiesta swung into the third-nearest spot and a smartly dressed woman leaped out.

Nancy Elizabeth Templar, Alice said to herself.

She started haranguing Reisinger, pointing to the marked spaces. Reisinger said something, a cool expression on his face, and went into the office.

Still mad, Templar snatched off a pair of driving shoes, replaced them with expensive-looking heels in olive green—the exact same color as her business suit—and followed him inside.

There were no more arrivals. By ten, Alice was busting for a leak. She considered re-using the empty coffee cup, then dismissed the idea, recalling the chamomile tea she'd had earlier. Too much volume.

That was the problem with stakeouts. They could drag on for hours. Days, sometimes. Did she really want to get back into fieldwork?

She was scoping out the muffler place, checking to see if they had a public washroom, and almost missed the next arrival.

The Porsche Cayenne swung into the lot.

The driver's arrival was clearly anticipated. Before he could even open his door, the two hired hands came out, followed at a more sedate pace by Reisinger. They stood around him as he locked his car, nodding then pointing to the gate and the camera on the front of the warehouse.

He was average height, not tall or short, but the others surrounded him like paparazzi. And when he headed for the office, Reisinger walked on his right, obstructing her view.

That wasn't what she was after. Still no positive ID. Not even close. She'd have to go in.

* * *

Within half an hour of docking, gantry cranes began unloading the *Pacific Ram*, winching up the heavy containers and moving them to designated areas on the dock. An optical reader in the cab cross-referenced the ISO code on the end of each container with the ship's manifest and the port's computer records to determine their disposition. The pale gray container was one of a dozen that went to a priority clearance area. There it was picked up by a lift truck and placed on a conveyor belt where it passed through gamma and neutron radiation detectors to check for smuggled nuclear materials.

It passed.

As it was moved to the marshaling yard, the port's

computer fired off a text message to the driver of a flatbed truck waiting in a lot to the south. He started his engine, waved to other waiting truckers, and swung his rig into the access lane. Ten minutes later, he passed again, heading the other way, the single gray forty-foot container clamped to the trailer.

THIRTY-TWO

Alice found a gas station, topped up her tank, and used the restroom to freshen up and change into something more businesslike. Then she drove back, straight into Hartley's lot and parked between the Fiesta and the old Impala.

Technically, taking the she guessed was reserved for Thaksin Metharom made her fourth in the pecking order.

She got out and headed for the office, not giving herself time for second thoughts.

The office looked like a regular office. A curved front counter topped in blue laminate stood in front of a couple of desks topped with computers, papers and the usual office clutter. The walls were beige. There were calendars and year planners and safety memos tacked to them. Fifteen feet back, the open area narrowed to a corridor with offices running off it. Patterns of light and shade suggested rooms on either side.

There was no sign of Hartley.

So much for that idea. March in, eyeball the guy, make an excuse and march out again.

Dammit.

Her heart kicked up a notch. It would have to be Plan B.

Her arrival hadn't been noticed. The tubby guy was on the phone, swiveled away, so Alice waited by the counter. A wire basket sat on one end full of US Postal Service envelopes. The padded kind. Prepaid, priority mail. Sealed, addressed and ready to go.

The tubby guy swiveled back to write something down, caught sight of her, covered the mouthpiece and called out, "Ms Templar. Visitor."

"Where's Russo?" Templar's head appeared over the top of a cubicle in the back corner. She saw Alice and got to her feet.

"Yes?"

"Hartley Imports, right?" Alice said.

"Correct," Templar advanced on her. "We're wholesale only."

"Yes, I know. The thing is, I've just started my own interior design business back east. I found you online and thought that since I was in LA for a few days I'd look you up. Maybe set up an account while I was here. Perhaps even look over some of your stock."

"Well, Ms..."

"Wong. Susan Wong." Alice held out her hand.

Templar ignored it. "As I was about to say, Ms Wong, we deal in genuine antiques through an exclusive dealer network, not the sort of contemporary pieces likely to interest an interior designer."

"I work with a wide range of clientele," Alice said. "Before I set up my own business I worked as a buyer for Wallace Streetfield on the Stacy mansion."

There was a piece about the Stacy mansion in *Antiques Today*. A twenty-four-year-old internet tycoon had spent forty million dollars refitting an old Santa Cruz estate. Cynics dubbed it "instant heritage" because he'd cornered the antiques market for months on end, buying up everything, seemingly at random.

Templar crossed her arms. "As I said, Ms Wong—"

"Perhaps I could speak with Mr Hartley. I did email him."

Templar's eyes narrowed. "And he replied?"

Alice gave her an indeterminate nod.

"Very well. This was way."

The guy on the phone watched approvingly as Alice walked around the counter. Did he recognize her from the store? No big deal if he did.

Templar led her down the corridor, past a computer room, a storeroom full of boxes, and a copy room where a large commercial copier clunked and hummed. There was a kitchen, a bathroom, then four offices. Two on the left, one on the right, and one at the end of the passage. Hartley's. The brass nameplate said so. It was ajar. Templar tapped and pushed it wide. He was on the phone. Before she could speak, he held up a hand to signify he was listening to something important.

That was it. That was all Alice needed. Her thumping heart kicked into overdrive. After twenty years of nightmares, he now sat ten feet away, a phone pressed to one ear.

Young One, not so young now. Still, the years had been good to him. Better than he deserved. His face was weathered, a little lined, his strong chin softened by a fleshy neck, but the clear gray-blue eyes still shone through. Eyes she remembered. Encouraging eyes. Smiling eyes. Eyes that masked the depravity of the man behind them.

He looked her over as he talked, and for one crazy moment Alice thought he recognized her. Had to force herself to remember it had been twenty years. That she'd been a child.

That was it. She'd got her ID. What more did she want?

The room felt airless. Alice felt vaguely sick. She turned to Templar to make some excuse.

Then he spoke. Not to her. Into the phone.

"One a month? Really? Hell, that's four times what we're doing now. Holy shit, if they can handle that we'll really have to step up our game."

He was speaking Thai.

Hartley swiveled to look out the window, to the front of the warehouse and the big steel roller door. "Arrived today and on its way, clean and cleared. ... Yeah, that's all sorted, thanks to Nancy. ... The Mexican special?" He laughed. "No, I haven't heard yet, but I imagine they're dealing with that as we speak.

"What time's your flight?" He swiveled back and made a note. "I'll send Benny. ... Yeah, sure Tak. And give my regards to Mr Ling."

The sound of the old tongue hit her like a bucket of ice water and Alice's head was clear before the phone was back in its cradle.

She took a breath and took in her surroundings for the first time. Another ordinary office. Comfortable, but bland. Wood-paneled walls, an executive desk, executive chair with an executive-sized computer monitor. The window overlooking the yard was shaded by a louvered blind.

There was an oblong table to one side surrounded by

six chairs. For meetings, she guessed. Beyond it stood a credenza, its sliding doors closed, its top scattered with papers. There were some golfing trophies on a shelf beside his desk. Ugly fake wood with gold plastic figurines on top swinging clubs.

Hartley got to his feet and held out a hand.

"Susan Wong," Templar said. "Says she emailed you."

Hartley looked at her quizzically.

The touch of his skin made her want to tear off her hand and discard it, but she forced a smile through clenched teeth.

"Oh really? Regarding what?"

He still had it. That look. That manner. That smile. Like you were the only one in the whole room. On the whole planet.

"About setting up an account," Alice said.

"An account?"

"I emailed you yesterday."

He frowned. Looked over at his computer. "I don't recall—"

"Oh, not again. I'm sorry, that may be my fault. I've been having problems with my service provider. They keep telling me it's fixed."

"What sort of account were you after, Ms Wong?"

Alice hesitated.

"You can speak freely in front of my colleague."

What the hell did that mean?

"Just a... regular account."

Templar regarded her challengingly. "Ms Wong says she's an antique buyer and interior designer."

Alice didn't demur, although she felt she should. But

say what...?

"I see." Hartley's gray-blue eyes closed down, like she'd failed some sort of test. "I'm afraid our dealer book is full at the moment, but if you leave us your details, we'll be in touch if there's an opening."

"Sure. Thanks. Sorry to have bothered you."

"No bother, Ms Wong."

Something passed between Hartley and Templar. A question, or perhaps a rebuke.

"This way, please," Templar said.

Alice followed her out.

* * *

The rule might have been first on, last off, but rules could be broken, especially when the order to break them came from US Customs and Border Protection. The skipper of the *Pacific Ram* knew better than to argue and assured the supervising officer of his full cooperation.

The ship's computer knew the exact location of the target container and the weights and dispositions of those around it. The information was relayed to the gantry crane along with details of the ship's current lading and ballast. Then it became a high school math problem: calculate the quickest, most efficient way to access it.

Within twenty minutes, a rectangle of sunlight reached below decks. Stevedores released locking pins on the blue container's corners, and the gantry crane whisked it away, delivering it to a separate, specially designated area on the dock.

A guy in body armor emerged from the shadows, checked the ISO code and the lead seal on the container's lockbox, and nodded to his companion. The second guy spoke into the radio he was carrying, two words, then he signaled to a waiting container lift truck.

The truck straddled the container like a giant insect, picked it up and carried it half a mile to the last of a line of wharfside sheds. The guys in body armor followed in the back of a waiting pickup, weapons at the ready.

The shed was a huge and empty—except for the line of police vehicles and CBP Tactical Unit trucks arranged down either side. There was even an ambulance and fire crew, well back, near the entrance.

The container was taken to the far end and positioned so its double doors opened into the body of the shed. The lift truck released its clamps and backed away, its reversing beep echoing through the building before the driver spun the wheel and drove away.

Someone hit a switch and the steel roller door closed behind it with a thunderous rumble. Then silence descended. A silence broken only by the low whine of the container's mechanical ventilation system.

* * *

Rosa had a day off. She'd woken with a temperature and a sore throat that had caused consternation in the household. There were calls to her school and doctor, and the rapid rearrangement of work schedules, but after a some junior paracetamol, a soothing drink, and a longer sleep, she woke mid-morning feeling fine and ready to play.

Annabel was working in the lounge, laptop on a side table, coffee cup in hand, so Rosa decided it was time for Bruin, her big brown bear, to become acquainted with their visitor. Alice had gone away for a few days, leaving her own bear behind with some of her things. She saw him sitting on the shelf in the spare room each time she passed. He looked lonely without Alice, so she took Bruin in to see him.

After introductions, the bears seemed to have a lot in common. Mr Tubble was older and wiser than her bear. You could tell because his yellow coat was faded in places. She took him down from the shelf and carried them to the bed, so they could be more comfortable.

Then she discovered that Mr Tubble was hurt. A seam in his back had split, and she could see some of his insides.

"Oh Mr Tubble, that must be sore!" She told him. "We better get you to the hostipul." She scooped him up and ran out. "Mommy, Mommy..."

* * *

Alice's mind was in a whirl as she drove out. Chevy guy was working on the gate, wearing overalls now, carrying a wrench. He looked up as she passed.

Russo, she figured. Templar had said, "Where's Russo?"

That made the tubby guy Benny: *"What time's your flight? I'll send Benny."*

Words, phrases, and impressions came back to her at random. She kept her mind on them as she accelerated away. Anything to avoid thinking about *him*.

It wasn't what she'd seen or heard, though. It was what she hadn't seen. She suddenly realized there'd been no antiques. And no catalogs, brochures, photographs or magazines about them either. Anywhere.

No odd shapes in bubble wrap awaiting dispatch. Nothing in the rooms she'd passed but cardboard boxes, computers, and copier machines. Nothing even in the boss's office. No little knickknack he'd picked up in Ayuttaya. No charming example of a seventeenth-century whatnot. Not even a framed print of a past treasure. Apart from a few golfing trophies, Hartley's office was as bland as the rest of the place.

Templar hadn't reacted when she mentioned the Stacy mansion either. Antiques weren't like used cars or whiteware. The market wasn't *that* big. You'd expect a dealer —even a wholesaler—to have an interest in action like that. Especially one specializing in Asian antiquities and period furniture. One of the mansion's highlights was a lavish Eastern room.

There was something else too. Something about the account.

You can speak freely in front of my colleague.

What sort of account had he been expecting her to ask for?

She continued on, mulling things over, then braked sharply at the next intersection as an articulated truck executed a lazy turn across half her lane. The long flatbed trailer scythed past her windscreen, a single gray container on its deck.

THIRTY-THREE

Ron Markham would have liked a name like Buck Duval. It was the sort of name they gave to action figures or movie heroes. Duval looked like an action figure too. Close-cropped hair, weathered features, and all hard muscle inside his CBP Tactical Unit uniform. With a name like Buck Duval you couldn't help but grow into a role like that. Who the fuck would call a kid Ronald?

Markham's boss, Watch Commander Dave Percy, introduced them.

"You the intel guy?" Duval held out a hand. He had a grip like an action figure too. So firm it might have been molded in plastic. "What have we got here?"

Markham sucked in his stomach and pointed to the container at the far end of the warehouse. "That was destined for Ensenada."

"Drug cartels?"

"Not a known affiliate. But down there, who can tell?"

"So what is it? Precursor chemicals? Lab equipment? What do you need my boys for?"

"It's people."

"Illegals?"

"Very."

Duval studied him. Markham didn't mind the scrutiny. He was enjoying the feeling of being in charge for once. Of directing a man like this.

"I intercepted a report suggesting this is more than just illegal immigrants. That one or more of their number are Islamic insurgents planning to enter the US via the Mexican border."

"Are they likely to be armed? Dangerous?"

"Unknown. All I can tell is that they're expecting to be landed some way south of here."

Duval nodded. "Then let's give 'em a warm Mexican welcome."

* * *

Alice pulled off the freeway and stopped at the first cafe she came to and ordered coffee and a proper breakfast, but when the food arrived she found she had no appetite. She picked around the sides of the plate and stared out the window.

There was a playground for little kids on the corner opposite. Swings. See-saws. Roundabouts. The moms stood in a group on one side, talking, while the kids ran about, laughing, swinging, twirling. A small Indian girl called out from the top of the slide, her voice shrill and insistent, and Alice suddenly remembered another little girl.

* * *

At first, she'd hardly missed him. There was so much to do,

so much to see, so much to learn. But six weeks after settling into the Kwann's home in Philadelphia they had a visit from the Devarajahs, Chatri's new family, a second-generation Indian couple with three bouncing sons and one all-too-pretty daughter. Chatri was already master of them all, especially the doe-eyed girl, who followed him about like a lost lamb.

"I despair of you, Chatri Juntasa," Alice told him in the backyard. He'd sent his new brothers off on a mission to raid a neighbor's lemon tree. "You have only just arrived and already you are stealing fruit."

He laughed. "Remember how you let me rob that poor man then showed me a pocketful of money?"

"We should have gone back and paid him."

"Yes, we should." He was suddenly serious. "I've missed you, Solikha."

"You're to call me Alice."

"I'll never call you Alice. You'll always be Solikha to me."

"Anyway, you have a new family now," she said.

"Grand, aren't they? Such kind people. I am so lucky. And it's all thanks to you."

He took her hand, squeezed it.

Alice/Solikha didn't know what to do, or even who she was right then. A Khmer girl from a village near Trasek Chrum, a Thai girl from Bangkok—because that's the language they were speaking—or this new person, this "Alice" she was still in the process of becoming.

"We can talk on the telephone," she said at length. "And Baltimore is only a hundred miles away."

She didn't take her hand back.

Chatri looked wistful. "It's not the same."

There were squeals and yells from his new brothers as they came bounding back over the fence, their arms full of plunder. But even that didn't break his grip. Little Lakshmi did though, with her doe-eyes and her mean right hook.

"Ow!" Alice laughed, surprised at the child's intense expression. She said to Chatri, "I bet you taught her that!"

* * *

The waiter brought more coffee and took away her picked-over plate. Alice dragged her eyes from the window.

She'd always prided herself on facing facts, but how objective could an individual ever be, especially about themselves?

She thought of Carla Ahearn, tormented by the memory of what had been done to her. How she might never recover from the trauma. For the first time in her life, Alice allowed herself to think the unthinkable—that she too might have been damaged.

But locked inside yourself, how would you ever know?

* * *

Lakshmi's death from leukemia at the age of fourteen almost finished him. Alice held him in the hospital car park and stroked his unruly hair. Chatri's sobs came in choking gasps, and the tears soaked the shoulder of her blouse.

For weeks afterwards, he walked around the campus like a zombie. Alice looked after him, mothered him, watched out for him. For the first time in her life, she felt she had a purpose. For the first time since the loss of her parents at the age of nine, she let herself reach out to someone. A tentative, uncertain reaching.

One night he reached back.

They'd been to a movie playing in the campus cinema, one her half-sister had recommended. A documentary about the physics of space-time. Serious stuff. Mind-expanding. Part way through they got the giggles and eventually fled to the sound of hisses and catcalls from the theater's more high-minded patrons.

They cut across the lawn. It was early winter. The wind was biting. No snow yet, but the grass was spiky with frost and crunched under foot. They huddled close in their heavy coats, still giggling.

Then suddenly they weren't.

In the shadow of the library building, Chatri kissed her. Long and languid. She kissed him back, losing herself in his embrace, feeling his desire for her, feeling her own for him.

It was difficult. Her roommate would be back. His too. It didn't matter. They'd make this sheltered corner their own.

The embraces and kisses and awkward fumbling went on for some time. Then he slipped a hand inside her coat and touched her. Alice froze. Something snapped inside, and she pushed him away with a startled cry.

"What is it, Sol? What's the matter?"

"Get away. Get away. Get away from me!"

It wasn't him she was seeing. It was that face. That friendly, smiling, deceitful face. The others too, leering at her in the darkness. At her small, cringing, naked body. A cavalcade of nightmares flooded in. Young One and what he did to her. Old One dragging her from the corner by the ankle and doing worse. The blood. The pain. Fat One with his belt around her throat. She screamed and fought, scratched and bit.

"Solikha. Solikha!"

He should have slapped her, brought her to her senses, but Chatri was too kind, too gentle. He tried to talk her round. Reason with her.

A campus cop came running. Seized him. Slammed him against the wall. Called for assistance.

Then another sort of nightmare started. Cops, counselors, campus staff. Talk of immediate expulsion. Right then. That night. She remembered the half-heard phrase: "Before his heels can even touch the ground."

She pleaded with them. It wasn't Chatri's fault.

Whose fault was it then?

"Mine." She stared at her hands.

"Yours? How?"

"Drugs," she whispered.

The lie came easily. She'd dropped a tab of acid. Had never tried it before. An experiment. It started out fine. Better than fine. People in the cinema would remember her giggling. How they had to leave. Then it turned nasty. A bad trip. Spiders everywhere.

Chatri didn't know. She hadn't told him. He was just trying to help.

That led to even more questions, but easier ones to answer.

No, Chatri hadn't supplied it.

Who had?

She mentioned the name of a girl expelled the previous

term. How she'd had it since then and hadn't tried it till tonight.

His room was searched anyway, all his things turned out. He stood in mute shock, watching.

Alice was reprimanded. Severely. Almost lost her scholarship. If it hadn't been for her grades, her obvious ability, the acclaim of her tutors and her outstanding record...

She stood, head bowed and barely said a word. She was truly sorry. It would never happen again. Ever. Yes, of course she'd see a counselor.

Counselors were easy. She'd been lying to them for years. The hard part—the impossible part—was telling Chatri, because that would mean telling him everything about what she really was and what she'd done.

He would hardly speak to her anyway. He blamed himself, thought he really had forced himself on her and was deeply ashamed. He was astonished to hear she'd taken LSD. But that was in his favor. It was imperative he not know anything about the lie. His genuine bewilderment when it was first put to him helped save him.

Then he apologized.

He apologized to *her!* It made her want to scream. Again. But what could she do other than reassure him that it hadn't been his fault?

Time healed. They moved on. Resumed their old friendship, their old ways. But not quite like before. It was never quite the same, never quite so easy. He started calling her his sister. At first, she was flattered, knowing how much he'd loved Lakshmi. Then she realized what else it meant. That there were certain things a brother and sister should not, could not share.

THIRTY-FOUR

"Jackson. Rodriguez." Buck Duval spoke quietly and two guys in body armor carried out banks of lightweight LED panels on tripods. They set them in front of the container, ten feet back, angled at forty-five degrees, then took up position either side of the steel doors.

Jackson took out a pair of side-cutters and removed the lead seal from the lockbox in the middle of the doors. Rodriguez held the lid open while his partner went to work on the padlock. Some sort of master key. It was off in seconds.

The two men stepped back awaiting further orders.

Ron Markham tugged on the armored vest he'd been issued. It was already tight, but he figured the tighter the better. He was positioned well back from any action, but if bullets started flying, you could never be too far back.

The location of the wharfside shed had puzzled him at first. It lay at the end of a long promontory, its back overlooking nothing but the wide blue Pacific. Now he realized it was an ideal spot for a shooting-range. The Tactical Unit team could machine gun the container if necessary. The only stray shot risks would be unlucky seabirds or fish hit by sinking chunks of lead a mile or two offshore.

Duval signaled to his men.

Each door was fitted with two vertical lock rods. The end of each rod was attached to a cam that hooked into knuckles welded to the top and bottom of the container. Two lock rods per door made a total of four closures.

The lock rods were turned by hinged handles folded flat against the container. The handles were held in place by simple catches. Jackson and Rodriguez released the catches on the outer lock rods, raised the handles and turned them ninety degrees to disengage the cams.

The creak and scrape of metal on metal echoed round the warehouse.

Two down, two to go. Jackson and Rodriguez moved to the inner handles.

This time, they synchronized their actions. Rodriguez started a silent, head-bob countdown. Three. Two. One. Go. They swung the handles out, then bounded backward, drawing the doors with them.

At the same moment, the lights came on flooding the end of the warehouse and the interior of the container with cold white light.

Markham could see already that the container was mostly empty.

"*Bienvenidos a México*," Duval called through a loud-hailer.

They came out in ones and twos, shielding their eyes from the glare. Men. More and more of them. Twelve, fourteen, fifteen. All men. All dressed in ragged, grimy clothes. Skinny. Asian. Fragile looking compared to the bulked up men in helmets and armored vests in the shadows that surrounded them, but Duval wasn't taking any chances.

"Get down on the ground! Get down on the ground! Get down on the ground!" he bellowed through the megaphone.

They didn't respond. Stood looking around. Dazed. Confused. Trying to see beyond the bright lights.

"Warning shot," Duval called, drawing and firing his sidearm.

The shot—high and wide—punched a neat round hole in the steel cladding at the back of the warehouse. It continued on, following the arc of its trajectory, eventually dropping somewhere into the wide blue Pacific. But long before it hit the water, the men dropped. Some to their knees with their arms raised, some prone on the cold concrete floor. One guy, who'd been supported by two others, was left to his own devices and fell heavily.

"Move in!"

The Tactical Unit edged from the shadows into the fringe of light, casting gigantic shadows. Seeing their weapons drawn and ready, the kneeling men imitated their prone companions and threw themselves to the floor.

A dog handler released a beagle. Someone adjusted the lights, so they shone deeper into the container. The interior was squalid, crisscrossed with lines of laundry and hanging blankets. It had a raised timber floor and bare metal sides. The dog went in.

Nobody moved. They waited as a stale smell infused the air. A mix of unwashed bodies, excrement and something else. Something sickly and sweet.

The dog returned to the entrance and gave a single

bark. Duval directed Jackson and Rodriguez in. Two others covered them.

They moved cautiously, half-crouched, swinging their weapons from side to side, knocking down blankets and laundry as they went, clearing the line of fire. Thirty seconds later they re-emerged, their postures relaxed, their weapons held easy.

"All clear, sir," Rodriguez called. "But we've got a body."

* * *

Alice left the cafe and returned to her car. The street outside was quiet, so she saw the red Ford Fiesta swing out behind her almost right away. At first, she didn't think anything of it. Then she recalled the cars drawing up outside Hartley Imports, and the look Hartley and Templar had exchanged when she asked to open an account.

Coincidence?

There was one way to find out.

She turned a corner and swung into the first parking spot she came across, forcing the Fiesta to carry on past. She glanced at the driver. A woman, but a brief look at the moving silhouette wasn't conclusive. The license plate was, however.

For something to do while watching the premises, Alice had noted down the plates of the cars parked out front.

Nancy Templar was following her.

She was easy to lose, but Alice was more cautious now as she returned to the backpackers. She had all afternoon to find a motel, but that wasn't what she needed. Not in her present mood. She knew she'd mope around an empty room. What she needed was a sense that there were other people on the planet, even if that just meant exchanging a greeting or a nod or sharing a mug of tea.

Besides, she wanted another word with Violet.

Tina, the reception goddess, had been replaced by the guy from the front desk. The guy with the dry lips and the sexual assault eyes.

He checked the register. "Only had ya down for one night."

"I came back."

"Making out, huh?" He licked his lips and looked her up and down.

"Oh yeah."

"I bet you are. Listen, if you want to save yourself a little money…"

Alice took the dorm room key and walked away.

It was still early. There were a couple of fellow drifters in the kitchen, faces she didn't recognize, but the place was mostly empty. She threw her pack on her old bunk, changed into her running gear, did some warm-ups, and headed out.

The air was warm and dry, the sky a steely gray.

It took a couple of blocks to loosen up. A couple more to get into her stride. Her ankle still bothered her a little. Nothing major. Something she could tune out. The smart thing would be to keep off it for a few days, but when did people ever do the smart thing?

The really smart thing to do would be to return the rental, go back to San Francisco and resume her vacation. Forget about Thomas Wilton Hartley. Put her past behind her, where it belonged. Get on with the rest of her life.

Yeah, that would be the smart thing.

Perhaps she could enroll in some sort of treatment program, like a Betty Ford clinic for the sexually abused. Not that she was sure she had a problem. Hadn't she just confronted her demon? Looked him in the eye and *not* fallen to pieces?

But there was a problem. She conceded that.

She found a path beside a long cement drain. Stormwater, maybe. Five feet wide, three feet deep, a muddy trickle in the bottom. Fenced along both sides for safety. The same galvanized steel mesh that surrounded Hartley Imports. The sight of it was all she needed to lock her mind on target.

What the hell did they need a warehouse for?

Something was up. That much was clear. The way Hartley's car had been surrounded the moment he arrived. The way the Impala guy—Russo—had been working on the gate. He hadn't arrived dressed for maintenance work. She remembered him getting out his car and shooting his cuffs.

Then there was Hartley, speaking Thai to someone called Tak—presumably Thaksin Metharom. He said something had just arrived and was on its way, "Clean and cleared." Whatever that meant.

The gate, the lights, the fence, the camera. Clearly something important. So important that a simple innocent account inquiry had resulted in her being tailed.

Clearly, she'd called at the wrong time

There was something she'd almost forgotten too. A name. Hartley said, "Give my regards to Mr Ling." For some reason the name was familiar. She'd heard it before somewhere, in another context, but it remained tantalizingly out of reach. Work, perhaps...?

Leave it. It'll come.

She ran on, following the mesh fence, knowing she should do the smart thing and forget all about him. Put her past behind her where it belonged and get the hell out of there.

But she also knew she wouldn't.

THIRTY-FIVE

After one final swaying lurch, all movement stopped. They waited in silence as the truck drove away. There was a low rumble followed by a bang that Kanya recognized as the sound of a roller door closing. Like the one she'd seen three weeks before, shutting out her last glimpse of Thai sunshine.

Faint screeches and popping sounds signaled the release of the latches, and a seam of light appeared around the edge of the container doors. Someone sighed. Footsteps moved away. A distant door banged shut.

Inside the container, no one moved. Then Kanya, who was nearest to the left-hand door, pushed on it gently, calling out.

No reply.

She pushed wider, called louder. No one answered but her echo.

The door swung back and slammed against the side of the container, making them all jump. Kanya stepped out, half-expecting to find they were back where they'd started, the last three weeks a cruel joke.

The others followed her in ones and twos, clutching each other for support.

The container had been deposited in an L-shaped space, its length occupying the long arm, leaving six feet spare on either side. The doors opened on a room twenty feet deep and forty wide with skylights set in the ceiling thirty feet above.

Kanya clutched her chest, feeling dizzy. After weeks in a box eight feet wide and eight feet high, the vast empty space was almost overwhelming.

Ahead was a motley collection of sofas and chairs. A lounge of sorts, like they'd seen in TV shows and movies. There was even a rug on the cement floor. To the right, beyond a large wooden table, was a kitchen area. Electric stove. Stainless steel benchtops. Refrigerator. Freezer. Cupboards stocked with cans of unfamiliar food. Beyond that, a partitioned space enclosed two toilets and two showers. A line of mattresses ran down either side of the container. Two-inch thick rectangles of rubber, each with a folded blanket on one end.

They wandered about in a daze, overcome by the luxury of the place. Proper seats. Running water. Fresh food. And so much space! After life in the slums this was like stepping into a dream.

Kanya caught Apinya's eye, and they moved to one side. They hadn't told the others about Namthip yet.

"What of the child?"

Eri ran around giggling with the other children.

Apinya said, "Not yet. Say her mother is sleeping. We need to talk to the people here. They will handle it."

"Are these for us?" Arisa called, holding up a pink plastic bag overflowing with discarded clothes. There were more bags piled behind it. Tops, skirts, pants, jackets, dresses, even shoes. The others crowded around. All they'd been allowed to bring was what they stood up in.

Katreeya, a sturdy, bright-eyed girl from Khlong Toey, snatched up a brightly colored top. "They must be. Isn't all the rest for us?" She held the top up against herself and swiveled to the others.

"Oh yes, very attractive." Apinya pushed to the front. "It goes well with your rats-nest of hair. And did you shit your smock and wipe it on your arms?"

Katreeya looked shocked. Apinya laughed. "Me also. Look!" She tugged at her own lank hair and held out her hands. "Look at us. We are all filthy. We all stink. And who's to wonder? We have been living like caged animals for weeks. New clothes won't help us. First, we must get clean."

The children were bustled off to the showers. Their squeals of delight encouraged the others who worked in relays, clearing and airing the container, bagging trash, emptying the piss containers and waiting for their turn.

Under cover of all the activity, Kanya and Apinya found a blanket and set to work with needles and thread, stitching Namthip's shrunken form inside it.

* * *

A fat *farang* came in an hour later, through a door in the cinder block wall that he closed and locked behind him. He pushed a cart that looked like an oversized shopping trolley. He didn't speak but gestured they should fill it with their trash.

As they did so, Apinya caught his sleeve, waved him

into the container, and showed him the body. He grunted, picked it up, carried it out and threw it in the trash.

It was early evening before their next visitor arrived. The glow from the skylights was fading. They'd switched on the lamps and the room was filled with the smell of cooking.

His arrival was announced by three sharp raps on the door. All turned to see a well-dressed, man with gray-blue eyes. A *farang*, but he spoke their language.

"Welcome to America."

There was a collective intake of breath. It was true. They'd made it!

"Although you have arrived safely, there is still a danger you will be detected, at least until we can provide you with the necessary papers. This door is locked for that reason. To protect you *and* to protect us. Going outside will put you in danger of arrest and instant deportation. What's more, you'll endanger the rest of your group too. You must *not* leave here unless you are accompanied by me or one of my people. Do I make myself clear?"

They nodded gravely. Very clear.

"Good." He smiled for the first time. It was like another light had been switched on. A warm and friendly glow seemed to fill the room. "Just remember, you're safe as long as you stay in here. Now, does anyone have questions?"

For a moment, no one spoke. Then someone said, "Our men, sir? What of them?"

"They, too, have arrived. From tomorrow, you will be taken in ones and twos to be reunited."

Another sigh ran around the group. Most had no other questions. Except Apinya.

"We... had a problem, sir. An illness..."

The man's face grew grave again. "So I understand. That's really why I'm here. Perhaps..." He gestured her to one side and said quietly, "There's a child, I believe."

"Yes, sir. Little Eri."

"Which one is she?"

Apinya pointed to a doe-eyed girl in a pretty blue dress sucking her finger.

"She hasn't been told yet?"

"No sir. Only that her mother is ill."

"Well, she's been laid out properly now and looks very peaceful. Her father's been sent for. I'll take her to him now."

"Oh thank you, sir. Thank you." Apinya had been dreading the task of telling Eri, and it was getting harder and harder to distract the child from wanting to see her mother.

The man smiled and beckoned to the girl. Little Eri came forward reluctantly, led by Kanya. He took her hand, said how pretty she looked, then scooped her up and carried her away.

* * *

Violet ambled into the kitchen wearing a T-shirt and cut-off jeans. Her hair was fluffed and she was still wearing make-up. With her slim figure and smattering of freckles, she barely looked fifteen.

"Hey, you're still with us. I thought you'd left. What's cooking?"

"Grilled squid skewered with cucumber and Asian

basil. I've made too much. You want some?"

"Sure. Great."

Alice pointed to a bowl. "That's the dip. Fish sauce, garlic, chili and lime juice."

"Are you a gourmet chef or something?"

Alice smiled. "I've got wine too."

They took an empty wooden bench in the quadrangle. There were a couple of guys in the corner, drinking beer. Another group on the recliners. Everyone was winding down.

"How was your day?" Alice poured the wine into plastic cups.

"Oh, pretty good."

"From the look on your face, I'd say it was more than that."

Violet's suppressed grin broke. "How about pretty spectacular?"

"Tell me more.

She leaned forward. "Keep a secret?"

"Sure."

"They signed me on the spot. I'm going to be a Vixen Pics' next *Little Girl Lost*. It's their most popular series. It means huge exposure. The website traffic alone is massive."

"That's fantastic! Congratulations." Alice raised her cup in a toast. "But why the secrecy?"

"This place is a bitchfest. Actors, you know? The competition's really tough, and people get het up. There was a girl here last quarter, signed up and singing about it. That night, in that very kitchen, she got splashed with hot oil. An accident." She emphasized the word with air quotes. "Second-degree burns. That's her career shot."

"Ow! Nice crowd."

Violet shrugged.

"So what did you have to do for your audition?"

"Really, it was dumbass easy. I got paired up with this guy Eric, and we worked up a routine beforehand. He's like six-five and huge. Makes me look tiny and about twelve years old. I was all, 'Gosh mister, what's that thing?' and 'No, no, you can't do that!'" She laughed. "They loved it, said the punters would lap it up. Signed me on the spot.

"They want to do a series, six or maybe even twelve parts. Call it *Violet's Travels*. Start simple and slowly build it up. Maybe me alone at first, then with another girl. Then oral, then a guy, then several guys, and so on. End up with a big group scene."

"You're happy with that?"

"I'm on my way, sister!" She held out her hand in a high five. "Look out for me in next year's AVNs."

"AVNs?"

"Annual awards. Adult Video News. They're like the Oscars of adult entertainment. There's also the XBIZ awards, but they're more like the Golden Globes."

"What do you get awards for?"

"All sorts of shit, just like the Oscars. Best film, best director, best actress, best music score. There's a whole sex scene category too. Best solo performance, best couple, best three-way. Stuff like that. There are even awards for spanking and foot fetish."

"You're kidding?"

"No, really."

"Foot fetish?"

"You ain't seen weird till you've seen this business."

Alice topped up Violet's cup, and they ate in silence for a while. The TV was on in the lounge. A newsflash about the interception of a container full of illegal refugees.

Cora-Jane walked past in a low-cut top, her high heels clacking on the flagstones. She gave them a dismissive look. Violet toasted her back. "Silly cow. She's like all the rest. Thinks it's just about getting noticed and getting laid. Moaning and groaning at the right times. *Uh-uh-uh*. Thinks her tits are all she needs. Doesn't seem to realize this town is full of them."

"So what is it all about?"

"It's a business. You've got to think of it like that. Treat it like that. You've got to participate for a start. Be a proper actor. Come up with fresh ideas. Improvise. Think about where you want to go and hustle, hustle, hustle. Make it happen. Don't just lie back and let them screw you.

"Know whose idea *Violet's Travels* was? Mine. I've been thinking about it for months. Soon as I had their attention, I put it to them. Hey, what about a series? Laid it out for them. Boom, boom, boom. Elevator pitch stuff, you know? That's what I mean. And they love that. Someone who can think and plan as well as act."

Alice raised her cup again. "To your first AVN."

Violet drank deeply.

"How about the others? How are they doing?"

"Tina on reception, she got signed. S&M, fake rape, pub-hum."

"Pub-hum?"

"Public humiliation. Not my scene. I know a few girls who've tried it, but once is enough for most of them. They cut and run."

"Is that the most extreme?"

"Pretty much. The real nasty stuff, the hangings and torture and snuff movies all come from overseas. No one does it here. At least, not for real."

"There much of a market for that?"

"There's a market for everything. Animals, kids, pooping. There are some real sick fucks out there. Like I said, you ain't seen weird till you've seen this business."

"Had bad does it get?"

"How bad can you imagine? If you've got the money, someone will supply it, either on video or for real. I hear the latest craze is to own your very own 'toy'—and we're not talking about dildos or blow-up dolls."

Alice frowned. "You don't mean real people?"

"If you've got the bread." Violet shrugged. "Then you can do what you like with them."

"Where do they come from?"

"People smugglers. Either across the Mexican border or from Asia somehow. A lot of people want to get to America, Alice. A lot of people will believe anything you tell 'em."

Violet finished her food and drained her plastic cup, thanked Alice, said she'd love to stay and chat, but had to get ready for a date.

"A date?"

"Yeah, Eric. The guy I told you about."

"Your co-star?"

"He's a nice guy. Really smart. Not like most of these steroid jocks." She jerked a thumb at the guys in the corner. "I know what you're thinking. We've been fucking half the afternoon, now we're going out on a date? But it's different. Work-life balance, you know?" She hesitated. "Besides, sometimes it's nice just to snuggle up to someone without all that other crap."

Alice watched her go, thinking about what she'd said.

"Hey."

It was one of the steroid jocks from the corner. He slipped into Violet's vacant spot and held out a hand. "Brad," he said.

"Alice," Alice said.

"How'd you go today, Alice?"

Alice waved her hand in a so-so gesture.

"Yeah, me too. Tough out there, huh?"

"Sure is."

"So uh..." He looked her over. "You wanna work on your routine? Get a little practice in?"

Alice looked back at him. Wide-set green eyes and curly blond hair. A great physique under his open-neck shirt. He was holding a beer.

"I'd love to, Brad."

"Yeah?" He grinned.

"Yeah. But I can't. Not right now."

"Oh? Why not?"

Alice gathered up her plate and cup, the cutlery and the wine bottle. "I've got something to attend to. A business something."

THIRTY-SIX

I t was after nine by the time she reached the corner of Mawney and Reeve. Traffic was light, the evening overcast, and the moon a slim crescent on the horizon. She wore a dark nylon jacket, black canvas shoes, black leggings and a close-fitting black top. With her olive skin and a navy blue baseball cap pulled down low, she looked like a shadow.

The industrial park was nighttime quiet. Pools of orange light from street lamps held the darkness at bay, but the roads were empty. Alice continued past Hartley Imports. Her impression of the morning had been right. Something was up. There were still two cars in the lot and lights on in the office building. The vehicles told her it was Russo and Hans Reisinger, Hartley's right-hand man.

Alice parked half a block away, switched off the interior light so it wouldn't flood the car when she stepped out and headed back to the warehouse on foot. She figured it was safe to leave the car unlocked. There was no one about, and she might need to make a quick getaway.

It wasn't just the office. Something was going on it the warehouse too. A narrow band of light was visible beneath the wide steel door. The gate, open yesterday, was now partly closed. Not all the way, but like a reminder to the last one out.

She slipped through, keeping close to the fence line as she approached the office. The front door was ajar and there was movement inside. Someone coming out. She pressed back against the mesh.

Russo emerged carrying a toolbox. He walked across the yard to the warehouse, holding out a hand as he went, like he was waving to someone. A moment later, he was bathed in light. Halogen lamps on a motion sensor fixed to the front of the building. Alice shielded her own eyes from the glare and made a mental note of the trigger point. He opened the workshop door beside the steel roller and stepped inside, calling out something as he went. A voice replied. He laughed and closed the door.

Thirty seconds later, detecting no further movement, the security lights went out.

Two cars meant two guys. And now she knew where they were.

She checked the windows of the office building anyway, just in case. The western end, the end that contained Hartley's office and overlooked the warehouse, was in darkness. The rest of the place was deserted.

Slipping in through the front door, she moved around the counter and dropped into a low crouch. Now that she was inside in the light, she'd be visible from the yard.

It still looked like a regular office.

Keeping low, moving quickly, she headed for the first available cover, the partitioned space Templar had emerged from that morning.

A dispatch area. The office's mail room.

There was a packing bench and a stack of padded envelopes. Printed mailing labels. Packing tape. A box of DVDs. Alice picked one out. The cover insert was deep maroon, printed to look like leather. The label, in a flowery old-fashioned script, read *The Connoisseur's Collection: Volume XIV*. Same legend on the spine. Nothing on the back except more of the printed leather look.

Alice opened the box. The disk was also labeled *The Connoisseur's Collection: Volume XIV*. Nothing else. Not even fine print or a copyright stamp. No insert. No other printed matter.

She took out the disk and studied it. It could be anything. Even a catalog of antique furniture.

There was a half-sheet of unused labels on the bench. The names were just names—P. Smail, M. Church, C. Lee—and the addresses were post office boxes from all over the country, but there were no business names or company names. The sort of names you'd expect in a company-to-company mailout.

Alice headed for the passage, taking a penlight from her pocket as she went.

The first room on the right housed a couple of computer servers, boxes of blank DVDs, and four DVD duplicators, each one capable of handling eight disks at once. Four times eight made thirty-two discs at a time. Say each disk took twenty minutes. That was ninety-six an hour or nearly eight hundred in a working day. Four thousand in a five-day week. Not a big operation, but big enough.

The room opposite was a storeroom, mostly stacked with cartons of blank DVD cases. Next to that was a washroom. There was a stationery cupboard, a broom closet, and the photocopier room.

Alice checked it out.

The machine was on standby. Its touch panel glowed in the darkness. A big machine connected to a trimmer and folder. There was a bin full of offcuts round the back, and the output tray held a stack of inserts ready to be added to the DVD cases. More of *The Connoisseur's Collection: Volume XIV*.

Next to the copy room was a canteen. A plain room with a linoleum floor and steel-framed chairs and tables. Sink bench, coffee machine, refrigerator. Nothing out of the ordinary except for a red-painted door that led into the warehouse.

It was locked and bolted. The bolts on this side were clearly meant to stop whatever was in the warehouse from coming through.

Presumably *not* antiques.

A sign on it read "Staff only. Strictly no admittance."

She moved on down the passage towards Hartley's office at the far end. There were two more doors on the left and one on the right, all ajar. Offices for Reisinger, Tak and Templar.

Suddenly the area outside lit up again. A blaze of light spilled through the storeroom window and into the passage behind. Someone had tripped the security light coming back from the warehouse.

Alice ran back and checked the window.

Two someones. Heading this way.

* * *

The gates of 1064 Presley Drive swung open and Ron Markham turned his wife's Malibu up the drive. At the top of the low rise, sheltered from a view of the road, was a long expansive house. Courtesy lights came on automatically. He continued past the guest's parking circle as instructed and stopped at the far end. As he did so, Thomas Hartley stepped from the shadows by the basement door.

"Evening, Ron."

"Thomas."

"You're right on time. Have a good day?"

"Yeah. It went off like clockwork."

"I saw the news. How does it feel to be a hero?"

Markham gave him an uncertain grin. "Pretty good."

"All part of the service, Ron. We look after our friends."

"How did things go at your end?"

"Like clockwork. Thanks to you."

Markham nodded.

Hartley saw he was sweating. Nervous. Not surprising.

"A little something to help you celebrate." He took a cooler bag from the shadows and held it out. "Champagne and caviar."

Markham wiped the palm of one hand on the front of his pants and took the bag. In his other hand, Hartley held out a key.

"So what's the deal?"

"Exactly what we talked about."

"Really?"

"Really. Like I said, we look after our friends."

"What about... complications?"

"There's no such thing, Ron. Ever. You have free rein. Whatever you like. And if there are any *complications*, well, she won't be missed."

Markham chewed his lip.

"First time, right? I still remember mine."

"You've done this too?"

"We all have Ron. You're joining an exclusive club."

Markham breathed in, then breathed out.

"A little nerve-racking, right? Exciting too. Intense."

"You got that right. Intense."

"That's what the champagne's for. Take your time. Relax. Ease into it."

Markham nodded and gripped the bag.

"You tell your wife you're pulling an all-nighter?"

He nodded.

"So take all night. The first of many."

"And it's really no holds barred?"

"No holds barred, Ron."

Markham looked down at the key. "What about... afterwards?"

"Close the door, leave the key in the lock and drive on out."

"I meant about—?"

"One of my guys will tidy up." Harley smiled. "All part of the service."

* * *

It was the pair of them, Russo and Reisinger. A casual walk back. Like they were finishing up for the night.

Alice slipped into the storeroom and hid behind the half-open door. She heard their voices in the outer office,

272

then footsteps in the passage. Russo walked into the computer room opposite and began popping drawers on the burners, gathering a stack of freshly cut DVDs. Reisinger followed him, stood in the passage outside so close to where Alice was hiding that she could smell his aftershave. He had a cellphone to his ear. He shut it off and slipped it in his pocket.

"Thomas has a job for you in the morning. A clean-up. His place."

"Clean-up or disposal?"

"Disposal, most like. But a small package."

"I'll bring my truck. Do it on the way in."

"No rush. Take your time tomorrow. It's been a long day." Reisinger held out a gray plastic key fob. "For the gate."

Russo took it, arched his back and yawned. "I won't be there before ten. Benny said he's got another one ready to go."

"There was a breakage in the shipment."

"Well, if this one's small enough, we can flush 'em both at once."

* * *

The basement reminded Markham of his Alabama boyhood. It was like a storm shelter. Foam filled 14-gauge steel door set in a 16-gauge steel frame. Two-by-four studs, half-inch drywall over three-quarter inch plywood. Solid. Soundproof. He knew the construction method well. His daddy had built storm shelters until he got laid-off.

The little girl wore a pretty blue dress. She was tied to

an iron-framed bed by one ankle and looked up at Markham with frightened eyes as he descended the basement steps. Sweet face. Big eyes.

He smiled back. Cute kid.

His old demon stirred.

She stared at him. She'd been crying. That was OK. She'd be doing a lot more of that before he was done with her.

* * *

Alice listened as they closed up the office and drove out the yard. She heard the second car stop, heard the drag and rattle of the gate, the clank and click of a chain and padlock. Then she remembered the alarm pad by the office door and Benny punching in numbers when he opened up. Not only was she locked inside the building, not only was the place alarmed, but she was also locked inside the yard. A yard with a high mesh fence and razor wire along the top. A yard with video cameras and lights and motion sensors. If there was any time to act, it was now.

She shoved a stack of boxes over so they spilled out into the passage. Nothing happened, so she dashed from the storeroom out into the darkened office, waving her arms like she was trying to fly.

She tripped on something in the darkness and bashed her thigh on the corner of a desk, but was rewarded with a loud undulating squeal from the alarm and flashing lights from the control box by the door. The piercing scream went on and on. She imagined the guy at the gate, just finished locking up. Weary, heading for home, now having to go back in and reset everything.

She ducked into an opening beneath the front counter and waited.

* * *

Markham had heard about the death spasm. Even seen it once. Supposedly. But the video quality was so shitty it was hard to tell if it was real.

The body went into rictus. Every muscle spasmed, fighting in a last desperate bid to hold on to life. That was the very best time, they said. The purest rush. Like crack cocaine. A good choke hold, a little care, and you could do it again and again. Work it steadily, keep on the plateau, then go all out in a final deadly rush.

* * *

Impala guy, Russo, came back into the office. He was a good employee. Didn't just reset the alarm and leave again, but came in to check the cause. Came in wary, holding a gun. A Ruger SR9. Compact, semi-automatic, brushed stainless steel finish.

Alice, dressed like a shadow, scrunched herself more deeply into the shaded recess beneath the counter as his black and gray striped pants passed within five feet of her.

He threw on the lights and cast about, but only in a half-hearted fashion. He wasn't *that* good an employee.

She guessed his thinking. He'd just closed up. Most

likely it was the banging of the door or the gate that had triggered the alarm. Not like it was 3:00am and there was a hole in the fence.

Alice slipped off her shoes. She'd move more quietly in bare feet.

Russo went through the office, glancing behind desks, gun at the ready in his right hand. He checked the partitioned space, then spotted the spilled boxes in the passage, muttered, "What the fuck?" and moved towards them.

Alice eased from her hiding place, slipped around the counter, pushed through the partly open door and raced out into the night.

THIRTY-SEVEN

It was after midnight by the time Alice got back to Stiler's. There was music and some shuffling shadows in the quad, comatose shapes in the lounge, a couple necking in the kitchen. Alice moved past quietly, heading for her room.

"Hey." A voice from the shadows. The steroid jock. Brad. The guy who wanted to work on his routine.

"Oh. Hi."

"Business sorted?" He was still holding a beer. Maybe the same one he'd been holding earlier, although she doubted it.

"Kind of."

"Black suits you."

"Thanks."

"But you look like you could do with some unwinding."

Alice said nothing.

"Want me to unwind you?"

Sounds from the necking couple intensified. She realized the shapes in the lounge weren't all comatose. Some of them were moving. Slowly.

Brad looked good, even in the unlit hallway.

Alice felt a pounding in her throat.

He put his beer aside. Moved closer. Slipped his hands round her waist.

Sometimes it's nice just to snuggle up to someone without all that other crap.

He ran a practiced hand up her spine. It felt good. She let herself give a little, sink against him and raised her own hands to his hips.

He had a bunch of keys hooked in the belt loop of his pants.

For the gate.

In her mind's eye, she saw Reisinger hand Russo the gray key fob and suddenly realized whose gate it must be for.

Alice pushed herself away. "Sorry Brad, I've got an early call."

* * *

It was an old habit, maybe more of that country girl stuff, but Alice woke one minute before the alarm she'd set on her phone. The display read 5:29. She canceled the alarm, eased out of bed, gathered up her stuff and tiptoed to the bathroom. Twenty minutes later, she was packed, in her car and heading west.

1064 Presley Drive lay in shadow. She drove past, U-turned, came back down the hill, and slotted in behind a parked car thirty yards from the gate.

She'd stopped twice on the way. Once at an all-night convenience store for a can of hairspray, and once at fast food drive-thru for a Styrofoam cup of coffee and a cardboard breakfast tray of food. She figured there might be more nutritional value in the packaging—and possibly more flavor too—but testing that theory would have to wait. She took out the hairspray, discarded the cap, gave the can a shake and stepped out the car.

Keeping to the shadows, she made her way down to 1064. From the uphill side, there was a ten-foot section of fence before the gate. It had the same spiked iron railings as the rest. Beyond it, the driveway led up to the house, curving slightly to allow for the in-swing of a vehicle coming up the hill, which meant the gate camera would be angled downhill too.

The camera was housed in an all-weather casing with a metal hood and sloping glass in front to protect it from rain and falling leaves. It had been there a while. There was ivy growing up its support column and over the back of the housing. It almost looked like a garden ornament.

Alice kept to the uphill side, reached through the fence, stretched as far as she could, then hit the nozzle on the can.

The spray had a range of about three feet, which was just about right. She waved it about and blew, carrying the sticky mist as far as it would go in the still morning air. Most of it missed the camera and settled on the ivy and the surrounding vegetation, but enough found the sloping glass plate in front to subtlety alter what the camera saw. On the monitor, it would look like mist or fog. There'd still be a picture, but a fuzzy one. Blurred outlines. No sharp details. Enough to obscure your identity.

She returned to her car, threw the empty can in the rental company trash bag and settled down to breakfast.

At Quantico, they taught the key to observational

fieldwork was to be in place early. Settle in, blend in, become part of the scenery. If the meeting was down for nine o'clock, be there at eight. If the perp was a high-profile underworld figure or a foreign agent who might have watchers watching for watchers, get there earlier. Seven o'clock or even six. It was a waiting game.

Alice didn't think Hartley was high-profile or a foreign agent, but she didn't know his routine. He hadn't arrived at work till after ten the day before, but that didn't mean he was a late starter. You couldn't generalize from a single instance.

Besides, there were other considerations. Did he have a wife? A family? Live-in staff or outside help? Someone maintained those grounds. There'd be a cleaner too, though she was pretty sure it wasn't the guy named Russo. *His* cleaning service was something special. Something that required a truck.

And he wouldn't be there till after ten. Alice wanted to be certain he'd be the only one around. So by 6:30 she was parked up, watching and waiting. Sipping lukewarm coffee and eating cardboard food.

* * *

Chatri woke with a stiff neck and a sore back. The sofa was all right for a Sunday afternoon nap, but he wouldn't want to live there.

He'd lived there last night though because Annabel had been very drunk. Raging and incoherent. He'd never seen her so bad. For the first time ever, she'd frightened him.

He'd arrived home late. Perhaps that was it. But he had called ahead. And twice during the day to check on Rosa. By mid-afternoon, she'd been well enough to go on a sleep-over at a cousin's in St Francis Heights.

Annabel, slumped at the breakfast bar, had roused herself blearily when he came in, and he managed to steer her to the bedroom. Then she'd come to her senses and slammed the door in his face. He went to open it, but something crashed against the other side. More things. Hurled from the dresser, he guessed. Things that shattered and broke. She shouted for him to stay away, and he decided not to press his luck. When he risked a peek thirty minutes later, she'd passed out diagonally across the bed. He threw a quilt over her, gathered some clothes for the morning, closed the door and retreated to the lounge.

Now he checked on her. Cautiously. The blinds were drawn and the room was in darkness. Best let her sleep it off. Sort things out tonight.

He showered, dressed, and closed the front door quietly. His car was parked in the driveway, but when he reached it, she came storming out behind him carrying an overnight bag and hurled it at him.

"Yours. Get out and stay away. Get out of my life."

The bag bounced off the roof and landed on the hood.

"Annabel?"

She looked a mess. For a moment he thought she was still drunk. Then he realized she'd been crying.

"What is it? What's wrong?" He advanced across the lawn.

"Get away from me or I'll call the cops."

"Annabel."

"I mean it. Keep away from me."

"What—?"

"You filthy pervert! You disgusting creep! You'll never see your daughter again, I promise you that. I'm calling a lawyer first thing. I want a divorce. And if you contest it, if you contest one single clause, I'll go to the cops and have them put you and your filthy pervert friend away for life."

"Annabel... I don't—."

"Get out! Get out! *Get away from me!*"

She ran up the steps and slammed the door. He heard the bolt rammed home.

He followed, knocked and called her name. No response.

People were leaving for work. Kids on bikes passed on their way to school. The old guy across the street was on his front lawn, unbagging the morning newspaper. He caught Chatri's eye. Chatri looked away.

He didn't know what to do. His car was sitting in the drive, the overnight bag laying on the hood. The guy across the street was pretending to study his newspaper.

Chatri walked back, picked up the bag and threw it in the car. He tried calling Annabel from his cell, but she wouldn't answer. He left a message. "I don't understand. What's happened? Please call me." Then he sat, trying to think of what else he could do, looking back at the house and the bolted door. Eventually, he started the car and headed for work.

* * *

Alice thought about Brad, the guy from last night. Why hadn't she gone with him, apart from the early start? In a sense, it would have been perfect. Ships passing in the night. No commitments, no comeback.

It's clean. Everybody's tested.

And yet that made it all wrong too. The commoditization of the physical act. Treating people as objects. Receptacles. Items to be used and then discarded. Sex without affection.

She drained the last of her coffee. It was cold and bitter.

The first departure came just after 7:00. A light blue Chevy Malibu, three or four years old. Kind of nondescript for such a swanky neighborhood. Maybe Hartley did have live-in staff.

The reflection of early morning sun on glass made it impossible to see who was behind the wheel, but she scribbled the registration on a notepad. California plates.

Her caution had been advisable. It turned out Hartley was an early riser after all because just after 7:40 his green Porsche Cayenne turned out of the drive. Or maybe he was just going down to the store for milk.

Did people in a place like that ever go down to the store for milk? He probably had his own dairy herd out back.

She waited. It wasn't milk. Or anything else. He didn't return. Neither did the maid or whoever it was in the blue Malibu. Two hours ticked past with no other sign of activity from 1064 Presley Drive.

The sun beat on the roof of her rental. Alice moved it back ten feet to catch the shifting shade of an overhanging tree. It didn't make much difference. It was still hot.

The two hours ticked past slowly. Two-and-a-half. Still nothing.

Coming up on 10:30, she saw a truck heading up the hill. A black Ford pickup with black glass windows. An F-150, maybe ten years old. Again, not the kind of vehicle you'd expect in this kind of neighborhood.

She watched through her hunting scope as it headed towards her, the cross-hairs focused on the outline of the driver. Hard to tell if it was Russo through the tinted glass, but something told her this had to be it.

She got out the car, did a few quick stretches on the sidewalk, then jogged across the road. Pausing in shadows twenty yards away, she pretended to retie her shoelace. She kept one eye on the approaching truck, timing her run to match his turn up the drive, then kicked off at a measured pace. The truck turned across the sidewalk twenty yards ahead. A motor whined. The iron gates swung back. The truck accelerated up the drive.

Alice pulled up the hood of her sweatshirt and put on a burst of speed. By the time she reached the closing gates, they were barely three feet apart. Keeping the hood up and her head down, she slipped sideways through the gap.

THIRTY-EIGHT

Ron Markham arrived early, took some clean clothes from his locker, showered and changed. It was his second shower of the morning, but the first time he'd really felt clean.

He balled up his clothes from yesterday and threw them in the trash. The little girl had coughed some blood onto his pants, and he'd run them under the hot tap in Hartley's basement before remembering his wife's wise words about blood stains: use cold water. Hot water set the stain and made it hard to remove.

He ran an electric razor over his face and studied himself in the mirror. The buzz seemed to continue once he'd switched it off. A strange sensation: a mix of fatigue, elation, relief and excitement. Like he ruled the world.

You're joining an exclusive club.

He took a sports jacket from a hanger in his locker. Like the shirt, it was new. Presents to himself. A little celebration.

He combed his hair, added some gel and swept it to one side the way Thomas Hartley did. He checked the mirror.

Looking good.

He straightened his collar, already thinking about the next time.

There was a note on his desk. His boss wanted to see him as soon as he got in. He screwed it up, threw it in the trash and made his way to the ninth floor.

Watch Commander Percy's office was a glass cube known to the troops as the goldfish bowl because Percy swam about in it in a sea of paperwork.

"Ron. Good morning." Percy gestured to a seat. "You're an early bird."

"Catches the worm, sir."

"We caught a lot more than that yesterday, thanks to your efforts."

"Any further progress?"

"Not from the suspects. Every single one of them is sticking to their stories. The same story, as it happens. They're all just humble economic refugees."

"IDs?"

"The computers have been churning through fingerprints and faceprints all night. Nothing yet."

"What about the body?"

"No ID on that either, apart from a Christian name: Arthit. One of them did confess to the murder though. A dispute over food supplies, apparently. Dwindling stocks. Things got a little tense. Guy threw a punch. A single unlucky blow. The ME confirmed it."

"So what about the hidden extras?"

Percy smiled and pulled out a report. "Now that's where it gets interesting."

The container had had a raised timber floor. Markham himself pointed it out. Usually, the steel deck was just overlaid with ply. Prying up the boards had revealed an interesting stash. Three AK-47s along with spare magazines and ammunition, a hundred boxes of what looked like prescription drugs, and dozens of bags of white powder.

"The lab's ID'd the drugs. Pseudoephedrine."

Markham nodded. "What about the bags?"

"Ammonium nitrate. Ninety pounds of it."

"Fertilizer grade?"

"Better."

"A good score."

"A great score, Ron. A fantastic score. A triple whammy. We got guns, methamphetamine precursors, and Grade-A explosive ingredients. You found us a terror cell all right."

* * *

There was still a chance she'd been seen, despite frosting the gate camera. A chance the arrival of the truck would alert someone up at the house to the fogged lens. A chance they'd see a blurred shape follow it in and come looking. Or loose some dogs. Alice liked dogs, but not that sort, and there was no point taking unnecessary risks. She found a tree near the front fence, climbed as high as she could and waited. Worst case scenario, she could swing across to a branch outside and drop back to the street. It was high, maybe twenty feet to the sidewalk, but a busted ankle was better than having your leg chewed off.

She waited ten minutes, figuring even a lazy guard would take five minutes to walk down from the house. When no one appeared, she climbed back down.

She kept to the south side of the grounds. It was away from the drive and offered cover with its line of bushy shrubs.

The house was single-story. Slate facade, gray roof, lots of big wide windows and tinted glass. The driveway split at the north side, one arm leading to a garage beside the house, the other to a guest parking bay out front. The black pickup was parked at the end of the parking bay, nose out, tailgate down.

Alice could see a door open at the end of the house. A service door of some sort, maybe. She eased closer then slipped back into the undergrowth at the sound of footsteps.

Russo emerged wearing track pants, scuffed shoes, and an old T-shirt. He had a pair of yellow rubber gloves on and was carrying what looked like a dry-cleaning bag. The sort they put over a suit or a ball gown. The sort that had a hanger at one end. It was only when he stepped out of the shadows that Alice realized he wasn't picking up the cleaning.

His words came back to her from the previous evening: *Benny said he's got another one ready to go. If this one's small enough, we can flush 'em both at once.*

What the hell had she stumbled on?

Russo threw the body bag in the back of the truck. An adult-sized body bag folded in half. Only partly filled. Light too, judging by the way he handled it.

He went to the cab, opened the passenger door and took out a mop and bucket, then headed back to the basement door and disappeared down the steps.

Alice watched him go then moved to the truck. It might

not be what she thought it was. All her training taught her not to jump to conclusions. It could be a dog or something.

She had to know.

The tray of the truck was high. She vaulted up onto it and squatted by the body bag. The end with the zipper was folded underneath. She turned it over.

It didn't feel like a dog.

She pulled down the zipper in one quick movement, revealing the head and shoulders of a small girl, the pain on her face locked in the rictus of death. She was naked, maybe five or six, and must have had a sweet face once, but it was bruised and battered now, and her neck was a mess. It wasn't broken, but the throat had been crushed somehow. Squeezed shapeless. Like an old-fashioned metal toothpaste tube.

Alice reeled back and almost gagged.

Then the phone in her back pocket rang. Loudly.

* * *

"Last night." Thomas Hartley threw a couple of memory cards onto Nancy Templar's desk. "From the basement cams."

"Useful?"

"Very. Check 'em out."

"Probably a bit tame for me."

"We don't all have your refined tastes, Nancy. But maybe you could put a thirty-second teaser together. In case CBP Officer Markham ever needs reminding that he belongs to us now."

* * *

The basement had originally run all the way under the house, but Hartley had had one end blocked off to make a room ten feet by twelve with A-grade soundproofing on the walls and ceiling. For an in-home recording studio, the workmen were told. Which it was. It had two cameras behind a large two-way mirror and a microphone concealed in a light fitting.

The room felt a little creepy with the outside door closed. Soundproof rooms often do because we're not used to complete silence. You start hearing things in a soundproof room, like the thump of your own heartbeat and the coursing of the blood in your veins. Which was why Russo left the basement door wedged open.

There was also the smell, but that didn't bother him. Dying bodies often voided themselves, and the girl had vomited too. But there wasn't much of anything. She was only a kid. It was easy work.

The other odd thing about soundproof rooms is that when the soundproof seal is broken, outside sounds seem amplified. The sigh of the wind. The creak of a tree branch. The melodic jingle of a mobile phone's ring tone.

Russo was supposed to have the place to himself. No gardeners. No staff. No chance of a chance discovery. Hartley didn't take risks. None of them did. So unless the squirrels had started carrying iPhones, there was someone out there. Someone who shouldn't be.

He dropped the mop and took the stairs two at a time, drawing his Ruger as he went. There was a round already in the chamber. He released the safety as he ran.

THIRTY-NINE

People were arriving at work, filing past the goldfish bowl. Markham saw the movement in the corner of his eye.

"Any clue who these guys really are?" he asked.

Watch Commander Percy flicked through a stack of paperwork. Affidavits. Reports. Photographs. "Same story all the way through. Like carbon copies. Like it's been rehearsed."

"Probably has been. Not a lot to do locked inside a container for three weeks."

"They all claim a guy in Bangkok offered them work in the States. Minimal deposit, balance to be paid out of their wages once they got here. The usual story."

"Slave labor."

"Essentially."

"But they were headed for Mexico."

"They claim they didn't know that."

"We got a name for the guy in Bangkok?"

"A Mr Tak. We've got our people there looking into it, but it doesn't look hopeful. Half the fucking population's called Tak-something or something-Tak."

"What about the Mexican connection?"

"The container was destined for a small-time hustler by the name of Salgado, suspected of people trafficking in the past. We dropped a team on him at dawn this morning. Our guys are still going through his place. The pseudoephedrine caught the DEA's attention. It's a possible link to the drug cartels. They want a piece of him when we're through."

"You mean there'll be anything left?"

Percy smiled.

"So the illegals: any family connections?" Markham's pulse kicked up a notch, but he had to know.

"Nothing. They won't talk about their families. None of them."

Not when their wives and kids were on the same boat and might have got through.

"Color me surprised. Just what you'd expect from a bunch of terrorists," he said aloud.

"That's just the thing, Ron. I've spoken to some of these guys through an interpreter. They'll talk about anything *but* their families."

"You think they might be hostages?"

"Maybe. Something certainly doesn't feel right about this. I get the feeling that at least some of them are genuine. That the actual terror cell may be much smaller, and they're using the others as cover. Three AK-47s for sixteen men doesn't figure."

"But how many and which ones?"

"That's what we've got to figure out."

"Well, they've had plenty of time for rehearsals. To practice their stories and get things straight between them. What's the bet they finger the dead guy as one of the terrorists? And maybe his assailant too."

"If that's the case, and their families are being held hostage, it's going to make them hard to break." Percy blew out his cheeks.

"A little Gitmo time might wear them down."

"Yeah, you may be right."

Markham smiled. That might be worth a bonus from his new friends. Getting rid of the men would mean they'd be even less likely to mention their women and kids.

"Oh, by the way Ron, you got a tie in your drawer?"

"A tie?"

"Yeah. The DFO's scheduled a press conference. The media picked up the interception of illegals yesterday, but we're going to break the terror cell angle eleven o'clock, in time for the lunchtime bulletins. I want you up there on the podium with us."

Markham's smile broadened. "I have just the thing in my locker. Sir."

* * *

Alice's mobile rang again. Loudly.

That damn alarm!

She'd turned the volume up because of her earplugs, because of Cora-Jane's snoring. But she'd woken before the alarm went off and canceled it, then forgotten to turn the volume down again.

Mistake number one.

There wasn't time to change it now. Or answer it. Or even shut it off. There was no time to zip up the body bag. Or replace it the way it had been dumped. All there was time to do was get the hell out of there.

She got the hell out of there.

She didn't know how far down the stairs went, or where they led, but she did know that Russo packed a Ruger. She'd seen it last night after she'd tripped the office alarm. Fully loaded, a standard magazine carried ten shots. Or seventeen, if he'd gone for the full-size magazine. But handguns were only really effective up close. Beyond fifty yards, they were just noisemakers. Sure you could hit the bullseye at twice that distance on a shooting-range, bracing, breathing, taking careful aim, but hitting a moving target when you yourself were moving was a whole different ball game. That meant her best defense was distance.

She leaped from the back of the truck and cursed herself in mid-flight, the phone still chiming in her pocket.

Mistake number two.

She'd launched from her good ankle, meaning she'd land on the one she'd sprained the week before. The one that was still tender.

She angled her foot the moment before she landed so her toes touched down first, then buckled her knee as the weight came on and threw her shoulders forward. She pitched over in a roll, spreading the impact and momentum through her whole body.

It saved her ankle.

And her life.

Russo saw the leaping figure as it sprang from the back of his truck. The deck obscured its landing point, but the angle and the speed of its departure told him all he needed. He dropped to one knee, aimed and put two quick rounds into where the upper body would emerge.

And missed.

Alice heard the shots, did one more shoulder roll, then sprang into the cover of some low bushes. The damn phone was still ringing! It was like a beacon screaming "Aim here!" She took it out and tossed it up the garden towards the front fence. Three more shots followed it. Low, this time, tearing holes in the undergrowth. Nicely spaced. The guy was good.

He moved quickly too. Came at a low run. The gun in his right hand, braced with his left.

Alice edged back towards the house.

The phone stopped ringing. Russo stopped. Everything went quiet.

Alice waited. If he was smart, he'd wait too. Call for backup. It was a closed yard with a high fence. Suicide to climb in front of a man with a gun. All he had to do was patrol it from a distance till his buddies arrived. Then they could drive her out into the open. Like herding sheep.

But that supposed she was still alive.

If he'd hit and wounded her already, even killed her, he'd look like a pussy calling for backup. Besides, it would take at least twenty minutes for them to get there from Hartley Imports.

He was a good shot. He knew he was a good shot, and he'd put three rounds right through the place where the cell phone last rang. Maybe it was psychological, but the sudden silence of the phone suggested another kind of silencing. And it was clear from the absence of return fire that the perp was unarmed.

Russo straightened from his crouch and came on, angled sideways, the gun still in a two-handed grip. He swung it smoothly left and right, edging towards the spot where the phone had stopped.

Not so smart.

Alice picked up a stone.

One thing Russo hadn't considered was that the leaping figure might not have been alone. The idea only occurred to him when he heard a faint movement ten yards behind him to his left. A *snick* like a snapping twig.

He spun left, dropped low and aimed. Alice came in from his right, which was now effectively his rear. She crossed the distance between them in three long strides, like a sprinter bounding from her mark. He heard the movement, half-turned back, and caught the well-aimed fourth stride on the side of his head. He went down hard, rolling sideways.

Alice skidded to a halt. The impact checked some of her momentum, but it still took another yard to stop and come about. By that time Russo was scrambling to his feet.

He looked dazed. He looked a mess. His left cheekbone was smashed and his head was at a funny angle. Dislocated neck, maybe. But he was tough, and he was operating on the life-and-death autopilot that keeps men fighting even when they know they're finished. And he still had the gun.

He fired, but it wasn't aimed. More a reflex action. Or a warning. Like shouting, "I'm still dangerous!"

Alice ignored it.

She lunged, spun and connected with the wrist of the hand still holding the gun. Heel versus wrist. No contest. The wrist bones gave, the gun went flying, and the impact spun him sideways. He fell again, grunting explosively with the pain. His neck, she guessed. This time, he didn't move or try to get up, just lay there on his side, breathing heavily.

Alice kept one eye on him as she retrieved the gun.

She picked it up, went back, stood over him and aimed it at his head.

"Who was she?"

He seemed to have trouble focusing on anything above her ankles, reluctant or unable to raise his head. Alice helped him by kicking his shoulder and rolling him onto his back. He cried out in pain and one hand came up to cradle his neck, got halfway and dropped again. Even that movement was too much.

"I said who was she? The little girl?"

He let out a long groan. Made words from the tail end of it. "Who the fuck are you?"

The first shot landed an inch from his shattered left cheek, throwing up a spray of dirt as the round tunneled into the earth.

"Who was she?"

"I dunno. Just meat."

"Meat?"

"Yeah, meat. D'you care where your steak comes from?"

"Where did she come from?"

"Where they all come from. Gook land. Meat from gook land."

The second shot thudded past his right cheek, practically scraping flesh. He winced.

"I make that eight shots," Alice said, weighing the pistol and running it up and down his sprawled form. "You any good at math, Mr Russo? Because with a ten-shot magazine, that leaves me two shots. I figure one in the kneecap, then a gut shot for good measure."

He stared up at her.

"A bullet in the kneecap is excruciating. Crippling, but rarely fatal. Gut shots on the other hand..." She shook her head. "I'd do it from the side here, angle it across, front to back. Maximum damage. Although at this range, a nine-millimeter parabellum's going to take out a fair sized chunk anyway. It's just that I'd hate to knick your spine and leave you feeling nothing before you died. Because you will die. Slowly and very painfully. By mid-afternoon, if you're lucky."

"Who the fuck are you?" he said again.

"I'll ask the questions. Now tell me about the little girl."

"I dunno. I'm just the clean-up guy."

"Who did that to her? Hartley?"

"Nah, nah, one of his marks."

"His marks?"

"Someone he owes a favor to. Someone he's setting up to do him a lot more favors in the future."

"Who? The guy in the Malibu?"

"I dunno. I'm just the clean-up guy."

"Do a lot of this kind of thing, Mr Russo?"

"Some."

Alice aimed the gun at his head, right between the eyes. Her face was blank. Expressionless.

The Ruger's trigger required a pull of five point two pounds force. Alice was putting about five point one pounds on it. Maybe five point one nine. It came that close.

She lowered her arm, said, "Where's your phone?"

"Side pocket."

"Get it for me."

He did as he was told, moving carefully so as not to disturb his upper body. His neck must've hurt like hell.

His keys fell out as he pulled out the phone. The keychain had the remote for the gates on it. The one Reisinger handed him last night. She picked up both, tucked the keys in her pocket, then dialed her own number.

A ringtone started in the undergrowth twenty feet away. Loud. She followed it, retrieved her phone, then returned. Russo hadn't moved.

"Tell me about Hartley's operation. I want to know everything."

"Hey, I'm just the clean-up guy."

"Then you're no use to me." She raised the gun again.

"Whoa, hold on. How do I know you won't kill me anyway?"

"You have my word."

Russo considered. What did he have to lose? Tell what he knew and he might just live. Keep schtum and die. No choice, really. Not for a thinking man.

"All right, all right. We bring 'em in from Asia."

"Who? What?"

"People. In containers. People wanting to come over here. To the States. Illegals. They even pay us." He grunted. "Stupid fucks."

"And that's it? Where did the little girl fit in?"

"No, that's not it. We bring 'em over separate. Men in one container, women and kids in the other. The men are disposable. Know what I mean?"

"And the women and children?"

"Some of them work for us, but mostly they're pre-sold."

"Pre-sold?"

"Yeah, big demand for fresh meat. Especially the kids

and teenage girls."

"Who the hell do you sell them to?"

"Gangs. The sex trade. Private individuals sometimes. You know, bankers, lawyers, judges. Anyone with money."

"Judges?"

"Hey, everyone likes to screw."

"How do you find these people?"

"They find us. Word of mouth. We're careful who we take. They start off as subscribers."

"Subscribers? To what?"

"DVDs. Thomas won't do online. Too risky these days."

Alice thought of *The Connoisseur's Collection: Volume XIV* and the mailing envelopes.

"And that's the work?"

"Huh?"

"You said 'Some of them work for us'."

"Yeah, movies, videos. The hard stuff, you know? It's what our subscribers pay us for. What they want. When we're done with 'em, we sell 'em off. Those that make it."

"*Make it?*"

"I told you, it's pretty extreme."

"You make snuff movies?"

"Nah, nah, that's a waste of meat. But it happens sometimes by accident, you know?"

"And Hartley takes part in this?"

"They all do. All four of 'em."

"Four?"

"Hartley, Tak, Reisinger and Templar. They've all got their specialties."

"What's Hartley's?"

"Kids. The little girls, you know?"

"Oh, I know all about that."

"Tak's straight. He's the meat finder. Reisinger's into guys. Nancy likes hurting people."

"What about the fat guy?"

"Benny? Him and me, we just do odd jobs. A little camera work sometimes."

"Odd jobs and camera work? That's it?"

"Hey, you know how it is."

"No, tell me."

Silence.

Alice raised the gun again.

"We take what we can get. Job benefit, you know?"

Alice stared at the prone man. Let out a breath.

"So, you going to kill me now?"

That wasn't her intention, but she had to keep him out of the way in case he warned the others. For a moment, she thought of dragging him to the basement and locking him in. Then she had a better idea.

"I might have done so already," she said, transferring the gun to her left hand.

She knelt beside him and reached around behind his neck. Russo lay very still as she ran her fingers up and down, from the top of his shoulders to the base of his skull.

She sat back and gave him a concerned look.

"What is it?"

"Severe dislocation of the fifth cervical vertebra. You still feel your hands and feet?"

"Yeah." He looked up, fear in his eyes. And not from the gun.

"You're lucky because your spinal cord is hanging there without any support. Maybe even over a jagged edge of

302

bone. Any movement, no matter how slight, could sever it. That would leave you paralyzed," she tapped the barrel of the gun against his chest, "from there on down for the rest of your life. So I suggest you lay very, very still, Mr Russo."

He swallowed. She got to her feet and brushed herself off.

"Job benefit, huh?" she said. "What, young, old?"

Silence.

"Young, I bet. Younger the better, huh?"

Russo said nothing.

She tucked the gun into the waistband of her pants and stood looking down at him. Then she lashed out with her foot and kicked him in the balls. Russo gave a strangled cry. He writhed and twisted, desperately trying to keep his head and shoulders still.

"Hurt, huh? That's a good sign. You should be pleased. Clearly your spinal cord is still hanging in there."

FORTY

The warehouse, the fence, and the preparations all suddenly made sense, and a plan came together as Alice jogged back to Russo's truck. She had to act now. Her sole advantage was surprise. They didn't know what she knew, and they didn't know she'd be coming. Yet.

There had been gunshots. If a neighbor had heard and called the cops, and the cops found the man lying in the front garden of 1064 Presley Drive, they'd contact Hartley. Paralyzed or not, Russo would warn him. Even dead, his body would put them on the alert.

Russo's day wear was in the truck, neatly folded on the passenger seat. Clearly, he planned to change once he'd finished the clean-up. Alice opened the door with the bottom of her sweatshirt, mindful of fingerprints.

There were shoes, socks, pants and a work shirt. The jacket was on a hanger in the back. She carried the pants, shirt and shoes to the lawn. He was taller than her, and broader, so they were all too big. She kicked off her running shoes and pulled on the pants—black and gray stripe, like yesterday—tucking them into the waistband of her shorts. Too long. She rolled up the cuffs. She put on his shoes and laced them tight, then slipped the shirt over her sweatshirt and did up the buttons. Her arms only made it as far as the cuffs. The guy was a gorilla. But that was good.

Back at the truck, she returned to the body bag and zipped it closed. Then she wiped down every surface she might have touched or stepped on using the shirt cuffs as cleaning cloths. Locard's Exchange Principle of forensic science said that every contact left a trace. When the cops eventually arrived, they'd find a murder scene and their prime suspect on the front lawn so the forensics wouldn't get too heavy. But there was no point taking chances.

She drew a breath, unlatched the tailgate and slid the body bag to the end. Picked it up and carried the little girl's remains back inside the house. She weighed almost nothing.

The oversized shoes made the narrow basement steps awkward, but Alice managed it without incident and set the body bag gently on the bed. Russo's clean-up was only half done. She averted her eyes, ran quickly back up the steps and closed the door.

The shockwave caught up with her, like the rumble of thunder after a flash of lightning. The room, the child, what they'd done... Suddenly she was nine years old again, back in a grimy Bangkok hotel.

She gripped the door handle through the sleeve of Russo's shirt.

No, she had to hold herself together. Other people depended on her. A whole container full of people. Speed was everything.

On her way back to the truck, she checked her phone to see who'd called earlier. Chatri. She might have guessed. It was a comfort knowing he was there, a mere button-push away. But she wouldn't push that button yet. She had to focus.

What would Russo do once he had the body loaded?

Cover it.

There was a fabric cover for the back of the ute, sitting in a corner of the tray. She closed the tailgate and hooked its elastic webbing around the outer edge. It made a good fit. Tight as a drum.

She put her running shoes in a plastic bag she found beneath the driver's seat. There was more ammunition in the glove compartment. The Ruger had a ten-shot magazine. She reloaded it, tucked another ten rounds in the pocket of her sweatshirt, then took a pair of sunglasses from the dash and put them on.

The gates opened at her approach, and she headed down Presley Drive, past the fine houses and the gated lives, heading for the freeway. Near the intersection at the bottom, Russo's phone rang. She checked it. The display read: "Benny (work)". The tubby guy at Hartley's calling from his desk. She let ring through to voicemail then called Russo's service to retrieve the message.

"Hey, it's me, you lazy fuck. Where the hell are you? We got a ton of work to do. Thomas says if we get done early, we can try a little product. So get a move on."

"Be there in twenty minutes," Alice told the phone as the message clicked off.

* * *

Annabel's lawyer called shortly before eleven o'clock. She'd done what she'd threatened; got on to it first thing.

Did Chatri have counsel?

Of course not.

He should get some.

Chatri hung up and called Annabel.

"Go away," she said before he had a chance to speak. "And don't ever call me again."

Then he tried Solikha. The phone rang and rang before switching to voicemail.

Chatri hated leaving messages. The whole electronic voice thing was too impersonal. You called people to talk to them personally, not via a machine. He hung up and spent twenty minutes trying to focus on work, failed, and called her again.

She answered this time, but sounded distracted. She was driving. There were highway sounds in the background.

"Sorry Chatri, I can't talk now. I'll call you back when I'm free. But if you don't hear from me by... say three o'clock this afternoon, I want you to call Chatsworth PD in LA and report a murder."

"*What?*"

"Tell them there's a body in the basement of 1064 Presley Drive. Have you got that?"

He scribbled a note. "Yes, yes, but—"

"Repeat it back to me."

"1064 Presley Drive, Chatsworth. Solikha, what the hell is going on?"

"Tell you later. Before three, I hope." She clicked off.

He pulled the phone from his ear and sat staring at the screen. He almost wished he'd just left a message the first time he'd called.

FORTY-ONE

Kanya had slept well, despite her excitement. Her first decent night's sleep in weeks. They'd arrived! Their new lives had begun.

They were all up early. Conscious of soon being reunited with their men, they resumed altering the clothes that had been left for them. Some of the children's things were OK, but most of the others were too big. But there were sewing supplies in one of the kitchen drawers, and they were all handy with a needle and thread. Kanya worked on a blouse with a silky, peach-colored fabric. Everyone said how much it suited her.

A rap on the steel door made them all look up. The first call already? They were hardly finished with their sewing. Perhaps it was just little Eri returning. The door opened and there was a collective intake of breath.

Mr Tak. What was he doing here?

"Good morning." He smiled at them. "I hope you slept well."

They returned the greeting and thanked him. Yes, they had. Most of them smiled back, but not all of them, Kanya noticed.

He was carrying a sheet of paper. He looked down and

read out a name. "Kanya Kajornchaiyakul?"

She stepped forward, uncertain, especially after what Namthip had told her about the man.

"Your husband will be here at two o'clock," he said, smiling. "Be ready please."

Relief flooded through her. For a moment she thought she might faint.

Tak turned to go.

Apinya said, "Excuse me, sir. The little girl, Eri...?"

"With her father," Tak said, and closed the door behind him.

* * *

The gate was closed when Alice swung into Hartley Imports, so she stopped the truck a foot away and sounded the horn. Two short taps. Nothing happened for half a minute, then Benny appeared from the office.

"What am I, your fucking slave?"

Alice watched from behind the black glass windows and revved the engine.

"Yeah, yeah, keep your hair on."

Benny threw the gate wide. Alice drove on in.

There were five cars in the lot. A silver BMW she hadn't seen before, parked beside Hartley's Porsche. Thaksin Metharom, back from Thailand, had pushed Templar and Reisinger down to third and fourth place respectively. A full house. As full as it was going to get without Russo.

Where would he go with a load like this? Not to the office, obviously.

We can flush 'em both at once.

She headed for the warehouse, spun the wheel, reversed and stopped with the rear end to the workshop door. Benny followed at a tubby trot.

Opening the driver's door would leave her visible from Hartley's office. She might be wearing Russo's clothes, but would only pass a cursory inspection. No point risking it. She waited till Benny unlocked the human-sized door beside the warehouse roller.

"What kept ya?" he called, starting on the deck cover as Alice clambered over the seat and readied herself at the passenger door. This way she'd keep the body of the truck between her and the office building.

Benny didn't bother with the sides of the cover, just the back. He released the tailgate and peered inside.

Alice kept low. She must have looked comical in Russo's clothes. The cuffs of the pants were rolled up round her ankles and the baggy shirt was bunched up at the sleeves. But when Benny looked up, he didn't laugh.

"What the f—" His voice died at the sight of Russo's gun.

Alice gestured towards the open door then followed him into the warehouse.

"Hands high," she said as soon as they were out of sight. She pressed the gun into the back of his chubby neck and patted him down with her free hand. He was clean.

"Get over to that bench. Stand two feet back from it. Spread your legs, lean forward and take the weight on your arms."

Benny did as he was told.

The unbalanced position gave her some leeway. If he

moved or tried anything, she'd have plenty of warning. She lowered the gun and looked around.

The warehouse had been partitioned into rooms. A high cinder block wall closed off the loading dock, and Alice found herself in what must have been some kind of office, now converted to a workshop. A space maybe twelve feet square. Beneath the barred window was an ancient desk strewn with yellowing newspapers and takeaway coffee cups, a broken chair pushed under it. Beside it, a filing cabinet that might have come out of the ark, and an ancient punch clock on the wall beside the door, the hands on its grimy face stopped at 9:14. Above that was a new extractor fan.

There was a second door set in the rear wall, diagonally opposite the one she'd come through. Next to that was the bench Benny was spread-eagled against. Apart from the fan, it was about the newest thing in the room, roughly made but solid. Beneath it was two fifty-five gallon barrels. Black plastic with yellow triangular warning signs: *Danger! Highly Corrosive*. The label beneath said they contained sodium hydroxide.

"Hey, ain't you that broad from yesterday." Benny was peering over one shoulder at her.

"Oh Jesus!" Alice muttered, spotting what was underneath the other end of the bench.

Three thirty-three gallon plastic barrels, side by side. Three feet high by two feet wide with big screw-top lids. The sides were ribbed and semi-transparent. They looked like before, during and after samples of some fiendish experiment. The one on the left was empty. The one on the right was full of a coffee-colored sludge. The one in the middle held a body.

It didn't look quite right at first. The semi-transparent plastic didn't help. The body had been packed down, maybe jumped on to make it fit. The torso and one arm were pressed against the side, a naked breast was clearly visible. The head was tilted back, the mouth wide, open.

Benny said he's got another one ready to go.

The body of a young woman.

If this one's small enough, we can flush 'em both at once.

The little girl.

Sodium hydroxide. Common name: Lye. Used to digest the tissues of dead animals. Or dead humans. It wasn't fussy. After a few hours in lye, a body would dissolve completely leaving a coffee-colored liquid. Such bones as remained would be powdery husks that turned to dust with a hammer tap.

"I said, ain't you that—"

Alice swung the Ruger and clubbed the fat fuck around the head.

FORTY-TWO

K anya squirmed as Katreeya pinched the back of the blouse and pinned it. "Don't make it too tight."

"You must let him see your shape.".

"After three weeks in a box, he will not care what shape she is," Fah called.

Kanya blushed. The others laughed.

"Make the stitches big and loose," Apinya said. "Easier to tear off."

More laughter.

Mai held out a flower. "For your hair."

"It's plastic."

"You think he'll notice when he's ripping off your clothes?"

Arisa said, "I wonder who'll be next."

"Could be any one of us. We should be ready."

Kanya slipped off the blouse, folded the fabric along the pinned line and found her needle. She'd promised to keep Namthip's secret, but what harm could it do now? She said, "I'm worried about little Eri."

"You heard Mr Tak. She's gone to her father."

"But she doesn't have one."

"Of course she does. He looks like Akara Amarttayakul."

"Better. That's what she told us."

"No," Kanya said. "His name was Akara, but he abandoned her. She had no man."

There was silence for a moment.

"But Mr Tak said—"

Kanya wondered if she should tell them the rest. About what had happened to Namthip.

"We will ask again," Apinya said. "Or perhaps you will find out this afternoon."

"Yes, yes, your Arthit will know. She probably lied and he looks more like a lizard."

The others laughed.

Kanya wasn't sure. She tried to remember if little Eri had ever mentioned a father. But Apinya was right. Arthit would know more.

* * *

Thomas Hartley sat at the head of the conference table, leaning back in his chair, watching his colleagues take their places. Tak at the opposite end, Reisinger on his right, Templar on his left. A good team, each with their own specialty, but it had taken his genius to combine their talents. Instead of a bunch of independents working alone, constantly looking over their shoulders, he'd created this, a corporation of sorts. They shared contacts, intel, resources, costs, and of course, customers. The profits were huge.

"Another successful shipment. And two days ahead of schedule."

"Except for one breakage and one... loss," Templar said.

"I prefer the term *investment*. And we sometimes lose one or two en route. Par for the course. Also, I'm reliably informed our second consignment is on its way to a Caribbean vacation. Guantanamo Bay, I believe. Well done everyone." He raised his bottled water in salute. "Especially Tak, who has not only arranged two more shipments for the next two months, but also set the current one up. And I do mean *set up.*"

"Any news of our Mexican friend?" Reisinger asked.

"A contact in Ensenada saw him being bundled into an unmarked van this morning. The timing suggests Homeland Security, but it may have been one of the cartels. Either way, he won't be resurfacing any time soon.

"So, first order of business. Keeping in mind we want to process this lot as quickly as possible, what have you got for me?"

Reisinger spoke first, picking up a printed sheet. "Two o'clock this afternoon: 'Lovely Lucy is eagerly awaiting the return of her boyfriend after a long sea voyage, but six bikers beat him to his prize...'"

"Oh Jesus, not bikers again?" Templar said. "What is it with you and those guys? You got a hard-on for the head honcho or something?"

"Fuck you."

"You wish."

"People, people. Let's keep this civilized."

"That's more than his fucking bikers do."

"Who've we got, Tak?"

Tak consulted a manifest. "Already organized. Name of Kanya. The others are dolling her up now. You know what they're like."

"Excellent. Thank you."

"Hope they've got a good First Aid kit for when Hans's Heroes have finished with her," Templar said.

"With plenty of spray-on skin in case she runs into Nancy the Knife."

"C'mon people!"

Tak said, "I suggest she not be returned. In any condition. We don't want a riot. I've arranged for the Talucci syndicate to collect her at five. At a discount. I said she should be usable within a week, so no broken bones, no cutting, no unnecessary bruising please," he said to Reisinger.

"Gang rape and sodomy OK?"

"Perfectly. But not the guy with the hammer. The one who likes to break teeth."

Reisinger scowled.

"You can have Russo on camera," Tak continued. "He and Benny can prepare the set as soon as they've finished with last night's clean up." He looked up as Russo's truck swung into the yard. From his end of the conference table, he had a clear view of the lot outside.

"Benny needs talking to," Templar said. "His so-called clean-up yesterday was shit."

Tak looked past her to the lot outside, realising he hadn't seen Russo yet. He'd parked up but hadn't gotten out.

Tak admired Russo. Russo was straight. A straight shooter too. He called him The Soprano because he reminded him of one of the characters in the old TV show, and his clothes and dress-sense amused him too. The man had something; a certain style.

Templar and Reisinger started bickering again. He

stopped listening. Russo still hadn't got out the cab. What was was he doing? That damn black glass.

"I might only have a tenth of your subscribers, but my revenue's still half of yours," Templar snapped. "My crowd are premium payers."

"They damn well should be for what it costs us in merchandise," Reisinger replied.

"What do you suggest we do with them once your hammer guy is done? Send them to an orthodontist?"

Tak saw Benny unhitch the end of the deck cover, drop the tailgate, peer inside then look up. He said something then backed away into the workshop, bumping the door jamb as he went.

Who was he talking to?

And still no sign of Russo.

A shadow passed between the tailgate and the door. A smaller shadow than he would have expected.

"Excuse me a moment." Tak got to his feet. On his way past his office, he stopped and took a gun from his drawer.

* * *

Benny hit the floor like a sack of flour. Alice cursed herself. A moment of weakness. The body in the barrel, the little girl in the basement, the thought of what these men did to people.

If you've got money, someone will supply it.

She'd let emotion steer her actions for a moment. Bad move. Benny could have been useful. Told her things. Acted as a decoy or hostage. But he was out cold now.

Blood ran down the side of his head, pooling on the cement floor.

Alice drew a breath. What now?

She looked around the workshop, figuring out the next steps in the process. Figuring out how much time she had.

Russo delivers a body. They'd get it in a barrel then top it up with lye. There was a hand pump on the bench along with a two pairs of industrial-strength rubber gloves and a couple of breathing masks. Little chance of anyone interrupting that till the barrel was sealed. Say, ten minutes work?

With her hands in the cuffs of Russo's shirt, she flipped on the extractor fan and opened the outside door a little wider. Fan and door were visible from Hartley's office. Both were clues there was nothing amiss.

She moved to the rear door, eased it open, then stepped into the warehouse, or rather, the remaining two-thirds of it.

The first third, the loading dock, was sealed off by a cinder block wall. Twenty feet from the rear, it turned a right-angle, forming an L-shape that went on another twenty feet. There was a steel door in the center of the L, bolted shut.

Alice moved towards it, guessing what was inside. Women and kids. Frightened women and kids.

For a moment, she had a vision of herding them out to Russo's truck and driving them away. But she didn't know how many there were. Then she remembered the locked gates.

Bad idea.

But she could give them a chance if things went wrong

for her.

She turned the key quietly in the lock. The door stayed shut, but they could get out now.

At the end of the L-shaped room was a storage alcove piled with furniture. A modern leather sofa, a chaise-longue, several metal-framed high school desks, an old-style blackboard, a dresser, and what looked like a disassembled four-poster bed.

Beside the alcove was a second room, low and squat. It looked like a bunker for storing dangerous goods. It, too, had a steel door. It, too, was shut.

On the eastern side of the warehouse were what looked like a couple of unfinished rooms. Alice recognized them as movie sets.

The first looked like the lounge and bedroom of a modern apartment. Fake wooden flooring, scatter rugs, coffee table, leather sofa. There was an unmade bed in one corner beside a pine dresser. The second set looked like the bathroom in a luxury hotel. Shower, tub, vanity and toilet. White tiled walls, gray linoleum on the floor. A potted plant in the corner. Garden hoses snaked in amongst the lighting rig, so some of the amenities actually worked. Probably the shower and bath.

There was a partitioned area in the front corner of the warehouse, a space not much bigger than a walk-in closet packed with monitors and mixers and video editing equipment. To the right of that was a short passage leading to the office block out front. The other side of the door in the kitchen she'd seen last night, only this time it was open.

Staff Only. Strictly No Admittance.

Five cars in the lot meant five people at work. One of

those was accounted for—Benny out cold in the workshop.

One down, four to go.

The warehouse was still and silent. No activity, no lights, just a kind of grainy twilight from translucent panels set in the roof. Clearly the other four were still out front.

As she moved closer, she saw movement in one of the monitors beside the mixing desk. The screen was divided into four, carrying four separate feeds. Security. Four different views from four different cameras. One she recognized. A high-up view of the lot outside. Russo's truck in the foreground, bordered by the fence and razor wire. But the other three showed a place she hadn't seen yet. An enclosed space by the look of it, with people moving about.

The inside of the loading dock.

She peered closer, found the control on the console and zoomed one of the cameras in on what looked like a domestic scene. A group of women chatting as they sewed and held up clothes against each other. She picked up a pair of headphones from the console and held one earpiece to her ear. Thai. The old tongue. Talk about a husband. The sound of laughter.

She stared at the screen a moment longer, then put the headphones back and turned to find Tak Metharom raising a pistol to her head.

FORTY-THREE

Ron Markham glanced at the two stars on the Director of Field Operations uniform. He was talking to Buck Duval. Markham straightened his back and squared his shoulders.

"Nervous?" Watch Commander Percy said.

"No, I'm good."

"Well these things always scare the crap out of me."

The Press Officer was a woman in her fifties. She'd introduce the DFO, who would tell the media about the latest development—the interception of a terrorist cell on US soil. "There'll be a lot of questions. I'll field them and direct them back to you guys. OK?"

They fell silent. Nodded. She checked her watch.

"Let's go.

* * *

"We have a visitor." Tak pushed Alice ahead of him into Hartley's office.

Reisinger leaped to his feet. "Who the fuck—?"

"Susan Wong, I believe. Interior designer," Templar said.

"How the hell did she get in here?" Hartley glanced out the window behind him at Russo's truck. "Where's Russo?"

"That's what I was wondering." Tak forced Alice into his vacant seat. "I went out to check and caught her snooping round. She was carrying this." He slid her gun across the conference table. "Looks like Russo's."

The others exchanged glances.

Hartley said, "Check the rest of the place. Hans, check the gate. We'll look after your prisoner." He went to his desk, took a gun from a lower drawer and aimed it at Alice's chest. A Glock 19. This one didn't look like painted plastic.

"So, care to tell me what you're doing here?"

Alice said nothing.

"How did you get in? Where's Russo?"

Alice said nothing.

Reisinger returned. "Gate's secure."

"Check on Tak."

But Tak was right behind him.

"She whacked Benny. He's coming round. No sign of anyone else."

"No Russo?"

He shook his head.

"You check the truck?"

"Empty. She appears to be on her own."

Hartley came around the desk, keeping the gun level. "Search her."

Templar grabbed her by the hair and dragged her to her feet. Forced her forward, bent at the waist, hands on the tabletop, legs wide. She made a thorough job of it. Patted her down first then tore open the loosely buttoned shirt, took the spare ammo from the pocket of her sweatshirt and threw it on the table. Then she pulled at the pants Alice had tucked into the top of her running shorts.

"What the fuck is this, a costume party?"

Alice had left her phone—and Russo's—in the cab of the truck, but she still had her driver's license in the pocket of her shorts. Templar hauled it out and threw it on the table with the ammo.

"Those look like Russo's clothes," Tak said as Alice tucked herself back in.

Hartley picked up the license, glanced at it, then looked again. He stared it for a moment, raised the gun and aimed it squarely at her head.

"What the hell is going on here?"

"What do you mean?"

He kept his eyes and gun on Alice as he tossed the license to Reisinger.

"Holy fuck."

Reisinger passed it to Tak.

Tak raised an eyebrow, said nothing and passed it on to Templar.

It seemed her name meant something to these men.

"Well now, Alice Kwann," Hartley said. "I strongly suggest you start talking."

Alice looked back at him. Said nothing.

Reisinger said, "What the hell is this, some sort of family crusade?"

And there she had it.

Give my regards to Mr Ling.

Hartley advanced. "It's got to be. Except this one doesn't look much like family. Not blood family. Unless the old man was screwing some of his foundlings."

"Didn't they adopt at some point?" Templar said.

"I believe you're right, Nancy. Is that where you're from, Alice Kwann? Adopted by good old Glenn and Mary? They like the gooks so much they had to get one for themselves?" He shoved the barrel under her chin.

Alice said nothing.

"You know what I think? I think you should've paid attention to what happened to mom and pop. We spent good money arranging that little accident of theirs."

Still Alice said nothing, but her brain was working overtime.

For years, in addition to their institute work, they'd been investigating a sophisticated people trafficking network operated by a secretive Thai gang. Their last letter mentioned a breakthrough. The identity of the man behind it; an apparently respectable rice exporter named Ling.

"One of Ling's people has agreed to talk with us next week," her stepfather had written. Two days after she read the words, her adoptive parents were dead.

Chatri had asked what they were doing down in Pattaya where the accident happened. It was over a hundred miles from their base in Bangkok, but only a half-hour's drive from Thailand's busiest port, Laem Chabang.

It suddenly all came together. A truck at an intersection. Early morning. A clear road. The driver should have seen them...

It seemed he had. All too clearly.

"How did you find us? Who tipped you off? Talk!" Hartley jammed the gun higher, forcing her head up.

Alice thought of her insurance policy: Chatri's call to the police if he hadn't heard from her by three o'clock. Not much consolation if she was dead, but it was something.

Tak put a hand on Hartley's arm. "First things first, Thomas. We need to find Russo."

"You think he's the link?"

"No, but he is the missing piece in the puzzle. If she did something to him, if he's lying dead or injured somewhere, who knows where that could lead."

"You're right." Hartley took a step back and leveled the gun at her chest. "Where's Russo?"

They mustn't find him. Not yet. Not before Chatri's call.

"Dead," she said.

"Where?"

"Side of the road. In some bushes."

"Where exactly?"

Alice shrugged.

"How?"

"I broke his neck."

"I don't believe you," Tak said.

"That's what the running gear was for. I pretended I was hurt and flagged him down. You should've warned him about stopping for hitchhikers."

"Why are you wearing his clothes?"

"They were in the cab and it seemed like a good idea at the time. Thought they might help me get in gate, but it turns out your boy Benny's dumber than I thought."

Tak said to Hartley, "That means Russo must be somewhere between his place and yours. He was on his way there to the clean-up. We know he didn't make it from the empty truck."

"That's still a ten-mile stretch."

"But most of it's freeway. Not many places to pull over.

Fewer still with bushes to hide a body."

"I'll get my people on to it," Reisinger said, glancing at Templar as he left the office. "Sometimes bikers have other uses."

"That seems to deal with the immediate threat," Hartley said, "but I still want to know how you found Russo in the first place. And how you found us. And who else knows you're here."

Alice said nothing.

"I advise you to talk, Ms Kwann. Nancy can be *very* persuasive."

Templar smiled and moistened her lips.

"Well?"

Alice said nothing.

"Bad choice," Hartley said. He looked genuinely sorry.

FORTY-FOUR

Templar had a gun of her own. She took it from the pocket of her business suit. It looked like a toy cut from half-inch thick titanium, except this toy was capable of firing a couple of .45s. Alice recognized it as a DoubleTap pocket pistol. Five inches long, two barrels in an under/over configuration, and less than a pound in weight. The perfect concealed weapon.

Hartley said, "I want answers Nancy, fast."

"I'll start with the pliers. Toenails and fingernails. Then maybe a blowtorch. Give the pokers a chance to heat up."

"One last chance," Hartley said to Alice.

Alice said nothing.

"Take her away."

Templar shoved the gun in the small of her back, steered her out the office, down the passage, through the kitchen, and into the warehouse. Alice could feel the barrel against her spine, angled slightly down. Best case scenario, she'd end up in the paraplegic ward in the bed next to Russo.

They crossed the warehouse, heading for the bunker on the far side. The woman was thirty pounds heavier and a good two inches taller than Alice. She had a gun, and she was in control of the situation, but there was something else too. Something in her breathing. Alice sensed it. Excitement, perhaps. Anticipation.

Nancy likes hurting people.

Perhaps a .45 in the back would be better.

As they passed the rear door of the workshop, Benny staggered out. His face was pale, and he clutched the wall for support. He stiffened when he saw Alice. Smiled when he saw Templar's gun.

"Welcome back," Templar told him, then nodded at the bunker door.

He went ahead, still unsteady on his feet, unlatched the door and drew it back. A sickly smell, sweet and cloying, drifted out as he hit a switch and fluorescent lights pinged on.

The inside of the door was padded and the bunker was double-lined. Alice saw tufts of soundproofing showing through a split seam.

There were manacles and chains on a rack by the door. A St Andrew's cross by one wall. Gags, whips, and ropes littered a bench on one side. In the corner was a wooden frame that looked like a medieval rack.

"Cozy," Alice remarked.

The other side of the room looked more conventional. A workbench and tool rack. A locker. Drawers and cupboards. A table and chair with an angled lamp over the desk. The tools had stencil lines around them so you could see where they fitted. None was missing. It might have been a home handyman's basement workshop, except for the photographs pinned to the wall above the desk. A large black and white showed an unshaven guy in a check cap. The color shots showed off some of his handiwork.

Edward Theodore Gein.

Alice knew all about Ed Gein. One of the textbook cases from her classes at Quantico. When they arrested him in 1957, police found his house filled with trophies and keepsakes. A wastebasket and lampshade made from human skin. A pair of lips on the drawstring of a blind. A face mask made from a real face. A corset from a female torso, skinned from shoulders to waist

Gein's source—apart from a couple of clumsy murders —were bodies he'd exhumed from graveyards around his hometown of Plainfield, Wisconsin.

"I see you're a fan," Alice said.

"Except that I prefer my trophies fresh."

She took a teak cigar box from the desk. It was finely made, with dovetailed corners and brass hinges. She opened the lid one-handed and held it out to Alice. The interior was lined with plush green felt. On it lay a crude belt made from female nipples.

"Just like Ed's," Alice remarked.

Templar smiled.

"I can see the appeal. The puckered skin matches your complexion."

Templar slammed the box shut. "Chain her up," she snapped at Benny.

Benny grabbed her wrist with his left hand and reached for one of the manacles with his right.

"Sorry about your head," Alice said to him. "But you must admit it's pretty thick and pretty ugly. Without this place, I bet you'd never get laid."

"Fuck you," he said, releasing the manacle and driving

his right fist into her stomach. It was exactly what she hoped he'd do.

Benny was still woozy from the earlier blow and lacked a little coordination. He wasn't fit, clearly didn't work out, but he carried a fair amount of weight. That meant the blow carried a fair amount of momentum.

Alice tensed her stomach muscles as it came in, doubling over and kicking backward lightly, timing the movement to the speed of his fist. To a casual observer, it looked like she'd taken the full force of it.

She doubled over, pulled free of his restraining hand and pitched forward, falling to her knees, clutching her stomach, groaning and gasping for breath. Templar muttered, "Oh, Jesus!"

A foot jabbed her shoulder. "Get up, you little bitch. We haven't even started yet."

Alice crawled closer, gasping and groaning. The foot came in again. Harder this time. Rounded toe to shoulder blade. "I said get up."

Alice gagged, making as if she was about the throw up on the shoes.

"Shit!"

Templar stepped back as Alice lunged from her crouched position and caught the heel of the backward-stepping foot. Templar was already moving, pushing with her left, relying on the right to take the weight, but when it didn't arrive she went down. Hard. On her back.

Benny turned in time to see her fall. A second later, Alice's head, driven with the force of two pumping legs, hit him in the solar plexus. He, too, went over backward, cracking his skull on the steel frame of the St Andrew's cross and clipping the board of manacles and chains. It teetered for a moment, then fell with a loud clanking crash.

Templar had good reflexes. She took the fall in her arms but still landed heavily, slamming the back of her head against the concrete floor. One arm, her right, her gun arm, didn't look too good. She'd smashed the elbow. Dislocated it, maybe. Alice added to her troubles by stamping on her hand before tugging the gun from her broken fingers.

The noise of the falling manacle board drew attention from the kitchen. Across the width of the warehouse, Alice saw Tak's face appear.

"Hey Nancy, keep your door— Oh shit!"

Alice fired as he slammed the steel door. The gun made a weedy pop in the sound-baffled room, but the ricochet that pinged off the closing door was real enough.

Alice ran towards it. There was a latch was on her side but there were bolts on the other. She could hear them being thrown as she hurled herself against it.

Locked.

Too late.

Now what?

FORTY-FIVE

Alice had a tactical problem. There were three men on the other side of the door—a door they controlled—and at least two of them were armed. Probably all three. In addition, the gate on the yard outside was locked, which meant she was now as much a prisoner as the women and kids in the L-shaped room.

If she could get to Russo's truck, she might stand a chance. Ram down the gate or go straight out through the wire mesh. But she'd have to get there first.

They'd be expecting that. Have it covered. The truck was parked side-on to Hartley's office, the driver's door facing his window. While the engine block might slow a bullet, a 9mm round would pass through a thin steel door like it was tissue paper.

So her best move was not the smartest move. Which made it a tactical problem.

From their perspective, they should have come straight out, all guns blazing. Templar's gun, the DoubleTap, was purely for personal protection. More of a toy than a real gun. With a good stance and a firm grip, you might hit a target at twenty-five feet on the range, but moving figures in a gun battle? Forget it. Plus, the thing only carried two rounds, one in each of its under/over barrels. And she'd already fired one of those.

But the guys behind the door didn't come out right away. She'd caught them by surprise. They'd be communicating, coordinating, arguing, maybe. She should use their confusion.

Alice ducked back into the bunker, checked the DoubleTap's grip and slid out the speed loader. There were two more rounds in it, but that was all. Three rounds total. One for each of them. Theoretically.

She reloaded the spent barrel and shook out her stinging hand. The damn thing focused all its recoil on the gun's half-inch width. Another reason not to get into a gunfight with it.

Their second best response would be a pincer movement. Activity at the kitchen door to keep her occupied while one of them ran across the lot to the open door of the workshop.

Templar moaned, tried to get to her feet. A quick kick to the side of the head sent her back down, then Alice hurried to the workshop.

The only way to see if anyone was coming was to stick her head around the open door. No way she was doing that. In addition to the guy approaching, they'd have someone at Hartley's office window, covering him, probably targeting the door right now. Then she spotted the humming extractor fan on the wall above the desk. She leaped up behind it, dislodging old newspapers and Styrofoam cups, and peered through the spinning blades.

Not much of a view and the angle was awkward, but it was enough to show the edge of a lengthening shadow moving around the end of the office block. It looked like they were going for option two.

She jumped down and searched for a place to hide. There wasn't anywhere except behind the door, but that was too obvious. He'd push it wide before he came in. Then she spotted the other possibility.

She pulled the broken chair from underneath the desk, crawled into the recess, then drew it back in place.

She sat crouched, perfectly still, straining her ears above the hum of the extractor fan. There was a faint creak from the workshop door. A soft thump as it was pushed back all the way.

Displacements? Plan of attack? Alice thought rapidly. Whoever was in the workshop would signal the guy in the office that it was clear. Office guy would join the guy in the kitchen to provide a distraction. The pair of them would take some pot-shots, make some noise, and try to keep her busy.

Which was exactly what happened next.

The bolts on the kitchen door slammed back and someone shouted for her to give herself up. There were a couple of shots and a rolling crash, like someone threw a trash can lid.

A stealthy footstep landed in front of her. Alice reached up and fired two quick shots, letting the recoil carry the gun upwards.

The bullets struck him in the chest and lower jaw. The guy went down.

The DoubleTap might look like a toy, but it was a nasty one.

It was Tak. He wasn't dead, but didn't sound far off it.

His breathing sputtered like a mistuned engine and blood bubbles frothed around his mouth.

He was carrying Russo's Ruger, an altogether more useful weapon. Alice dropped the DoubleTap and helped herself. She checked the clip. Fully loaded. Ten rounds. Just as she'd left it.

There was an old Chinese Type 77 pistol half-in, half-out of Tak's jacket pocket. The thing he'd stuck against her head in the control room. Not a great weapon, and the ammunition could be hard to come by. The Ruger was a better choice, even though it hadn't done Tak or Russo much good.

The takedown and the toy gun's pops had gone unnoticed over the noise of the diversion Hartley and Reisinger were working up at the kitchen door. Alice figured she could sneak back the way Tak had come and take them from behind, but that was risky. Especially when there was an easier way.

She edged into the storage area and fired two quick shots into the roof.

The Ruger's retort was substantial, like a teacher slamming down a ruler to silence an unruly class.

The noise from the partly open kitchen door stopped.

Alice covered her mouth and called out gruffly, "*Chǎn ying ter!*" Got her!

"*Kun nâe jai?*" Hartley's voice. You sure?

"*Dtaai pǒm kít wâa,*" Alice said. Dying, I think.

They didn't know she spoke Thai.

Reisinger was first through the door. The shot hit him in the temple and took off the back of his head. Hartley, standing four feet behind and to his left, caught the spray of blood and brain matter in the face. He reeled back as Alice rushed the door and kicked it wide.

He still carried the Glock, but it wasn't pointing anywhere in particular. He was clawing at his eyes with his free hand, trying to clear his vision when Alice cannoned into him.

He dropped the gun, staggered, slipped in Reisinger's blood, and fell.

Alice snatched up the gun, aimed Russo's at him and said, "Game over, Mr Hartley."

* * *

Nancy Templar heard the shots as she swam back into consciousness, then the voices speaking Thai. They'd got the bitch. Something about her being dead or dying. She knew that word. The women she worked on said it a lot: *Please let me die.*

Pity. She'd been looking forward to a little fresh meat. One that wasn't already half-dead after Reisinger's goons were through with them. A challenge too, making her talk.

Perhaps there was still hope. Perhaps she was only wounded. Perhaps she could still get something out of the bitch. After all, Templar was very good at keeping death at bay.

Spurred by the thought, she got to her feet and moved to the doorway of the bunker. Then she saw the bitch was still alive. Saw her from behind, braced in a two-handed stance as she shot Reisinger and rushed the kitchen door.

The sight of Reisinger's head coming apart told her she

had to act fast.

She snatched up one of the fallen manacles and raced across the intervening space, swinging it like it was nunchuks.

FORTY-SIX

"Hush, what was that?" Apinya called. "Did you hear? It sounded like gunshots."

They'd all heard.

Kanya, closest to the door, pressed her ear against it, then stepped back in surprise.

"It's unlocked!"

The others stared at her in alarm. Even the children stopped playing.

"Some mistake," Apinya muttered, joining her, checking it, then opening it a fraction.

"They said we must not go outside," Fah wailed.

"Ssshh!"

"But—"

"It's not outside," Kanya whispered peering through the gap. "There is more building."

Apinya opened the door a fraction wider and they listened. Silence, then the sound of muffled voices. One carried clearly: *"Dtaai pŏm kít wâa."*

Apinya quickly closed the door again.

"You hear?"

They all had. Someone had been hit. Someone was dying.

Another gunshot sounded and they all jumped.

"What do we do?" Fah whimpered helplessly.

* * *

Templar's charge took Alice by surprise. The swinging manacle clipped the barrel of Russo's gun and ripped it from her hand, while the charging form slammed into her shoulder, forcing her to leap over Hartley, still sprawled on the floor.

The leap saved her from the upswing of the manacle, but Hartley kicked wildly at her legs. Alice, wearing Russo's shoes, wasn't as nimble as she usually was, and slipped on the bloody floor.

Hartley scrambled to his feet and dived after her, pinning her face down on the bare linoleum. He slipped one arm around her neck and rolled sideways, carrying her with him so that they sprawled on the floor like a pair of lovers.

He snarled, his face still streaked with Reisinger's blood. "*Now* I believe it's game over, Ms Kwann."

He tightened the arm around her neck. Little points of light danced across her vision.

Templar hurled the manacle aside and reached for Russo's Ruger.

Alice still had Hartley's Glock in her left hand, the hand twisted underneath her, but she'd picked it off the floor like she was picking up litter and held it by the barrel, not in a shooter's grip. Her instinct was to drop it, free her arm, and use it to help in her fight for air. A temptation she struggled to resist.

Suddenly the constriction stopped. Hartley released her and kicked back, scrambling to his feet. Templar had retrieved Russo's gun and now had it aimed squarely at her head.

Alice sank back on her side. No one spoke for a moment. They were all out of breath. Then Templar waved her to her feet. "Get up, bitch. I'm going to make you pay for what you've done."

Alice pushed herself into a sitting position, keeping her left hand behind her, still gripping the Glock awkwardly. She could see Hartley looking around for his missing weapon. He was only seconds away from concluding she must have it, but pulling it out now would be suicide. Any sudden movement and Templar would fire.

"I said, get up!"

* * *

"They told us we must not go outside," Fah said again.

"But those shots—"

"You will endanger us all!"

"It's not outside," Kanya insisted. "It's still warehouse."

"Then why did they lock the door?"

"Why did they unlock it? Someone is hurt. You heard."

Apinya held up her hands and the argument ceased. There'd been no more sounds for at least a minute now.

"I have a solution," she said. "We must do what Mr Blue Eyes said. Stay here. But we let them know we do not have to. Yes?"

The others considered for a moment, then nodded

340

their agreement.

* * *

The voice came out of nowhere. Loud, but uncertain. Fractured English. "Hello? You there? Everything OK?"

"I thought Tak said she was alone," Templar hissed at Hartley.

The momentary distraction was all Alice needed. She hurled the Glock at Templar's face and dived after it. The woman flinched and raised a hand instinctively as Alice took her in a low tackle.

Templar went over backward—again—landing on her damaged elbow and gasping at the pain. Alice tore the gun from her left hand, pushed back, aimed and fired.

The bullet caught her just below the ribcage on the right-hand side. Templar screamed and kicked at the floor, as if she could kick herself away from the wound.

Alice swung the gun at Hartley, frozen in surprise at the sudden turnaround.

"You were saying?" she said, waving him back against the wall as she retrieved the Glock.

Templar's cries came in low bursts each time she gasped for breath. Her legs twitched. Blood welled over the hands she had clamped against her side. It looked like she was holding herself together.

Hartley said, "We should do something."

"Why? Looks like she's having a blast. Better than a red-hot poker, I bet."

"Who the hell are you?"

"I'm the flower of death, Mr Hartley. And I'm finally in bloom."

She directed him to his office where she checked the drawers of his desk for other weapons before waving him down into his executive chair. She checked the Glock. Two rounds left in the magazine, one in the breech. Plenty. She pocketed the Ruger.

"What do you want?" he said. "We can make all this go away, you know. I have money. What can I do?"

"How about you bring my parents back from the dead and restore all the lives you've wrecked over the years?"

He looked at her uncertainly. Didn't reply.

Alice thought of the final scenes in Hollywood movies. The villain cornered. The protagonist delivering a heroic speech. The villain making one last dash before the killing shot...

She thought of the movie in her mind. The one she'd played to herself for the last twenty years. The one where she told him who she was and what he'd done to her. The one where even he choked up and showed remorse.

Fuck that.

She fired.

The shot snapped the curved plastic arm of Hartley's executive chair just above his left knee. He scooted backward, half-rose and raised his hands.

"One thing," she said. "Who killed the child?"

"Child?"

"The one Russo was cleaning up."

"I... I don't know what you're talking about."

"At your house, Mr Hartley. In the basement of 1064 Presley Drive."

"It wasn't me. It was a customer." He settled back in the damaged chair.

"Drives a blue Malibu?"

He stared at her, his silence giving her the answer.

"I... don't know who he is. These guys never use their real names."

"Bullshit. This was someone special. This was someone who warranted particular attention. Someone you owed a favor too. Or someone you were buying off. Why else would you let him past those fine iron gates of yours, Mr Hartley? Why not entertain him here?"

"I don't know what you're—"

She fired again.

The bullet slammed through the seat between his parted legs, punching a hole through fabric, foam, seat base, carpet, and timber floor. On the way, it sliced a neat semi-circle through a fold in Hartley's pants. He lurched backward again, partly from the shock and partly from the impact and momentum.

"Markham. The guy's name's Markham. Works for CBP."

Alice nodded. "So that's where he fits in. I should have guessed. Thank you."

Hartley stared at her and swallowed.

The third shot hit him between the eyes.

FORTY-SEVEN

Alice stepped back and looked around the office, taking a long slow breath. Her driver's license was lying on Hartley's desk. She picked it up and used the cuff of Russo's shirt to wipe around the spot. Locard's Exchange Principal. No point taking chances.

Hartley's right arm twitched. A muscle spasm. It meant nothing. You could tell at once he was dead. The spread of blood, bone and brain matter running down the back of the executive chair was a clue. But no matter how catastrophic the injury, death was never instantaneous. It was a process, like everything else. Different bits died at different times. His nails might keep growing for hours yet. His hair too—the bits of it that were still attached to what was left of his skull.

What else had she touched?

She looked around. Double-checked. There was bound to be some trace of her presence—a hair or two, flakes of skin—but her job now was to present a credible crime scene. One that didn't lead forensics to look for other suspects.

She took the Glock by the barrel, wiped it clean, and retraced her steps to the kitchen.

Templar had kicked herself into the corner. There was a broad bloody smear beneath her skirt, and her shoes were ruined. She was still holding herself together, her breath coming in short gasps, like someone in the throes of coitus. The puddle of blood beneath her was growing steadily. She looked up, her face wretched, as Alice knelt beside her.

"I've decided to be merciful." She held out the Glock, the barrel still wrapped in Russo's sleeve. "Here. There's one round left."

Templar took it in a trembling, bloody hand. Her left. The fingers of her right were smashed.

Alice rose and walked towards the door into the warehouse.

She heard the click of a dry-fire and looked back.

Templar had her arm outstretched, aimed right at her. She continued working the trigger uselessly.

"Guess I miscalculated." Alice shrugged. "Sorry."

On her way back, she stopped at the control room. Ignoring the feeds from the L-shaped room, she concentrated on the other screens. How much of this place was wired? How much of what had just gone down had been recorded?

Not much, it turned out. The external camera was still on, but all that had caught was a hunched figure in Russo's clothes emerging from the passenger door of his truck and hustling Benny inside. It was a wide-angle lens. The action was at the bottom of the frame. Magnified, there was little detail in it, but she'd be going out that way, so she shut the camera off.

She crossed to the door of the L-shaped room and paused, considering whether to open it and make a speech.

Tell them what had happened. That they'd be all right. That the authorities would look after them. But what was the point? They'd be free soon enough. And she didn't want them seeing the mess she'd made. Not young women and little kids. Instead, she just relocked it and went back to the workshop.

Tak was dead. The sucking chest wound sucked no more. She retrieved the DoubleTap and checked on Benny in the bunker. He was still breathing. He didn't look good, but he'd do for an hour or two. She took his hand, wrapped it around the gun, rubbed the barrel against his cheek as if he'd scratched himself with it, then slid it away across the concrete. Something for forensics to find later.

* * *

Chatri answered on the first ring. Alice checked the rearview mirror. The gate was locked, the office and workshop doors closed. It looked like just another quiet day at Hartley Imports. Benny's gate key lay on the seat beside her. She gunned the pickup down Reeve Road.

"Solikha?"

"Yeah, it's me. I'm OK. No need to make that call."

"What the hell is going on?"

"Later Chatri. I'm in the middle of something. Do you have access to the DMV?"

"Of course. It's a test system, but the database is only a few weeks out of date."

"I need a registration check. California plate." She gave him the number of the blue Malibu.

"Hold on." A clack of keys. "It's registered to an Emmeline Ann Markham in Culver City."

His wife's car.

Alice memorized the address.

"Solikha, I need to talk to you."

"Can it wait, Chatri? I'll be home tomorrow."

"I don't have a home anymore."

"What? What are you talking about?"

"Annabel. She found the tape."

* * *

Her first stop was 1064 Presley Drive. The remote let her in. Alice parked the truck where she'd found it and carefully wiped down everything she might have touched. She stepped out, took off Russo's pants and shirt, folded them neatly and placed them back on the passenger seat where she'd found them. She did the same for his shoes, swapping them for her runners, and placed them back in the footwell.

She did one final check, closed the door, then went out to visit Russo. He was where she'd left him, lying very still. His eyes flicked open and tracked her as she approached.

"What the fuck?" he said, squinting. The sun was in his face now. He couldn't see her clearly. "You back again?"

"What d'you mean, back again? I haven't left. It's only quarter of eleven."

He scowled

"Time passing slowly for you, huh?"

"I thought I heard—"

"That truck go past? Yeah, I thought it was coming in

here too."

He blinked. Looked confused.

The time and the suggestion of another truck would help mix things up when he was finally interviewed.

"I've got one more question before I go. If you get it right, you get a prize. Where does the feed from the gate camera go?"

"What's the prize?"

"I don't kick you in the head."

He seemed to think that was worthwhile. "It's off. Hartley turns it off before I arrive. You think he wants evidence lying around? You think he's stupid?"

Alice paused a beat. "I think he's dead."

"Huh?"

"Templar killed him. Then you killed her and Reisinger. Don't you remember?"

"What...?"

More confusion.

"You've qualified for a bonus prize. Here."

She wiped the Ruger and pressed it into his hand. His fingers curled around it in a reflex action. There were still four rounds in the magazine, but the safety was on, and she knew that he knew if he fired it, the recoil might cripple him for life. Still, she backed away quickly, slipping into the undergrowth.

The keys were in the ignition of the truck, but she still had the remote. The gates swung wide, and she headed out into Presley Drive, downhill at a steady jog, past the front fence, checking the street and neighboring properties. No one about. No one had seen her exit.

Fifty yards on, she did a little circuit and headed back

uphill towards her parked car, slowing as she passed Hartley's gate. She wiped down the remote and flicked it over the fence as she passed the driveway. It would look like Russo had dropped it.

It took an hour to find a suitable public phone. There were plenty in the malls, but malls had surveillance cameras and Alice preferred to remain a mystery. She finally found one outside a 7-Eleven. By then it was almost two hours since she'd shot Templar. Given her rate of blood loss, she'd be dead by now. Good timing. Alice called it in.

"A small girl's been murdered in the basement of 1064 Presley Drive," she said in her best Southern accent. "There's a man on the lawn who knows all about it. He'll need an ambulance. I think he was responsible for a shoot-out at an office on the corner of Mawney and Reeve. There are women and children in there, locked in the loading dock. Y'all go careful, you hear?"

She hung up the phone and wiped down the receiver. They'd figure out the rest.

* * *

With time to kill, Alice returned to Reeve Road, parked up, and watched Hartley Imports. There was already one police car there when she arrived. It was soon joined by three more, one unmarked. Vehicles continued to arrive as the afternoon wore on. Detectives, forensics people, social workers. Then an LAPD police bus for the women and kids. She watched them filing from the warehouse, shielding their eyes, looking bemused.

Then the press arrived. Time to go.

It was evening by the time Alice reached Culver City. There was a party on at the Markham house. An open patio, lights strung around the lawn out back, people milling about. Music. Alice slipped some jeans over her shorts, put on sunglasses and a baseball cap, and stood out on the sidewalk looking in, uncertain. But only for a moment. The image of the little girl in the body bag came back to her and spurred her on.

She walked up the driveway, past ornamental shrubs and a neatly trimmed lawn, stopped at the front door and rang the bell.

A middle-aged woman she guessed to be Emmeline Ann Markham answered. She took one look at Alice and said, "Please, no more reporters. Ron's very tired, and we've got friends over."

"I understand," Alice said, "but if you mention it concerns a Mr Thomas Hartley, I sure he'll want to see me."

Emmeline Ann Markham gave her a doubtful look and left her standing at the door. But she didn't close it.

Alice could see the concern on Markham's face the moment he stepped into the hall. He was wearing shorts and a Hawaiian shirt. He was fleshy and pale. He looked tired. Like he'd been up all night.

"Mr Markham?".

Who are you?"

"A messenger."

"From Thomas?"

"Kind of."

"What do you want?"

"I've come with a warning."

He said nothing, but his eyes widened.

"Your wife's blue Chevy Malibu was seen leaving 1064 Presley Drive early this morning. The police are there right now."

She watched the color drain from his face.

"The clean-up guy screwed up. Your forensics are all over the place. You're on tape too. There are security cameras up and down Hartley's drive, and he's currently spilling his guts to the cops. Just thought I'd let you know. Good night."

Alice turned and walked away, back up the driveway, past the neatly trimmed lawn and ornamental shrubs. Markham stood looking after her for a long time, then softly closed the door.

Alice returned to her car.

Customs and Border Protection officers usually carried Heckler & Koch pistols. Alice didn't know if that included desk jockeys like Markham, but the blast she heard from the front bedroom of the house sounded more like a shotgun.

FORTY-EIGHT

It took ten minutes for the police and ambulance to arrive. All that time Alice sat staring out the windscreen, seeing nothing, feeling nothing. When the sound of sirens finally roused her, she started the engine and drove away.

She drove and kept on driving, heading north, found the I-5 and let the empty miles grind her down till she could barely keep her eyes open. Then she found a freeway exit, a quiet residential street, a shadowed patch between the streetlights, inclined her seat as much as it would go, locked the doors, balled her jacket for a pillow, and laid back and slept.

She woke in the early hours, feeling like shit—as she knew she would—but at least she was feeling something. The sun wasn't up yet, but she could see it behind a range of hills to the east, pushing away the night sky and washing out the stars.

She unlocked the door, got out and stretched. The air was morning crisp, refreshing. She cricked her neck and took a long slow breath. Then another. Then another. Then she smiled.

She got back in the car and switched on the ignition.

She needed gas. She needed to pee. She needed some damn coffee.

* * *

Chatri was waiting for her at a coffee shop on California Street. He looked rumpled and worn.

"Tell me what happened."

He told her.

"It's all my fault," she said.

"Rosa shouldn't have gone into your room. You weren't to know she'd find the tape."

"I should have fixed that stitching."

"And I should have locked the camera away. Then Annabel couldn't have watched it."

"Did she watch much?"

"Enough, clearly."

"But you told her, right? Who's it was? What it was about?"

"I didn't get a chance. Not between her calling me a filthy pervert and threatening to call the police. She'd been drinking. She was in a rage. Retreat was the best option. I've tried calling her since, but she won't answer. Yesterday I heard from her lawyer. She wants a divorce, her terms, uncontested, or she'll hand the tape to the police. I could get ten years for possession of something like that."

"It's not yours dammit, it's mine. I shouldn't have involved you in the first place. I should have done my own dirty work."

After a pause, Chatri said, "Isn't that what you've been

doing?"

Alice said nothing. A cable car rumbled past the window, heading for Van Ness.

"More secrets?"

"What do you mean?"

"You're full of them, Solikha. Only now am I coming to realize that."

"It's the job. You know how it is."

He shook his head. "It's more than that. It's always been this way with you."

She said nothing.

"Some secrets never come out, and no one ever guesses. Some stay locked away for years, and when they're revealed it's too late to do anything about them. And some, though they're never told, leave people guessing. They see the gaps, pick up clues, and fill in the details for themselves."

"Sounds like what I do for a living."

"I'm starting to see the appeal of it."

"What does that mean?"

"I broke my promise, Solikha. I didn't watch the first five minutes of the tape. I watched it all. Or rather, I fast-forwarded through it. I couldn't..." He shook his head. "But I saw what they did to you, those men. I saw a terrified child brutalized by callous beasts. And I saw something else. I saw the Solikha I grew up with. The woman of secrets. I started putting my own picture together."

Alice said nothing.

"It's not complete. Never could be. A sad, misshapen thing. A jigsaw with half the pieces missing. But some of them fit together. The bigger ones."

"What... pieces?"

"Your obsessive dedication. The way you can blot out the world and focus on just one thing. Whether it's learning a new language or working your way through college. Or your job. How you never take a vacation. At least till now. And even then... That message yesterday. To call the police if I didn't hear from you. You're still working, aren't you? On this Long Tom person?"

Alice said nothing.

"Then there was Perry O'Reagan, the homosexual man you dated all through college. That arrangement you had. A good ploy. It worked. You fooled everyone. Even me. You broke my heart, you know."

Alice swallowed, drew a breath, went to speak, but he held up a hand and continued.

"And a certain night on campus. You and I, and its aftermath. The girl who, till then, had vehemently opposed all drug culture suddenly admitted she'd been dropping acid. I could never make that out. Till now."

Alice bit the inside of her lip. Tasted blood.

Another cable car rumbled past.

"It wasn't you, Chatri," she said length.

"I know that now. But maybe if you'd trusted me."

"I couldn't. I couldn't trust anyone. Not even myself.

He said nothing.

"Do you know what it's like, holding yourself in check, always? Especially at the times you're supposed to be most relaxed—talking to counselors and psychologists and trauma specialists? You build walls and barriers and fences topped with razor wire, and pretty soon even you can't find your way out again."

"I understand that much, Solikha. I saw what those men did to you. But you must have realized that's what all those counselors were for."

"Oh, I knew what they were for. But I couldn't tell them everything."

"I don't understand."

"I couldn't tell them what happened after the video ended."

He stared at her. "There's more?"

"Did you not wonder why I was only interested in the first man on that tape, not the others?"

"Now you come to mention it..."

"Because I knew they were already dead. Because I killed them."

"What? When?"

"Right after they finished filming."

Chatri frowned, then half-laughed. "But you were nine years old."

"There was a knife. They'd been cutting up fruit. I was frightened, desperate. I grabbed it. I stabbed the first guy in the leg and hit the femoral artery. As he leaped back, I lashed out and caught the second guy here." She marked a line across her throat. "Two lucky blows.

"The second guy's name was Joseph Lewis Moncrieff. He's buried in Sacramento. I know that because I stole his ID. Remember that money? I took it from his wallet.

"When Glenn and Mary rescued us, what could I do? What could I say? I'd just escaped one nightmare. A Cambodian peasant girl, illegally in Thailand, killer of two American tourists... Can you imagine what the authorities would have done with me?"

"Glenn and Mary would have protected you."

"I'm sure they would—at the risk of their whole operation there. But how could I tell them when I didn't speak the language? It would mean trusting an interpreter. I couldn't risk that. Then, later, when they wanted to adopt me, do you think this country would have taken me in after killing two of its citizens?

"Secrets, Chatri. It's like you said. Some never come out. Some shouldn't."

He reached across and clasped her hand. "But this one's out now. And I understand."

"It doesn't help though, does it? Not now that I've wrecked everything."

He said, "You and I, maybe we'd never have worked out anyway. Too much history, hmm? Besides, you nudged me in another direction. A path that led me to Annabel and Rosa. I have a daughter, Solikha. She is beautiful. I love her. I love them both."

Alice nodded slowly. "Then you need to tell them that."

"How? I can't. Not now."

She drew her hand away and said, "Maybe you can't, but maybe I can."

FORTY-NINE

It was after nine when they arrived at the house in Westlake. They found a park up the street and walked down. The lock on the front door had been changed. Chatri didn't have a key, but he was sure the sliding door out back would be open on such a mild night.

They saw Annabel through the uncurtained window. She was at the table, her chin resting on one bunched fist, studying a scattering of legal papers. There was a wine glass in front of her and tear tracks on her cheeks. She reacted immediately when she saw them, hurried to the door, tried to lock it, but Chatri beat her to it.

"We just want to talk," he said quietly, blocking the door with his toe.

"I'm calling the cops." She moved to the phone on the opposite wall.

"Annabel. Please."

Something in his tone made her pause. And perhaps the fact that he didn't try to come inside.

"We have nothing to say to each other," she said.

"Perhaps not. But Solikha does. To both of us."

Annabel's eyes narrowed as Alice came forward. Her nostrils flared. "I'm not having that... whatever she is...

anywhere near me. Get out. Go away!"

"It's about the tape," Alice said.

"I bet it is. Going to fall on your sword for him, are you? Going to say it's all your fault?" She gave Chatri a derisive look. "Is that the best you can do?"

Alice moved closer.

"Keep away!" Annabel's hand tightened around the receiver. "I'm not having you anywhere near my house. Or my daughter."

Alice stopped. "I understand, Annabel."

"You understand nothing, you filthy, vile—"

"You still have the tape? You've watched it, obviously. But you might want to look at it again. Look closely this time. At the little girl being raped. That little girl was me."

Annabel's eyes narrowed, staring at Alice. Alice stared back. Then something snapped inside, and she couldn't help herself. Tears, twenty years' worth, started of their own accord and wouldn't stop.

Village girls did cry after all.

* * *

It was almost midnight by the time Alice finished, but neither Annabel nor Chatri looked sleepy. It wasn't the coffee. They sat side by side on the sofa, their eyes fixed on her, hanging on every word.

There was a long silence when she finished, then Annabel said. "There was something about that Markham guy on the news this morning. Hero yesterday, dead today. Some sort of accident."

"Cleaning his gun in the middle of a party, no doubt."

"But the others," Chatri said. "Won't the police be looking for you?"

"I hope not. I hope I've given them a credible scenario. Hartley was shot with the Glock in Templar's hand. She and Reisinger with Russo's Ruger, still in his possession. It'll look like revenge, especially when they find Russo on Hartley's lawn."

"And the other guy. The Thai?"

"Tak's in the workshop. Shot with the DoubleTap, which they'll find in the bunker with Benny. There's some of Benny's blood on the workshop floor from when I knocked him out, and Tak was shot from a low angle. The most likely explanation is that Tak knocked him down and Benny pulled a gun."

"What about the mysterious informant? And the person who took down Russo?"

"They'll stay a mystery, I hope. There's nothing to connect me. Besides, the cops have a lot more work ahead of them. Bodies in barrels, a dead child, a room full of sex slaves. The whole smuggling operation. Videos of previous victims. Hartley's subscriber database. It's going to be a huge operation."

"You deserve a medal," Annabel said.

"No way I'll ever get one."

"Would you settle for a hug instead?" Annabel stood up. "Come here."

They embraced. Chatri joined them. A three-person hug that turned into a clumsy three-person dance around the living room. Before they knew it, they were all laughing with relief.

A small voice at the hall door said, "Mommy, Bruin says you're making too much noise."

"Well bring him in, poppet. He can join us."

"Daddy!" Rosa gave an excited cry as she spotted her father. She ran to Chatri, and he scooped her up into his arms.

* * *

Rosa insisted Alice take her back to bed.

"Bruin made a card for Mr Tubble," she said, taking a piece of paper from a table in the corner of her room. "It's a get well card cos Mr Tubble's sick. He's got a big hole in him. Will he get better, Alice?"

For a long moment Alice couldn't speak, just stood staring at the card. "Get well soooooooon!" followed by a smiley face. Eventually, she said, "Maybe not right away, Rosa. It's going to take a little time. But I'm sure he'll get there in the end."

Author's Note

Researching *Payback* took me into some dark places. The story is fiction, but the facts behind it are carefully researched and disturbingly true. I hope you enjoyed it.

Best wishes, and thanks for reading,

Geoff

About the Author

Geoff Palmer is an award-winning novelist and technical writer based in Wellington, New Zealand

You'll find him online at:
www.geoffpalmer.co.nz

On Facebook:
facebook.com/geoffpalmerNZ

On Twitter:
twitter.com/geoffpalmer

*

Also by Geoff Palmer

The Bluebelle Investigations series:
Private Viewing
Private Lives
Private Nightmares

The Forty Million Minutes series:
Too Many Zeros
Lair of the Sentinels
The Man with the Missing Jaw

Standalone novels:

Telling Stories (a novel)
Payback

Nonfiction:
How to Write a Book: 12 Simple Steps to Becoming an Author

Made in United States
North Haven, CT
19 October 2021

10424453R00215